OUR FATHERS' SHADOWS

Jack Fuller

OUR
FATHERS'
SHADOWS

Jack Fuller

William Morrow and Company, Inc.
New York

Library of Congress Cataloging-in-Publication Data

Fuller, Jack.
  Our fathers' shadows.
  I. Title.
PS3556.U44097   1987   813'.54   87-22047
ISBN 0-688-07452-9

Printed in the United States of America

First Edition

1   2   3   4   5   6   7   8   9   10

BOOK DESIGN BY MARK STEIN

For Kate and Edward

> *. . . mankind decays so soon,*
> *We're scarce our Fathers' shadows cast at noon:*
> *Only death adds to our length: nor are we grown*
> *In stature to be men, 'til we are none.*

—JOHN DONNE

ONE

THE INHERITANCE

1

For as long as Frank Nolan could remember there had been an odd old book on his father's shelves that told the story of life in these parts during the age of ice and after. His father always said a man had to know where he'd been before he could have any idea where he ought to go. It was typical of Sam Nolan to see himself as a process stretching all the way back to *Australopithecus* and forward to forms of life unforeseen. No wonder none of his children believed he would ever die.

When Frank was a boy, he liked to pull the book down and look at the maps that showed the ancient shape of the land in a shade of green like new grass growing and the waters of Lake Michigan as blue as a smokeless, prehistoric sky. He would trace with his finger the original shoreline and see how much of what now seemed solid had once lain submerged. Matching colors to legend, he could figure out the precise depth of the lake in places where today tall towers rose into the haze. He had learned from his father about the merciless cycle of things: ashes to ashes, all the seasons of the globe. And so on rainy days he planned escape routes, drawing the way into the glacial hills miles inland, just in case the ice and floods should ever come again.

Years later, he borrowed the book from his father and for the first time read the text. It told of great, extinct beasts that once roamed the land, the terror of the *Tyrannosaurus,* the tiny swimmers whose fossils now pocked the stone formations beneath the soil. He saw his childish pencil tracings and remembered all his naive, protective plans. And it seemed fitting somehow that the courthouse where he worked had been built on the deposits of the dead. He imagined the twilight, predatory depths, the shimmering creatures that cast their own light, the blind persistence of worms. And on certain evenings in the fog he could almost see their ghosts still prowling the blighted streets: familiar, unevolved.

But in the daytime no flight of imagination could make the place other than what it was. The criminal courthouse stood flanked on one end by a railroad siding and on the other by Cook County Jail. For security the wall was high, jutting out in places like the bastions of a castle, giving the whole complex the look of a place prepared for siege.

The courthouse had been built on a grand scale during the Depression, but it was showing its age. On the exterior, the detailed stonework had eroded, sharp corners going soft, statues staring down as faceless as men condemned. Inside, the high walls of the lobby were discolored by the smoke from advocates' cigars and the acid of countless perjured pleas.

On the stairs, the very gravity of the place seemed to draw a visitor toward the center of the step, where the marble was worn deep by generations of lawyers and judges following the path of least resistance. Ordinarily the big, decrepit courtrooms stood empty, except for a small knot of people murmuring up in front before the judge. To hear them at all, a visitor had to move to the first row of pews, crane his neck, and concentrate on every word.

Frank Nolan's voice never rose as he made his argument. He spoke in the calm, detached tone of a man who is confident that he will be heard. But he had not forgotten the way as a boy he had worried about the cycles of violence and decline. Beneath the restrained, formal words of his arguments and offers of proof, he felt himself locked in a mortal struggle of law against every brute impulse. Oh, yes, the solemn drama of justice.

"I'm afraid it isn't a mouse, your honor," Nolan said as he peeked into the empty jury box.

"Christ on a cross," said the judge as a big gray shape darted out and then retreated.

The court reporter bolted, knocking over her machine. A long white strip of paper marked with illegible notations slid zigzagging across the floor. The public defender and the police matron both edged toward the exit. Only the defendant remained unperturbed. She was a wiry, olive-skinned young woman in a tight T-shirt and hot pants. Nolan had already forgotten her name.

"Beeg fugging deal," she said. "I seen beegger rats plenty of times."

The judge was coming off the bench with a minimum of ceremony, but he stopped when she spoke, raising himself to his full, magisterial height and settling his wrinkled robes.

"I bet you have, sister," he said. "But you'd damn well better watch your language in my courtroom."

Nolan made one last effort to get the hearing back on track.

"The state is ready to go to trial, your honor," he said. It was no use.

"Recessed until two p.m.," said the judge, slapping his hand on the far rail of the bench in lieu of his gavel. "And Frank, for Chrissake have somebody get rid of the fucking rat."

Nolan waited until the judge had closed the door to his chambers, then he went up behind the bench and dialed the maintenance office.

"Harry?" he said. "Nolan. We've got an intruder in Morelli's court. . . . Yeah, another rat. . . . I don't care if you have to promise it immunity, just get it out of here, OK?"

As the matron led the defendant away, Nolan went to the jury box and looked over the scarred wooden panel. The rat was rooting around under one of the chairs, paying Nolan no mind.

"Leave it alone, Frank," said the public defender.

"That's what I like about you, Lonigan," said Nolan, "your universal compassion."

Lonigan looped his free arm over Nolan's shoulder and led him to the counsel's table, where Nolan picked up a stack of unfinished work.

"Friend of the friendless," said Lonigan, "who have nowhere else to turn."

"See, that's where you always go wrong," said Nolan. "The rats have found their niche. We're the ones who are out of place."

They stepped into the corridor. Most of the other courtrooms were still in session, and lawyers and clients huddled at the doors. The long hallway echoed with footsteps and deals.

At the corner they ran into the Deacon, a lanky court buff who always dressed in a preacher's stark wardrobe of black and white like some quaint notion of right and wrong.

"Anything good today, fellas?" he asked.

"Nothing on my call but a parade of ladies, Deacon," Nolan said. Then he lowered his voice to a wrathful whisper. "Harlots."

"Ain't like you, Mr. Nolan," said the Deacon, "chasin' a bunch of skirts."

"Only in election years," said Lonigan.

"Lonigan here has a client who claims she offered herself to Officer Jacobson of the Fifteenth District vice unit for love," said Nolan.

"There's a pretty good murder in Lawrence's court," said the Deacon. "No offense, Frank."

"None taken," said Nolan.

"You'd think we'd all find better things to do with our time," said Lonigan, running his finger along the manila edges of his files, which buzzed like a zipper coming down.

"Look," said Nolan, "if it were up to me, I'd let them do it for love or money or any other reason they pleased. And as for the dirty movies, if a person wants to pay three bucks to spend an hour and a half staring up somebody's asshole, it's OK as far as I'm concerned. Proctology, Lonigan. Nothing but a little group proctology. What was that last defendant's name?"

"Gonzales."

"Right," said Nolan. "Now you take Miss Gonzales, for example. The way I see it, she's not such a bad citizen. She doesn't hit anybody over the head. Her rates are quite reasonable, when you consider that she's selling off her youth. It's not her fault that she is only capable of one thing that has any economic value. Sure, maybe she has a dirty mouth, but think of all the places it's been."

"I didn't know you felt that way, Frank," said Lonigan. "I really didn't."

"I'm just saying," said Nolan.

"Something's gotten into him today," said the Deacon.

"Tell you what," said Lonigan. "I'll plead her guilty if you'll pop for a suspended sentence."

"Are you kidding?" said Nolan. "No way, Pat. What's law is law."

He left them and went to wait for an elevator. As the cars crawled slowly in their shafts, he leaned against the bare stone wall and found himself counting off the floors on the dial above the doors. The brass arrows pivoted like sweep second hands, the numbers rising and falling, passing him by.

It was one thing to come down on the hard guys, another to come down on everybody just because that's the way gravity pulled you. He thought about taking the Gonzales woman's plea. His orders were to make sure the hookers saw the inside of the jail before going back onto the street, but technically this requirement had been met. She had done a couple of weeks in County waiting for her hearing. In other circumstances, it would have been a simple equation, an admission of guilt in return for a sentence of time already served, putting another win in the state's attorney's conviction column and freeing up a cell for the next offender in the queue.

But he didn't trust his judgment anymore. He hadn't been thinking straight. He found himself going light on somebody just because he didn't have the energy to bear down. Then he would come on as strong as a man with a grudge in a case that wasn't worth the effort it took for the clerk to read off the docket number. The only way to carry the caseload was to lean away from the weight, and he struck bargains with time every day. Yet he could not shake the feeling that no matter how many shortcuts he took, time was running out.

"You goin' up?" asked the elevator operator.

"Yeah, Joe. Thanks."

The inner door was only a cross-hatched gate, and the floors slipped downward, each marked in white. Three, four, five. The passing of years.

"This is it, Mr. Nolan."

When Nolan stepped out into the hall O'Neill was standing there smiling, as if he had been lying in wait. Nolan nodded and tried to step past him.

"I thought you had a long call this morning," O'Neill said, blocking the way.

"Morelli saw a rat in the courtroom. Sentenced it to death."

Nolan edged away from the elevators. O'Neill followed.

"That's going to put you in a hole," he said.

"I'll push like hell this afternoon. A lot of them have been sitting around County waiting for their cases to come up. I can move them like lightning."

"Cheap, Frank. They must be mighty cheap if they don't even have pimps to make their bail."

"Lonigan's the PD. He'll go for time served if I can just cool Morelli down."

"What's wrong with Morelli?"

"When one of the hookers saw the rat, she called it a big fucking deal. Morelli delivered himself of a brief lecture on the dignity of the court before he hauled ass off the bench. He's going to be in a hanging mood."

"How long's the recess?" asked O'Neill as they passed through the outer office and into the room with all the cubicles. A janitor was dusting the asphalt tile floor with cleaning compound and pushing the mess around with a broom.

"We're out until two," said Nolan.

"Good," said O'Neill. "I got another one for you in the meantime. I was going to send Talley, but I'd rather have you on it. The judge and the vice dick are already lined up. It's a joint up on Dodge. Eros Unlimited."

"Give me a break, Terry."

"There's a film and a live act. The papers are already drawn up."

"If it's all the same to you, I'll stick with the hookers."

"Lots of men would give anything to have your job, Frank, going to movies in the middle of the day," said O'Neill. "Maybe it'll be a good show."

"Makes me look at my wife funny when I get home."

"Hell," said O'Neill. "You might even learn something."

Nolan turned toward his cubicle.

"Meet the vice dick in Judge Zacharias's chambers in half an hour," said O'Neill. "The great jurist will go along with you to the theater to swear out a warrant if the show gives him an erection. He isn't too bright, but I think he can handle it."

The doorknob balked as Nolan twisted it. He had to give it a shake, rattling the frosted glass.

"Oh, and by the way, Frank," said O'Neill, "make sure you pay close attention to the coming attractions."

O'Neill was pleased with himself. He laughed and laughed.

"Frank, you're too serious," he said when he finally settled down.

Nolan opened the door, threw his file down on the cluttered desk, and kicked his wastebasket into the wall.

He tried to read the documents, but he couldn't concentrate. He tried to call Laura, just to see if they could talk. But she did not answer the phone. He drank some coffee, and his hand shook with the weight of the Styrofoam cup.

Talley poked his head in just before it was time for Nolan to leave.

"I hear you're stuck with the blue-movie detail today," he said.

"Guess so."

"O'Neill didn't trust me with the reporter."

"Reporter?" said Nolan.

"Guy from the paper's going along on the bust. Just think, Frank, you're gonna be a star."

Talley came in and sat down on a rickety wooden chair next to Nolan's desk. He was new in the office, just out of the service.

"Don't worry about O'Neill," said Nolan. "He's got a thing about youth."

"I'm not that much younger than you."

"You are the way O'Neill counts it. Life begins at the courthouse door. He'll get used to you soon enough. Then you'll wish he hadn't."

"I'm sorry you got stuck with this," said Talley. "I really am."

"Don't worry about it."

"You hate vice, don't you."

"It's a living," said Nolan.

Talley got up and was half out the door when he stopped and turned back.

"How's your dad?" he asked.

Nolan closed the file on his desk and pushed himself upright, his knuckles pressed against the wood.

"He's back in the hospital," he said. "They've got him on the gas again."

"Sorry to hear that, Frank."

When Nolan's sister was trying to take care of their dad at home, the doctors had told her to ration the gas as if it were an opiate because pure oxygen is the most addictive substance in the world to a man whose lungs are going bad. Now they were leaving the hose on him all day long. They didn't even try to get him to breathe the honest air.

"They have any idea what it is?" asked Talley. "The big C?"

"Not cancer," said Nolan. "It's been coming on him for years. Doctors don't know what the hell they're dealing with."

It could be this, they had said, and it could be that. It could be any damned thing. But he only remembered one of the possibilities. They had said it might be an inherited condition.

The doctors didn't put any particular emphasis on it, but ever since Nolan heard them say it, the idea had preyed upon him. Whenever he was alone, he found himself counting off time in his head. He was twenty-nine years old. When his father was twenty-nine, Nolan was ten. Now his father was forty-eight, and he was dying. Such a young man, the neighbors said gravely. It wasn't right.

Nolan had to face the fact that if the disease was genetic, he might have it himself. Sometimes the symptoms appear quite early, the doctors had explained. There were many cases that showed up in adolescence, and that was particularly hard; the kids are so vulnerable to disability and the loss of hope. But hope was always frail, no matter what your age. Nolan felt cut off, alone. He could not even talk to Laura about it. She was eager to have children, but how could he consider it until the medical question was resolved? She wondered why he seemed so distant lately, and he could not bring himself to explain that it was as if he bore the instrument of their suffering within him, his doomed, defective seed.

He had to get a handle on all this soon, because his imagination was making awful leaps. He had even noticed certain things in his sister's behavior: trouble opening locks, fingers rebelling, a tendency to bump into furniture. Their father had been that way during the earliest stages of his illness. When Ruth called on the telephone the last time, Nolan had thought he heard a slight slurring of her words, but that might only have been the sound of tears. She was barely past adolescence herself. His kid sister trying to hold it all together. Only twenty-two years old. Too young. Too damned young.

He caught himself taking a deep breath and letting it out slowly. Talley was watching.

"Must be hard on you, Frank," he said.

"I'm late," said Nolan, picking up the Eros Unlimited file. "I've got to go."

Detective Bullock drove. He was tall and emaciated, and you could tell that he spent most of his days in moist, dark rooms. Nolan sat up front next to him. The judge and the reporter were in the back.

The plan, Bullock explained, was to go into the theater separately and meet at a prearranged spot inside. It would be no problem, he said, because these joints rarely filled up until noon.

The main feature was called *Low Blow*. Without referring to his notes, Bullock briefed the judge on what he would be seeing, scene by scene. "Male number one performs cunnilingus on female number three. Female number two fellates male number two to ejaculation . . ."

Abandoned tenements stood along the street like the ruins of an ancient battle. They weren't good for anything now except to hide a man when he took a needle or a woman, or when he just lay down to die. Nolan did not know whether anything but death was strong enough to stifle the itch of male number one and male number two anymore. It was as if evolution was running in reverse, and the only hope of holding it in check was the law.

When Nolan had first begun to study the legal order, it had seemed the most magnificent of all man's works: a vital organism as complex and adaptable as language, passed down from generation to generation, honored and improved. But when he took the job in the criminal courts, he discovered that the law they practiced there was just as crude as the instincts it was supposed to tame—hunkering down like a cornered beast, heaving in the tainted air and producing its excrement with a dull sense of disgust.

"This movie have any story to it?" asked the reporter.

"Same one over and over again," said Bullock.

"You see, son," said Judge Zacharias, "it's much easier if there's nothing in the film but sex. Otherwise it might have redeeming social value. You never know."

"The judge will decide whether it's obscene or not," Nolan explained.

"I don't know what obscenity is and I'm not so sure about art," said the judge, rising to the challenge, "but I know what I like."

The reporter started writing in his notebook. The judge's grin vanished.

"Don't quote me, son. We're all friends here, aren't we?"

Before long they came to the theater, which was nestled between a grocery and a Laundromat. The marquee was an unintelligible jumble of letters, some genetic code that stirred men's glands. The most important letter was X.

Inside it smelled of coffee and damp wool. A tall, middle-aged man with a single small earring took Nolan's ticket at the door. The judge and reporter had gone in first. Bullock was to bring up the rear.

A young girl stood behind a counter selling popcorn and candy. She was smoking a cigarette and blowing bubblegum spheres, pink membranes that burst in puffs of gray. He caught her eye and then gave it back before she offered more. On the way into the darkened hall he passed the doorway to the toilet, and the scent was urine overwhelming pine.

The judge and the others were on the right, watching the screen, where someone was licking something belonging to somebody else. Nolan crossed in front of them and took a seat. Within a few minutes, Bullock arrived.

"Shit," he said. "They changed the sequence from yesterday. We have to sit through the short subjects."

"They don't seem so short to me," said Judge Zacharias, and in the dark Nolan could not tell whether it was out of impatience or envy.

Nolan had to force himself to watch male number one in missionary position with female number one. It wasn't that female number one was unattractive. She had a lithe little body and disconcerting eyes. And despite himself, he felt the automatic stiffening of desire. But when an enormous appendage came into view and she took it, he closed his eyes.

He only opened them when he heard Bullock saying, "Good, good," and flicking through his notes.

"I think we're in luck," said the detective. "The film will be on before the live act, and we can watch them both before making the bust—that is, if your honor approves."

"I am not going to prejudge it, young man," said Judge Zacharias, looking over to make sure that the reporter had taken down every Solomonic word.

The music changed to "Girl from Ipanema." The crude title scrolled up on the screen.

"This is it," said Bullock.

Nolan made himself concentrate, just in case he had to swear out an affidavit or testify at the hearing. The film was the usual round robin. Female A with Male A. Female A with Female B. Female A and Female B with Male A. An exercise in permutations and combinations.

Still, it was a better movie than the first. The actors and actresses seemed to show real excitement. There was no plot, of course, but each episode was like a simple short story, rise, climax, and fall. Again the images caused a reflex in him; he tried to push it down. Then, enter the little girl.

She was no more than ten years old, blond and naked. She watched the goings-on intently, and in closeups she smiled. Then, in a shot so tight you could not tell who it really was, someone with smooth and innocent skin did something quite mature with her mouth.

"You didn't say anything about a child," said Nolan.

"Female D," said Bullock. "Didn't I tell you about that? Real jury appeal, no?"

Nolan could not keep his eyes off her, the strange, forsaken look on her face, the way she tried to please the camera, as if it were a parent withholding his love. He knew that it was impossible to follow these things back and find the wretches responsible for making them. But that only inflamed him. What kind of law was it that could not even protect the children?

When the film finally ended in a Gorgon's head of limbs and members, the screen rolled up and the curtains opened fitfully to the first bars of "Misty."

A woman walked out onstage fully dressed and stood before a set of three full-length mirrors that looked as if they had been taken from a tailor's shop. With much idle caressing of herself and no sense of the dance whatsoever, the woman slowly stripped.

When she finally bared her breasts, Nolan heard rustling in the row behind him. He turned to see a man in a business suit, his face pained, a newspaper moving rhythmically in his lap.

Judge Zacharias noticed it, too. He announced that he'd had enough. But Bullock settled him down. They had to wait until the end, he said, or else the arrests wouldn't stick. Just then the woman on the stage got rid of her G-string and made a few passes at her haunches with her hands before the curtain closed and it was over.

Bullock went backstage to grab the dancer while Judge Zacharias authorized the warrant and Nolan pinched the manager. But Nolan could not take any of it seriously except the little girl. To him she was the victim of a culture in shambles, one that bought the lie about good being what feels good after, and then forgot about the after. He nearly ripped the paper when he signed the line on the arrest form.

It was not long before Bullock led the dancer in from her dressing room and announced that she had given her name as Linda LaBelle. She said she was twenty-two, but up close you couldn't tell whether that was five years too much or ten too little.

"I shoulda stayed in bed," she said.

When two uniformed policemen arrived, Nolan, Bullock, and the reporter went upstairs to get the film. On the landing stood a pair of huge fake Oriental pots that must once have been for atmosphere. Now they were full of a sickening liquid. Cigarette butts and litter floated on top.

"Lord, give me comfort," said the projectionist when they stepped inside his booth and showed him their badges. Then he remembered his training. He pulled out his wallet and handed Bullock his union card.

"Don't worry," said Nolan. "You're not under arrest. We just want the film."

As the projectionist set the big machine spinning, Nolan looked around the booth. On the walls hung old calendars from auto-parts firms and posters of motorcycles doing wheelies. A Harley owner's manual lay on a table along with some biker magazines.

"You drive a cycle?" said Nolan.

"Fast as I can," said the projectionist.

"My brother drives one, too," said Nolan. "He's nuts."

"Excuse me, Frank," said the reporter, "but aren't you going to arrest this man?"

The projectionist stiffened and went for his wallet again.

"Take it easy," said Nolan.

"I don't get it," said the reporter.

"Watch," said Nolan, and then he turned back to the projectionist. "Tell me something. Doesn't the little girl in the film kind of bother you sometimes?"

"In the film?" said the projectionist.

"Right."

"Lord of mercy," said the man, "I never look at them films. I just thread 'em, flick on the machine, and sit back until I have to change reels.''

Nolan took the reporter by the elbow and pulled him aside.

"They're taught to make sure they know nothing about what they're showing," he said. "How're you going to prove intent?"

The projectionist handed over the reel, and Bullock checked a few frames against the light to make sure the man hadn't made a switch.

"I get a receipt or something?" said the projectionist. "I don't want nobody docking my check to pay for this piece of shit.''

Bullock gave him a copy of the warrant and then slipped the film into its can. When they got back downstairs, they found the dancer straining against a pair of cuffs.

"I mean," she said, "there's nothing wrong with the human body. It's a gift of God. Who are you to tell me I can't offer it to anybody I fucking please.''

"All depends on the terms," said one of the uniforms.

"I got rights, you know," said the dancer. "You don't arrest those fag ballet stars with their cocks bulging out like sausage under cellophane.''

"I always wondered about those guys, Ray," the cop said to his partner.

"You think I'm fair game because I'm a woman," said the dancer. "Nazis!"

"That's enough, lady," said Ray. "I fought the sons of bitches.''

"Why don't you take off the cuffs," said Nolan. "We aren't dealing with Dillinger here.''

"If they bolt," said Ray, "it's our ass.''

"I'll take the heat," said Nolan.

When Ray went behind the dancer to undo her wrists, a silly smile came over his face. He stood there for quite a while, grinning.

"Hey, honey," he said, laughing now. "Technically speaking, what you're doing with your hands is assaulting a police officer. But I can't say I don't like it.''

The elevated train came to a noisy stop at the station next nearest to the courthouse. Nolan had let the others go to lunch without him. He had told them he had work to do, but actually he had something else in mind. As he came through the turnstile, he checked his watch. There was still nearly an hour before he had to be back in court, plenty of time to check up on Sam Harrison.

The sky was overcast and the wind brisk, but it did not look like rain.

Nolan walked quickly down the main drag, past the barred windows of the storefronts, the boarded-up shooting galleries, the empty three-flats just waiting for the torch. There were still some businesses operating here, and Sam Harrison had opened his counter near a warehouse, an electronics factory, and a couple of dingy garages. People from the courthouse never strayed this far away for lunch. But Nolan was drawn here from time to time anyway, and not because of the food.

The neon sign in the window was flanked by red Coca-Cola ads. Steam from the grill gathered on the glass and ran down in sparkling little streams.

"Well look who's here," said Harrison when Nolan stepped through the door. "I was wondering when you'd come poking around."

"I thought I'd see if your tacos had gotten any better."

"Shit," said Harrison. He wiped his big, calloused hand on his greasy apron and held it out. Nolan shook it and sat down on a stool. "What's been going down?"

"Nothing, Sam. Nothing at all."

"The hell," said Harrison. "Last time you was in here, pretty soon you start showing up in the newspaper and those drawings they got on TV. Big case. A whole lot bigger than mine was, that's for sure."

"Now I'm raiding cathouses and dirty flicks."

"The man who put away Sam Harrison?"

"The very same."

"Here, let me get you something. Specialty of the house."

He got a plate together and put it before Nolan, who picked at the lettuce and fries.

"How's the family, Sam?"

"The boy's in first grade. He just won some kind of prize for doing his letters right. The girl's reading better than her old man already. Diana's got another in the oven."

"You just don't know when to quit, do you?"

"I ain't quitting ever. That was the deal. I'm straight and I'm gonna stay that way."

Harrison had been a defendant in Nolan's first big felony case. He was one of four men picked up for an armed robbery of a grocery store. The manager had come at them with a gun. There was some shooting. The manager died. The charge was murder.

The first time Nolan interrogated Harrison, he had a feeling that this guy was different from the others. Nolan spent some time looking into his background. He checked up on the family, the wife, the kids. It wasn't like a punk to stick with his responsibilities the way Harrison had. Harrison's lawyer wanted to get him probation for his testimony, but Nolan wasn't having any of it. He was ready to cut a deal for a guilty plea only so long as Harrison did at least a year of hard time. Don't worry about the family, Nolan had told him, there are ways we can take care of them. And after you go down, I'll do what I can to get you set up again. Trust me, he said.

For some reason Harrison had.

"You own this joint free and clear yet?" Nolan asked.

"Twenty-eight more years. Hell, you know that. You got me the loan."

"Looks like business is good."

"Can't complain."

"Say hello to Diana and the kids, OK?"

"You didn't even finish your taco."

"Even with a friend, Sam, you've got to draw the line."

The walk back to the courthouse was a long way in the cold. The wind rasped at his face and sneaked up under his coat. He leaned into it, hands in pockets, moving steadily ahead. In an alley a couple of bums squatted on a doorstep. Two more lay curled up nearby on the ground, flat green bottles poking from their pockets. You could always tell how bad it was from the shape the body took on the sidewalk. When the end was just beginning, a wino curled up like a fetus, conserving the body's heat against the pavement. Later, when his blood was supersaturated and hopelessness was crystallizing in long, choking fibers in all his veins, he would lie flat on the ground, giving in to it. You knew a man was a goner when you saw him lying as he fell, bottle in hand, sprawled out lengthwise. Pretty soon he would be John Doe naked and gray as the concrete slab in the morgue. And the cause of death was always listed as natural.

When Nolan had first joined the office out of law school he had been called to a murder scene one morning before dawn. Two defeated drunks lay crumpled up at the forgotten end of an alley. Their pockets had been turned out by somebody whose need must have been great to have killed for so little. Each had a bullet in the back of the head.

Pretty soon a deputy coroner joined the other celebrants of their passing.

"Murder-suicide," he said.

Nolan protested. "Look where they were shot," he said. "We can't even find the gun."

"Kid," said the slack-faced deputy, "somebody just gave them the only kind of injection that could cure what ailed them. Call it murder and you got another case to work. Call it murder-suicide and it's more like what it really is—nothing canceling out nothing."

Nolan had lost that one and a lot of others after. He had won quite a few, too, and there were even some special cases like Harrison, but not nearly enough of them. You did what you could, day by day, and tried not to ask what you were supposed to be accomplishing. You bargained murder to manslaughter, life to four years. A plea was worth a discount; a jury trial would send a man up for the max. Inform on a buddy, and maybe you could walk. Five give me five do I hear seven give me seven do I hear nine. Going once going twice going three times. Sold. One little piece of pure justice.

Nolan was still shivering when he reached his office. He rubbed his hands together, blew on them, flexed his fingers. Then he lifted off his heavy coat and dropped it on the chair.

"Might as well keep it on," O'Neill said, sticking his head into the cubicle. "I've been looking all over for you."

"They wanted to tell war stories," said Nolan. "I gave it a pass."

"I have another one for you."

"Morelli's expecting me in court at two."

"Forget it," said O'Neill. "I'll get Talley to cover. I want you on one that's going down right now."

"You can't raid a cathouse in the middle of the afternoon."

"Forget that shit. This one's a dead kid they found up near Old Town."

"What's the age?"

"Eight, ten, I don't know for sure yet."

"How'd the kid die?"

"Beating's the way I hear it."

"What are you doing to me, Terry?" Nolan said, slumping down in his chair.

"Putting you back in action, my friend," said O'Neill.

"Child abuse. Don't do me any favors."

"Just get moving, OK?"

"What is it, Terry? Did I hassle some politician I shouldn't have, or what?"

"Cops think they've got the guy who did it," said O'Neill.

"The kid's evil stepfather, right?"

"He's holed up in a building in the high-rent district. He's taken hostages. He wants to make a deal."

"It's sounding a little better."

"Did I tell you who the victim was? The granddaughter of Aaron Pricer, the guy who runs the bank. She was his favorite and now she won't be bouncing on his knee anymore. Naturally the man wants blood."

"Was there a ransom demand?"

"Get off your ass and find out, will you?"

"Don't give the whores to Talley," said Nolan. "I want him with me."

"I knew you'd understand."

2

O nly after she heard Frank turn the lock behind him that morning did Laura permit herself finally to get out of bed. She gathered her clothes from the closet and drawers and headed for the bathroom, which his long shower had left humid and warm.

She had awakened as soon as he did, feeling his weight lifting when the clock radio clicked on, a voice telling of some disaster far away. She had listened, eyes closed, her back turned toward him, as he bolted out of bed and shut it off then stretched and scratched before padding out of the room. She must have gone back to sleep, because the next thing she knew, she felt his lips on her cheek, the smell of shaving cream on his face, his hand resting lightly on her covered shoulder.

She had almost turned to him then, reached up and embraced him and told him it was all right. But she managed to hold herself back. She did not want to face him again this morning. She did not want to give way. Sleep had softened her feelings, made her frail to the mysterious strength of his refusal. She needed time and light to be prepared to meet him.

And so she had waited, hopelessly awake now because the act of spurning him gnawed like an undigested lump of food in her belly. She had listened to his familiar sounds: the hiss of steam from the kettle, the ring of its bouncing top, the snap of the toaster. He fed himself out of pure habit these days. He had lost all his appetites. She had only one hunger, and he had none.

When he had finally gone, Laura got up and went into the bathroom, shivering on the way, though it was not so very cold. Her shower was quick. She did not need to wash off his smell today.

It had surprised her when they were first married how fragile his desire, like hers, could be. The smallest hesitation on her part could dampen it. But until quite recently he could always rise if he sensed that she was eager. Now no matter what signals she sent, he denied her, and she did not begin to understand why.

She caught a look at her reflection in the long mirror on the door. Laura had been taught not to gaze upon her body, but this time she paused. She wasn't as firm as she had been in college, but you had to look closely and critically to notice the thickness of her hips, the slackening of her thighs. She thought it must have been the piano work that kept her in shape, the way it forced her to carry herself upright, the pressing of pedals, the dancing fingers, wrists, and arms. She was going to be thirty-three after the first of the year, three years older than Frank. In many ways, he was the older one, aged by sheer exposure, like a piece of unfinished wood. But she was the one who appreciated the approaching limits they faced.

She dried herself with her towel and got into her clothes. Of course, there was still plenty of fertile time, and the odds of birth defects did not begin to rise sharply until later. She knew the risks; she had been studying them in all the books. But scientific knowledge could not change her feelings, slake the need that went so deep that, like thirst, it overcame all others. It was a yearning that cried out in every cell. And now, whenever she heard that a friend had become pregnant, she sank into a kind of mourning.

But she could not even discuss it with him. When she had approached the question last night, his shoulders stiffened, his eyes dropped down.

"I'm not ready," he said.

"It might do your father a world of good if we could tell him a grandchild was on the way."

She regretted it as soon as she said the words. She could see that in some strange way the two things had come into conflict for him, birth and death, that for her were as harmonious as any song she knew.

"It's taken everything out of me," he said. "I can't think of anything else right now."

But she couldn't either, the possibilities dying within her, tiny voices that whispered as they expired.

"I'm talking about joy, Frank," she said. "About carrying on. He'd say the same thing if you asked him. I know he would."

"He says a lot of things."

"Ask him. Just ask him."

"Don't you dare," he said.

It had been futile to go on. She was looking for a chord that would bridge both keys, but the dissonance was too powerful. He banged away in anger, and he did not seem to care how it sounded.

They had gone to separate rooms at first. He said he had some reading to finish. She needed to study a new score. And when they were in bed, he said nothing about it. Nothing at all.

She was angry with him, and yet she had to admit that she was not helping very much either. It was selfish, expecting him to put her mourning before his own. She could not really appreciate what he was going through, because her own parents were both still healthy. Foolish, headstrong woman. She should be helping him through this thing, and instead she was pushing him away.

Don't do this, Laura, she told herself as she combed her hair, pulling the brush roughly through the tangles. Don't make yourself sympathize. When men say they do not understand women, it is not frustration. It is just a game they play so they will never have to try. That is their way, Laura, *his* way. You can play it too, but not if you meet his reasons.

Ugly thoughts. She pulled the knots out of them, painfully, one by one. He had been mean. That was true. But she had not been much better. She had been about as accommodating as a Beethoven finale, rushing headlong to the end. The strength of her need must have frightened him. Perhaps he was even afraid that she would trick him in bed, go secretly unprotected on a fertile day.

Laura slammed down her brush on the countertop and bared her teeth to the glass. Simply imagining that he might suspect her of such a deception was enough to drive off every conciliatory impulse in her. Of course she would never trick him into conceiving a child. She was careful even at times of the month when she knew deep in her belly that she lay empty. He ought to trust her at least that much.

She took a tissue from the box on the toilet and wiped her eyes. Their house had always been free of deceit, and if now he did not feel safe anymore, it could only be because she had failed to reassure him. Instead she had barreled ahead. Of course it frightened him. It was the same quality that drove her at the piano, the sheer determination to make the thing exactly the way she wanted it to be.

Laura remembered the day they were supposed to get their marriage license. He had been buried under final examinations all week, and so they had put it off until the very last day. That morning he had awakened with a miserable case of the flu and had spent several hours shuttling from the bed to the bathroom. But somehow he managed to take his last test anyway so he could graduate on time. When it was over, she was waiting for him with the car. He was pale and exhausted. She tried to comfort him, but she did not suggest that he ought to go straight home. Not quite yet. He lay in the back seat, moaning, as she drove to City Hall and parked. Supporting him by the elbow, she led the way into the building and found the proper line. They waited for forty-five minutes, Frank bearing up in silent misery, until they reached the window, presented their papers, and signed on the line. Frank joked about it later. He said that the clerk who served them must have thought he was the most reluctant groom in the city. But she felt guilty about it anyway, about the awful strength of her will.

Laura finished putting on her makeup and left the bathroom without another look at herself whole. He was hiding something from her. She had to reach it and touch it and make it better somehow. She went to the kitchen and poured herself a cup of coffee from the pot he had left warming there. Then she moved into the living room and sat down at the piano. Children. Their children. She touched her fingers to the keys and heard them laughing. High, lovely voices. If only she could listen to them closely enough, perhaps they would tell her how to give them life.

3

The Mars light on the roof of the squad car ahead of them cut a pair of raddling spirals in the haze as Nolan and Talley dodged through traffic. The whining siren echoed off stone.

A radio station was already broadcasting live from the scene, musk to all the gapers who had nothing better to do on a cold afternoon than mill around and hope that somebody died. The announcer said the gunman was a black male, thirty to thirty-five years old. He had taken refuge in a third-floor apartment, from which he had opened fire on the police. He was threatening to kill three hostages if the authorities made any move.

"There's going to be a crowd," said Nolan.

"The incident began," said the announcer on the radio, "when two uniformed police officers, responding to an anonymous telephone call, spotted the unidentified gunman acting suspiciously in an alley. . . ."

"Ever see somebody acting suspiciously, Talley?" said Nolan. "Here's how to tell. Just think of somebody trying to disown a fart."

"When the police approached, the man fled," said the announcer. "One of the officers gave chase. The other found the beaten body of a child partially hidden under a pile of rags in a trash can. More later, but first this word from Little Sizzler sausages."

"What's it sound like to you, Frank?"

"I don't like the fact that he's shooting at the police. That tells you he means business."

"I don't care what anybody says," said Talley. "When somebody's shooting, he's always shooting at you."

"You must've been one tough kid on the streets."

"I'm talking about the army, Frank. When I was a kid, my parents wouldn't even let me watch *Naked City* on TV."

"My brother's in the army," said Nolan.

29

They wheeled around a corner and saw the roadblock. The cop in the escort squad stifled the siren, pulled over to the side, and switched off his Mars light. He waved and gave them thumbs up as they passed. With their credentials pressed against the side window, they rolled through the roadblock slowly.

On the other side of it was one of those in-between streets that had seen better times and was on the way to seeing them again. Some of the buildings had already been renovated—sandblasted clean and fitted out with polite brass knockers and wrought-iron fences that wouldn't keep out a dog. Others were still untouched, blackened by soot, the woodwork dry and gray. Their yards were strewn with debris—rusted bedsprings, broken chairs, upended barrels. Beside one front walk stood the decapitated body of a plaster jockey, still holding out his ring.

Nolan parked the car and found a police lieutenant who pointed up the street to where the squad cars were congregated.

"Who are the hostages?" Nolan asked.

"A man, a woman, and a kid," said the lieutenant. "Stupid bastards opened the door when he banged on it. You'd think they was from out of town."

Nolan and Talley made their way to an alley where they could move up out of the apartment's line of sight. But the last fifty yards were in the open. They made a dash and came to a stop behind a squad car.

"Whose heroes are you?" asked a portly sergeant crouched against the fender. "I have trouble keeping them all straight."

"State's attorney's office," said Talley. Nolan was still gasping for breath, little pinpricks of light dancing before his eyes.

"What good is going to law school if they send your ass into places like this?" said the sergeant. "I told my kid, look, you get a law degree and set yourself up in something clean, like matrimonial work. There's a lot of money in busting up families. Get yourself an office, a desk, a pretty little girl outside in case you want to bust up your own someday."

"Is anybody working the alley where they found the body?" asked Nolan.

"Crime lab's there, I think. It's somebody else's problem."

"Who's the suspect?"

"Nobody knows for sure. Only good look we got was when he was at that second-story window, the one that's broken there. Then he starts shooting."

"Anybody hurt?"

"He's a piss-poor shot," said the sergeant.

Nolan looked up at the rooftops on either side of the street. He couldn't see them, but he knew the sharpshooters were up there waiting for a clear target and the word to fire.

"You going to take him out?" he asked.

"Ain't my draw," said the sergeant. "But if you have problems with it, you'd better find the deputy superintendent pretty quick, because if I were him I'd say nail the fucker."

Somebody shouted, and all the cops on the street began scurrying for cover. Nolan looked up and saw a shadow in another window, indistinct behind the dazed amber reflection of the sun.

"Damned glare," Nolan said.

"He uses the woman or the kid as a shield," said the sergeant.

Talley was up on one knee, peering out over the hood.

"What are the demands?" Nolan asked.

"The usual. A car and money. A break on the prosecution."

"What did you tell him?"

"We promised to go easy in court but not to bring around the car. Didn't want to offer anything we'd have to deliver."

"That where the bidding stands?"

"Far as I know. Somebody's on the phone to him, I think. Appealing to his better side. That's how we're taught to do it now, when there ain't a clear shot."

It was deathly still on the street, except for the squawk of the radios and the sound of distant traffic. The squads were bunched up, and cops huddled behind them, some smoking, some nervously fingering their holsters, dreaming of jobs that began and ended at a desk.

Nolan saw the window burst before he heard the rifle crack. A woman screamed. The cops were up off the ground in an instant, rushing the door.

"They better've got him," said the sergeant.

The street came alive with activity. Squad cars rolled. Cops ran this way and that. Then a uniformed officer poked his head out of the window. He was smiling like the guy who found a ten-dollar bill.

"The creep's dead!" he shouted.

When Nolan and Talley got inside, the woman was sobbing. Her husband held her by the shoulders and said it was all right. Upstairs, the boy was trying to sneak back into the room where the stiff lay sprawled next to a bed.

Blood pooled on the hardward floor, and the men were careful to step around it as they did their business. The bullet had gone in below the left eye and messed up his face pretty badly. A crime-lab camera flashed.

"You have an ID on the guy?" asked Nolan.

"Just from his wallet," a detective said. "So far all we've got is a name. Monroe Williams, address unknown."

"I thought I recognized him," said Nolan.

"You must run in funny circles, counselor," said the detective.

"I sent him away a few years ago. I didn't know he'd gotten out."

The camera blinked again. People walked in and out. Nolan got the information he needed, made a few notes on the layout of the apartment, and then found his partner and led him back into the street. When they reached the car, he told Talley to drive to the place where they had found the child.

"Can't we leave that to the dicks?" said Talley.

"This won't take long."

"What's the point?"

Nolan grunted as Talley started the car and pulled away.

The alley was near the projects, not too many blocks from the fancy condominiums where the dead girl's family lived. The police had both ends blocked off. The building on one side was boarded up. On the other side was a row of empty storefronts with a few apartments still occupied upstairs. The trashcan was about halfway down the block.

"I hear they got the animal that did this," said the uniform who was standing guard.

Nolan looked into the can. There was nothing in it but some old newspapers. A smear of blood on the metal was the only evidence of what had happened.

"Crime lab take anything?"

"Took pictures," said the uniform. "Wagon took the body."

"Were these things on top of the stiff or underneath?"

"Beats me," said the uniform. "The pictures'll show."

The papers were all afternoon turf editions with the scratch sheets torn off. The most recent was dated two days before.

"Better empty this stuff out and log it in," said Nolan.

"The garbage? I thought the case was all wrapped up."

"How often do they pick up trash around here?"

"In this neighborhood?" The uniform laughed. "What's the percentage? They can vote these empty buildings any way they want."

Nolan led Talley around to the front. He tried the first door and found it open. Upstairs only one apartment was occupied. The lady of the house answered his knock. She gave her name as Sophie Zabrinski. And she said she didn't know a thing.

"Do you live here alone?" Nolan asked through the six-inch crack between the scarred door and its frame.

"Just me and my old man."

"Could we speak with him?"

"Sure," she said. "And when you find him, you tell him I got the locks changed."

"Do you play the ponies, Mrs. Zabrinski?"

"That's his game."

"When exactly did he run out on you?"

"A day ago. He must of won some dough and decided to drink it all himself."

Nolan pulled out his notepad again and put down a word or two. You had to start by straightening out the times. What came first and when. Maybe it would lead you to something, and maybe it wouldn't. But unless you got set on the details, you'd never know what you were dealing with.

"Did you throw any newspapers in the trashcan out back?" he asked.

"Sure, that and some of the bum's clothes."

"When was that?"

"Last night when he didn't come home."

"Do you pitch the papers every day?"

"Pretty near."

"And was the barrel empty last night?"

"I didn't pay any attention."

"Have you thrown anything else out since?"

"I look like a maid or something?" She tried to close the door, but he blocked it with his shoe.

"Just answer me that one," he said, "and then we'll leave you alone."

"I ain't been in the alley since," she said. "I been a little under the weather. You know how it is."

"Thank you very much," said Nolan.

"Just leave me out of it, OK?"

They tried the other doors, up and down the street. Nobody had anything more to say than Mrs. Zabrinski. Most had less. Nolan told Talley the next stop was the morgue.

"Wouldn't it be easier just to let the cops clean this one up? All I see is a police shooting board to make the death of Williams clean. Nobody's even going to ask questions about it. The guy was a killer."

"Look," said Nolan. "Whatever else you do or don't do, you always have to see the body. You have to get right with the dead."

*   *   *

The morgue was closer to the courthouse than to the crime scene, but it was an easy drive through the deserted midafternoon streets. They parked in a place marked RESERVED and entered the drab corridors that smelled of disinfectant. Dr. Tomanelli had his office in a far corner. He was a big, round-faced man, with wire glasses and a fall of hair that made him look like Ben Franklin without the smile.

"Tony," said Nolan, "I want you to meet a new man in our office. Bill Talley. Tony Tomanelli. He's the guy who really runs the joint while the coroner gets all the glory."

"Some glory," said the doctor. "Tell me, who appreciates a good autopsy anymore?"

"You don't have a constituency, Tony. That's all there is to it."

"You want me to give your friend here the grand tour?"

"I came to ask a favor "

"Name it."

"Hurry up on the Tatum girl, will you? I want an estimate of the time of death."

"I thought they caught the guy who did it. I thought the wagon brought in his body, too."

"Just curious, Tony. That's all."

"Anything I should be looking for?"

"Nothing in particular. Something just doesn't seem right."

"Cops aren't going to be happy to hear that," said Dr. Tomanelli, unwinding the wire of his glasses from behind one ear and then the other. "They think they had a good shooting."

"I'm not saying they didn't," said Nolan. "I'm not saying anything at all."

"Except hurry."

"That's it."

Nolan looked past Dr. Tomanelli out the window. The sky was thickening, clouds rolling in under other clouds. He checked his watch. There was still time to make one more stop, but they had to finish the business here first.

"You mind if we have a look at the victim?" Nolan said.

"Your friend ever seen one of these before?"

"He was in the war."

"I never had trouble looking at the dead," said Talley. "It was the ones who were still moving that tore me up."

"This kid's all right, Frank," said Dr. Tomanelli. "Reminds me of you, before you lost your heart."

He ordered up the body and offered them coffee while they waited. Talley had a few sips, then excused himself and made a trip to the men's room.

When he was gone, Nolan asked the doctor what he knew about a thing called ataxia. He leaned over the desk and whispered the word.

"Little girls with bruises and fractures do not die of ataxia, Frank."

"This is something else," said Nolan.

"Ataxia is a name they give to symptoms. It's the loss of muscular control."

"Will it kill you?"

"When it gets the lungs or heart it will."

"What causes it?"

"Depends. The word covers a lot of ground."

"Infection?"

"You can't rule it out. They used to think every ataxia was caused by syphilis. Just like now they'll tell you cancer is because of something you did wrong."

"What about heredity?"

"You never know."

Talley returned as the telephone rang. Dr. Tomanelli had a short conversation and then announced that the corpse was ready. He led them down the hall to a small room that had a row of chairs facing a wide, curtained window. When he opened the drapes, there she was: a tiny, lost child laid out on a cold metal table. A hanging scale swung slowly above her head.

"Jesus," said Talley.

"You all right?" said Dr. Tomanelli.

"Yeah. Sure. She's just so little, that's all."

"What was she wearing when they brought her in?" asked Nolan.

The doctor checked the papers on his clipboard.

"Looks like she was naked, Frank."

The whole body was blue, but the bruises were darker, almost black. Nolan rubbed his fingers together slowly as if he were rolling a pebble between them. The face was the worst. It had been struck so hard and often that it had lost its shape. She might have been a pretty child, but now she was hideous. Maybe that was the way it had to be. To take a bright and smiling child and kill her just like that was unthinkable. The killer would first turn the sweet, innocent child into a howling, pained animal. And then he could do to her whatever he wanted.

"If you had to guess, Tony . . ."

"We'll know by tomorrow."

"Sexually molested?"

"I wouldn't bet against it, would you?"

Nolan put his hand on Talley's shoulder and turned him to the door.

"Give me a call when you're finished, OK, Doc?"

When they got outside, Talley's ashen face began to get some of its color back, and Nolan took in strong, steady breaths.

"I think you feel responsible for what happened to that little girl," said Talley.

"I was wondering when you'd get to that."

'That's why we're chasing all over the city. If you'd put this character away for good, then he wouldn't have been out and the little girl would be alive. You dealt him, didn't you?"

"I went the limit," said Nolan. "I put twelve in the box, and the jury came through for me. There were four defendants. I gave one of them a break, but it wasn't Williams. Funny thing about that. I saw the fourth guy just this morning. He's the only one I took a chance on, and he's still straight. I asked for the max on Williams, but I didn't get it. See, he didn't pull the trigger. When the shooting started, he ran. His record wasn't too bad, all cheap stuff—petty theft, possession of pills, nothing more. The judge went light on him."

Nolan stopped, rubbed his hand across his mouth.

"But sure," he said, "I feel guilty. And you know what that does to me? It gives me an itch. It's bothering hell out of me. It makes me jump around like a fool."

Talley gave him a ride to the Tatums' place but didn't go inside. Nolan watched the car pull away, then he walked up the long sidewalk to the big converted mansion. It had once belonged to one of the finest families in the city, ornate as hell, like so many of the buildings they put up just after the fire. Somebody had split the house into three separate units, one per floor, judging from the mailboxes in the doorway. Nolan ran his hand along the wall. It was actually covered with plush, like something you read about.

He identified himself to the doorman and took the elevator to the third floor. A man was waiting for him at the top.

"I'm Aaron Pricer," the man said.

Pricer was a large man, balding, and he wore a pin-striped suit and freshly polished shoes. Years ago he had probably looked bookish, but his power pretty much excused any awkwardness in his manner. He spoke as if his teeth were wired together, and his voice was very soft, the way a man's can be when there is plenty behind it.

"What is it that you want?" he said.

The apartment wasn't as fancy as it might have been. There were homey overstuffed chairs in the living room, a plain old couch and family photographs in Plexiglas frames. The only sign of wealth was an array of electronics gear along one wall: speakers, complicated receivers and amps, an expensive tape deck flanked by two microphones. In a corner across the room a low shelf bulged with thin volumes of Dr. Seuss, Curious George, and Richard Scarry, their brightly colored spines reflecting the sun. A red plastic basket on the floor held a collection of toys and dolls. Pricer caught Nolan looking at it, and it was as if Nolan had stolen something from him.

"Where is your daughter now?" Nolan asked.

"She's in bed resting."

"The husband?"

Pricer's eyes slid down to the floor.

"He's away on business," he said. "We haven't been able to reach him yet."

"What kind of business?"

"Sales," said Pricer.

"Selling what?"

"A line of menswear."

"Looks like he must do pretty well."

"I help them," said Pricer.

"Does she work, too?"

"We decided that it wouldn't be best for the child." Another man might have balked, but Pricer did not. Nolan respected that.

"Who's we?" he asked.

"Linda and her husband," said Pricer. "I don't see what any of this can add."

"Just background, sir," said Nolan, and for a moment he was all deference and sympathy because otherwise he knew the banker would freeze up.

"What I can't understand is how anyone could do such a thing." Pricer seemed to expect Nolan to provide some answer. This was a man who quite obviously was used to having things explained.

"I can't say, sir," said Nolan. "It could have been money, but that doesn't tell us why she was worked over so badly."

"An animal," said Pricer. He moved to the window and parted the drapes. The light did not warm his face.

"When did you last see the child?" asked Nolan.

"I can't recall exactly what day."

"Roughly."

"About two weeks ago, I think. Linda had brought Susan downtown to shop. We couldn't have lunch. Some damned meeting or another. But they came up to the office. Susan loved to look out the window at the lake."

"She was all right as far as you could tell?"

Pricer turned.

"Of course," he said. "What exactly are you saying, Mr. Nolan?"

In fact, he wasn't saying anything in particular. There were just certain questions you had to ask.

"Formalities," he said. "You understand."

"Yes," said Pricer. He pulled off his glasses, and without them his eyes seemed old and tired. "I suppose I do."

"When did Susan disappear?"

"I'm not too clear on it," said Pricer. "Linda has blamed herself so. I didn't want to add to that."

"Of course," said Nolan.

"From what I can gather, she left Susan here in the apartment yesterday afternoon to get a few things at the store. When she returned, the door was open, and Susan was gone."

"Did the doorman see her leave?"

"There's a back way. It opens onto the alley. I didn't even think to talk to the doorman."

"It isn't your job," said Nolan. "Did Linda call the police right away?"

"That's what's so devastating for her. She went out searching for Susan. She thought she might just have gone to play in the park."

"How long did she wait?"

"She never did call for help. You have to understand. Linda wants so much to show that she is sufficient. I suppose that is my fault. It is difficult when you have had a certain success. There are expectations, no matter how hard you try to see your child on her own terms."

"She was afraid to call for help? Afraid of what people would think of her?"

"She was apparently out all night looking for Susan. She must have been hysterical. I don't know what she could have been thinking."

"You can't be sure it would have made any difference even if she had notified the authorities. They don't usually get involved right away. Most kids who run off come right home."

Pricer shook his head and pulled at the loose skin of his throat.

"She didn't run away, Mr. Nolan. She never ran away. It was just that she could not seem to understand that there was anything in the world that would do her harm."

Nolan picked up a photograph from an endtable. It showed the whole family. The little girl's face was obscure because she was looking back toward her granddad. He was looking at the camera.

"Did you know Monroe Williams?" Nolan asked.

"I certainly did not," said Pricer.

"How about Linda and her husband?"

"I can't imagine how."

"And there were no threats or ransom demands?"

"None that I heard about," said Pricer. He rubbed his palms flat against one another. "Do you have children, Mr. Nolan?"

"No, sir."

"It is so hard to protect them."

Nolan did not even pretend to join in the pain, because he knew it was indivisible.

"I think I'd better talk to her now," he said.

"Couldn't it wait?"

"Sometimes it's easier to go through this immediately," said Nolan, "before the numbness wears off."

"She won't be able to tell you much, I'm afraid."

"Anything might be of help."

"Help with what, Mr. Nolan? The man who did this is dead."

"Yes," said Nolan. "But it is always possible that there were others."

"You believe that?"

"I don't believe anything until I've gone through the motions," said Nolan.

"And it is up to you to decide?"

"Among other people."

"I suppose you are right to withhold your judgment. I had just assumed . . ."

"It's probably a pretty good assumption, Mr. Pricer. Don't get me wrong. These things usually are just what they appear to be."

Pricer turned stiffly away from him.

"Come this way," he said. "Be gentle with her, Mr. Nolan."

He led the way down a corridor hung with tasteful prints. In the bedroom, Susan's picture stood on a chest of drawers in a ceramic frame the shape of a heart. She was a pretty girl, not at all shy of the lens. Her mother lay facing the wall on a big four-poster bed.

"Linda, darling," whispered Pricer, touching her shoulder lightly. She startled and turned. "Mr. Nolan here needs to ask you some questions."

"I lost her," said the woman. "She was the only thing I ever gave you, and now I've gone and lost her."

4

R uth shut the door of her father's study and sat down at his cluttered desk. The portable tape recorder was all set up. She didn't even have to plug it in. He kept the blank cassettes in a box in the top drawer. She slipped one into the slot and snapped it shut. There was no use searching for the tapes he had made, because she knew they were gone. She could only guess what he had been up to. The man had always loved a mystery.

She sat down on his worn old chair and picked up a book that lay beside the machine, a volume of Roman philosophy, then punched the record button and let the dead white leader wind around the spool.

"Can anybody hear me out there?" she said. "Is this thing set right? Here, I'll put the volume up. Whoops. That probably got a little thunderous. I'm not exactly a model of dexterity. These quarrelsome hands."

The needle bounced around just short of the red the way it was supposed to for best results. It struck her as appropriate somehow, always verging on excess, like a brief, happy life.

"I want this to be an oral history," she said, "a family album. I thought all you latter-day Nolans might find it interesting someday after we're gone. Is anybody out there listening?"

Before they had sent him to the hospital, her father had holed up back here day after day speaking his mind into the machine. She could hear his voice, the frail coughing, but he always caught her when she sneaked up close, and so she had never been able to make out the words.

"I have a feeling you might already have gotten some of this from Dad," she said, shifting slightly in the chair. "It's amazing that he had the breath for it, sick as he's been. Not that he's gotten morbid or anything, though Lord knows he had reason to be. . . .

41

"Excuse me for a second. I guess sometimes I get a little morbid myself."

She left the tape running as she wiped her nose and eyes. It was a strange and scary business, inheritance, the way it made you think of all the things you couldn't change.

"I don't mean to correct him, you understand," she said. "I mean, Dad is quite capable of holding his own, thank you very much. But I know him well enough to guess that whatever he said proceeded from a . . . well, from a rather cosmic level."

Her fingertips touched the red buckram book and gently ran down the lines along its broken spine.

"I just thought it might be useful to fill in a few of the more mundane details about who we are. I'll leave it up to him to say why.

"Let's begin with my parents. They married quite young, as you may already know. That was during World War Two. My father was drafted, of course. Healthy as an elk, he used to say, and twice as horny. My mother hated it when he said that.

"She was working as a seamstress in a store where he landed a job as a stockboy. She was a little older than he was, but she claimed that even at eighteen he gave the impression of being very, very wise. I guess he operated on the cosmic level even then.

"Somewhere around here there are pictures of the two of them, he in his new uniform, she all aswirl in the fashion of the time. If you look closely, you'll recognize them. You'll see the way his brows meet over the bridge of his nose like a cowl, the distinctive shape of her nose. I'll bet anything you've got those brows. Of course, he would probably say these similarities don't tell you very much. He's not interested in what people are given but rather in what they make. Don't dwell on the accidents of flesh, Ruth, he'd say. They're as superficial as blood."

A little smile came to her lips as she imagined him delivering the lesson. It was his smile.

"He always claimed that he volunteered for the infantry because if you are going to do a thing, you might as well do it to the hilt," she said. "He has never talked much about the war. I don't know whether he had any sense of his own mortality then or whether that only came later. But I do know that he was in a powerful hurry to get married. And before he shipped out, he had left my mother bearing a son. My mother said he seemed driven to have a child, like a body with a fever. Mother may even have colored a little bit, remembering it.

"In her own way, she was as full of contradictions as he is. There were times when she could be insufferably pious, but she did not entirely deny the earthier parts of life. I wonder whether she gave herself to him before their wedding or whether she waited. It wasn't something I could ask her about, because by the time the question dawned on me, she was in her own cosmic phase. That was what split them apart, like a star exploding in the void.

"But whatever anybody thinks about what she did later, you have to remember how much strength it must have taken to handle things while he was away. She had her baby all alone, brought him home to an empty apartment, raised him. She made do on Dad's small enlisted man's allotment. It was no wonder that when Dad finally came home, he decided to settle down and earn a living rather than take advantage of the GI Bill. She encouraged him to go to college, but he was stubborn about it. My mother said he came back the very same man who had left—only more so.

"I suspect that in the beginning they didn't even discuss the religious matters that finally helped break them up. But I don't know how she could have failed to recognize the rugged streak of self-reliance in him, the way he turned away from the sources of solace she increasingly came to depend on. I have asked him about this, but he has always been evasive. I think he worries that I might turn sentimental on him someday myself. I hate to have to say this, but I believe it is only because I am a woman."

Yes, Ruth thought, he probably saw a little of his wife repeated in his daughter, no matter how hard she tried to prove otherwise. But she forgave him his doubts, because secretly she shared them, as if they were part of her birthright.

"From all I can gather, he was never a churchgoer," she said. "His own parents were divided on questions of faith, his mother a Catholic, his father a lapsed Protestant. He went to Catholic school because both parents believed in the nuns' birchrod discipline, but on Sunday he stayed home with his father. And it did not take him long to learn that it was better to give away the little statuettes of the Virgin Mary he won for perfect catechism than to bring them home. In his father's house, he said, the Mother of Mercy was the patron saint of argument.

"I've often wondered whether in the beginning he realized what he was getting into when he fell in love with my mother. Maybe this particular area of contention was bred into him, like the shape of his brow, some deep, unrecognized compulsion to repeat. Maybe their differences drew them together, complementary angles. But where does that leave us? We're stuck with a little of both of them, I guess: our father's fascination with the real, our mother's wild yearning for something beyond. That's quite a straddle, let me tell you, especially when you have loved them both.

"But don't get me wrong. We were not an unhappy family. Lord knows, there was more than enough affection, even in my mother's fool, doomed flight from us. We never had much money, but my father was not a failure. Some people make things or reputations. Others simply make a life.

"He had a talent for words, and he tethered it. He wrote whatever men of affairs would pay for: advertising copy, speeches, executive résumés. If there was any poetry in them, it certainly eluded me. But there was poetry in him, all right. Oh yes. Dark, sweet verse that talked right off the page."

She switched off the machine and sat back in the chair for a moment. It was hard to avoid making this an elegy, but she wanted it to be more than that. The point was for once to try to put all the pieces together and see what they made. When they had put him into the ambulance and carried him away, it had suddenly seemed important to her to get these things right—for future generations and for his memory, but also in the silence of his home, for herself. She pushed the button of the recorder again and went on.

"I was the last born, behind Frank and Jason—Jake to everyone except my mother—and I am told that my brothers doted on me. That is not exactly the way I remember it. I was the ground on which they played out their differences. If we had been a democracy, I would have held the deciding vote. But I didn't choose between them: reliability versus adventure, duty versus romance, Frank against Jake. Truth was, I favored them both in different ways. And I didn't want to take a side, any more than I did when my mother and father were making competing claims. I was stranded, like an ass midway between two bales of hay.

"And then they went veering off, first my mother, then Jake. I felt abandoned and ashamed. We could not hold them. And what made it even worse was their reasons, which were opposite. My mother was chasing her beliefs; Jake claimed to believe in nothing. She wanted God; the devil made him do it. When I read the poem that said the center does not hold, it was like a family chronicle.

"In a sense, though, I guess it was the center that forced them both away. My father was always so damned reasonable, it drove them absolutely nuts. With Jake, it was the usual antagonism. He was wild, and my father wanted to tame him. He saw only emptiness, and when my father tried to fill it, Jake just opened the space between them even wider.

"But with my mother, the energies were different. She wanted a kind of solace that he just could not abide. He never attacked her beliefs directly. He simply cross-examined them. 'Isn't this all there is?' he would say in a tone of perfect acceptance that must have infuriated her, his hand sweeping left and right toward the kitchen stove with its wired and taped handles and the old refrigerator that would not make ice. 'Isn't this enough?' She did not debate him. She just fell silent, an unaccountable smile on her lips, summoned up from a place his arguments could not reach, a bright, clean place as serene as a grave. That was how it always worked, his enthusiasm and her serenity. I guess I was deceived by that smile, because until the day she left I always thought she had the upper hand."

Ruth took a heavy breath. Now she had come to one of the hard parts. Her father would have been able to get through it, no matter how much pain it caused him. He would have been able to tell the story plainly, the precise words that had been said, leaving out all that came later, the things they wished they had told her, that might have held her back. If he could do it, Ruth thought, she could too. She leaned a little closer to the mike and lowered her voice.

"I knew something was wrong when I found my mother boxing up her books one morning after the boys had gone off to school. My bus came later, so I stood there watching her as she put all the strange volumes away. Nowadays they would not seem so odd: Hindu sages, Lao-tze, visitors' guides to Zen. But back then they were more than eccentric. They were terribly sad.

" 'Think of what you're doing, Sally,' my father said, kneeling down next to her and rearranging the books to protect their spines. 'You have to have some idea where you're going.'

" 'I'll know it when I find it,' she said.

" 'Well, Christ,' he said, 'then you'd better take the car.'

"Before I left the house, she took me aside and told me that she loved us as much as she loved anything in the world. But love is not easy, she said. It has to begin deep within, and this was what she had to discover, where love began.

"I did not understand it then. And even now, after reading all those books myself, I still do not. But I don't think I expected her to be gone for long. And when my father told us later that she had died trying to return, I knew that it must be so.

"God, this is awful. I didn't really mean it to be this way. I mean, we aren't that different from any other family, are we? Only more so."

This time when Ruth stopped the tape, she stood up. Before her were his books, row after row of them and not a one to tell you how to go on after a thing like that. They had recovered the volumes her mother had carried away with her and put them up there on the shelves, scattered among all the others like ashes.

Ruth sat down slowly and collected her thoughts, then pushed the button.

"Maybe I'd better get onto a different tack," she said. "I mean, you have to understand about my father. I don't blame him for what happened. It's just that he loved to make sweeping gestures, anything that would make us think or laugh, which to him amounted to the same thing. He meant no harm. I think it was his mischievous energy that caused all the trouble, but it came from a sound and generous heart. He could be awfully annoying at times, but later when you looked back on it, you had to grin.

"I remember the evening I went out on my first date. I was a little late in blooming, and so I didn't start going out with boys until I was in high school. By the time I did, I had given the idea so much thought that even if the earth moved I would have measured it with a seismograph and been disappointed if it registered less than seven point five on the Richter scale. Anyway, Dad was more than a little nervous about the prospect of entrusting me to the care of an adolescent in the first throes of testosterone poisoning. He grilled me without respite about the lad I was going out with, what he looked like, what he wanted to make out of his life. I answered as best I could. The boy, if I remember right, was a little shorter than I was, wore a bite plate, and thought he might make a career in chemistry. If his intentions were honorable—as, to my despair, I was sure they were—it was probably just because he had a father, too.

"Anyway, that night I heard Dad padding around in the front room as I bathed and dressed and made up my face. I was probably pretty glum, getting myself together. Talking about the boy had taken a lot of the mystery out of it, and I was of the age when nothing can taint a thing more than approval. The doorbell rang while I was in the bedroom. This, I thought, was only right. A gentleman caller ought to be announced. I waited, door closed, for my father to come and call me out to my destiny. But instead of a knock, I heard a fanfare. It was like a damned coronation. My father had put a march by Handel on the record player and turned it up full blast. I was mortified. I raced out of my room to see

Dad embracing the poor kid at the front door. Grabbing my coat, I pulled
the boy away and just about leaped out into the cold.

" 'I'm sorry,' I said, 'He gets a little excited sometimes.'

" 'What's with the banner?' he said.

"He pointed and I saw the curtains on the picture windows parting.
Behind them hung a huge, lettered sign. 'Do us proud,' it said, as if I
were going off on a crusade. If the earth moved at all that night, it was
only when I stamped my foot on the sidewalk. The boy was so spooked
that he did not know whether to kiss me or salute. He did neither. And if
you asked my father about it today he might just say that this was exactly
the way he wanted it."

5

*T*he clock on Nolan's desk had his father's name etched in brass at the base. It had been a Christmas gift from one of his father's clients. The house was filled with such useless presents of granite and silver and glass, and the children had their pick of them.

The fancy clock was as out of place in Nolan's cubicle as it had been on the dusty, cluttered shelves in his father's study. Its delicate blue face peeked up among the toppling piles of file jackets, flanked by empty coffee cups permanently browned at the bottom by sediment and ash. At one corner, the in box overflowed into the out. At another stood a framed photograph of Nolan and Laura arm in arm, smiling, taken at somebody's wedding years before.

When O'Neill entered, Nolan did not even look up.

"You could have called, Frank. Didn't you have any dimes?"

"The Tatum woman was too upset to talk," Nolan said. "I didn't call because I didn't have anything to report."

"I wouldn't say that. The cops seemed to think you were up to something."

"It was a good shooting, Terry. They don't have anything to worry about. I would have signed off on it on the spot, if they'd asked me."

"You sure took your time about coming back."

Nolan's chair squeaked as he turned and pointed at the clock.

"It's not so late," he said.

O'Neill picked up the clock and set it back down.

"This old thing isn't right, Frank. You know that. It runs slow. It's winding down."

He moved Nolan's wadded-up trenchcoat and made a place for himself on one of the chairs.

"I might have had something to tell you, you know," he said. "I might have had something important."

"More tits and ass," said Nolan. "I know the docket."

O'Neill rubbed his eyes with stubby fingers.

"Frank," he said, "there was a call from your dad's doctor."

O'Neill hesitated, and Nolan's deepest fears rushed in. He was sure that it was finally over, and he was suddenly struck silent with the numb relief of loss.

"He said your dad is holding on," O'Neill said at last, handing him a little pink sheet with the doctor's name and number on it. "But he wants to talk to you."

"Something about the Tatum case isn't quite right," Nolan said.

"The doctor said as soon as possible."

"I've got a funny feeling about the guy they shot," said Nolan. "And the little girl's body. I think it might have been in the garbage can all night."

"Forget about it. The case is wrapped up tight, Frank. Look, I know you want off vice. Maybe in a week or two I can spring you. Don't worry about anything until then. Just take care of your old man."

A phone began to ring in the distance. O'Neill turned toward it.

"Go ahead, Terry. Take the call."

"Just a few weeks," said O'Neill, standing.

"You should have seen what they did to that little girl," said Nolan. "Williams?"

"Somebody."

When O'Neill was gone, Nolan picked up his phone, then set it back down again. He went to the secretary's desk and felt the coffee pot. The little light was out, but there was still some warmth coming through the glass. He poured a cup and brought it back to his cubicle. As he sipped at the thick, tepid liquid, he rearranged some of the mess on his desk. Then he finally dialed the number.

"Dr. Erdman's office," the woman said.

"This is Frank Nolan. Is he there?"

"Doctor wanted you to stop by."

"Should we set up a time?"

"Could you come by right now?"

"This afternoon?"

"Doctor said it was rather urgent."

"Is anything wrong?"

"Not at all, Mr. Nolan."

"It'll be a few minutes, OK?"

"I'll tell him to expect you."

He took one more sip of coffee and left the rest for the cleaning ladies to worry about. He hauled on his coat and pulled one file out of the litter on the desk, quickly slipping it into his briefcase and snapping the latch closed. It was the file on Williams, from arrest to imprisonment. The sheet noting that the man had gone out on parole wasn't there. Probably still in the distribution system. Or maybe it had been placed in the wrong jacket. Williams was a common name. It was easy to make a mistake.

Dr. Erdman's office was downtown in the Northwestern University hospital complex. There was nothing particularly fancy about it: plastic chairs, posters asking patients kindly not to smoke, magazines strewn around, none of them new.

The receptionist took Nolan's name without comment. Was she the one he had talked to? He tried to see if there was pity in her expression, something she did not want to let on. But she just smiled and went back to her billing.

Nolan sat down near a plaque inscribed with the Hippocratic oath. It was a new version that excused abortion from the ancient imperatives. He admired the artful language, the way it avoided right and wrong.

He had not been waiting long when the hallway door opened and a young woman entered with a boy in tow. She announced herself to the receptionist and then, though he seemed old enough to do it himself, began to extricate the boy from his parka. She pushed and pulled to get the bulky thing off the boy's uncooperative arms. The fabric seemed caught on something. Nolan reached over and held the sleeve.

"Thanks," she said, and then she laughed. "I'm pretty used to it by now, but it's always a battle."

"Momma," said the boy.

"It's all right, Billy. This is Mr. . . ."

"Nolan. Frank Nolan."

"Say hello, Billy."

The little boy quickly hid behind the woman's skirt. Then he peeked out, finding courage enough to show a single eye.

"How old are you, Bill?"

"He wants to know how old you are, Billy. Won't you tell the nice man?"

The boy began to breathe deeply, shaping his mouth around a word and trying to blow life into it.

"Thuh. Thuh. Thuh," he said. His whole body heaved with the effort.

"That's all right," said Nolan.

"Thuh. Thuh. Theven," the boy finally said, and then he smiled that wonderful eager, innocent smile that retarded children never have the wit to lose.

"Seven," said Nolan. "You're a very big boy for seven."

"Eleven," said the woman.

"I'm sorry," said Nolan.

The boy nuzzled up against her and circled her waist with his arms. She reached out and brushed the hair from his eyes.

"Mrs. Mueller," said the receptionist. "Doctor is ready for you now."

"Goodbye, sport," said Nolan.

The woman took the boy's hand and waved it for him. Nolan waved back.

When they were gone, Nolan investigated the receptionist's face again.

"I could come back tomorrow," he said.

"He'll be with you in a few minutes," she said without looking up from the bills.

"I didn't realize there was that much demand for his specialty."

"If you'll excuse me," she said.

Nolan had been reluctant when Dr. Owen had first suggested bringing in the specialist. How could a new man give his father the same care and understanding as a family doctor who had known them for years? But Dr. Owen was insistent, and he left it up to Nolan to get his father's consent.

There was no way to refuse, but Nolan had undertaken the assignment without much optimism, knowing that all his father's prejudices would be arrayed against him. Sam Nolan had a brief against the professions, especially men of medicine.

"Parasite!" he would holler at Dr. Owen. "Look how he sucks my blood."

And Dr. Owen would get that martyred look on his face and snap the rubber strap from where it bound Sam Nolan's arm. The dark arterial blood would pulse into the tube.

"Someday, Doc, that well's gonna run dry," Frank's father would say.

"That it will, Sam," Dr. Owen would reply, hoping his patient would get philosophical, because then it would be easy to talk as friends. "It's only a question of time."

Nolan had talked with his father about the specialist during an earlier episode in the hospital. His father still had enough breath to speak that time, the voice to object. Nolan had approached the subject cautiously, trying to put as little weight on it as he could. His father's response had surprised him.

"I ever talk to you about the mitochondria?" he said. His words were as soft as flesh. The slurring was more pronounced than ever. But Nolan had grown accustomed to that. They understood one another, always had.

"Never met the gent," he said.

"Oh yes you have. You've got some in you. Everybody does. They're little fellows who live in our cells. I mean that literally. They've camped out there, reproducing when we reproduce, dying when we crap out. But they're not really us, in the usual sense. They have their own unique DNA, and it is coded differently from our own. By any useful standard, they seem to have an identity apart."

Nolan did not even ask him what he was driving at. His father always had some destination in mind, even when he seemed to be wandering around lost.

"These little mitochondria critters," his father continued, "they help in oxidation." He tapped the big green cylinder of gas next to the bed and watched his son to see if the reference had bitten. It had, but Nolan kept his head high anyway. That was the way his father would want the thing played. The man in the hospital bed smiled.

"That isn't the half of it," he said. "Take the organelle. There is a considerable body of opinion that holds that these little fellows who show up in our cells are really a form of bacteria that colonized us somewhere along the line. And, why, the flagella and cilia of the intestinal tract, some very smart folks think they might originally have been independent spirochetes that decided to get into our act."

He waited for a time to catch his breath, and Nolan looked away so they could both pretend that it was not necessary.

"I have seen it asserted," said his father slowly, "that since our bodies are aswarm with these alien beings, the idea of a man's having a unique identity might just be a conceit. It might be more appropriate to think of ourselves not as singular but as plural, as a community."

He took a sharp, shallow breath that was as deep as they got anymore, then he pressed on.

"That's where the new doctor comes into it," he said.

"Maybe we should just forget about him," said Nolan.

"I'm not finished yet," said his father.

Nolan felt both edges of the words.

"Well," his father continued, "I guess we'll have to let old man Owen call in whoever he wants."

"You could refuse."

"If it were only for me," his father said. "But remember the mitochondria. The organelles. I have responsibilities. I've got to think of the family."

The receptionist called Nolan's name. For a moment, he thought he had been weeping. But when he wiped at his eyes, his finger came away dry.

"Dr. Erdman will see you now," the woman said.

He hurriedly gathered up his overcoat, and she led him down a corridor to the office at the end. He could hear little Billy crying behind one of the closed doors.

"Please have a seat."

The small office was choked with plants. The afternoon sun only reached a few of them. Shoots rooted in water. Succulents lazed in the shade. Rows of peas basked under a grow lamp. The chair was uncomfortable. A large leaf tickled his neck when he tried to lean back. A hidden clock ticked somewhere in the thicket, and he heard doors in the corridor open and close.

He arranged his coat on his lap and occupied himself at first by trying to translate the Latin words on the diplomas that hung on the wall behind the desk. Then he dug into his coat pocket for something to read. All he found was a bill for his credit card. He glanced at the brochure advertising flight insurance, then threw it away. Finally, he opened his briefcase and pulled out the Williams file. The words were written in his own hand, surer in those days, every letter carefully formed.

"I'm sorry to have made you wait," said the doctor as he slipped through the doorway and took the papers out of the clip that hung beside it. "I hope you'll excuse the profusion in here. I'm trying to grow hybrids. They're not nearly so difficult as the higher species. The plants submit to my ministrations in silence. They only know how to turn away from the darkness."

"I'm a little worried," Nolan whispered.

"Please don't be," said the doctor. "I told her to make it clear to you that there has been no change. I'm sorry if she left you in suspense about that."

"I got the message," said Nolan. "But sometimes that's the lie you tell."

"His condition is stable," said the doctor, linking his straight, thin fingers at the tips. "We have tried some new therapy techniques."

"Have they done any good?"

"It is a very imprecise matter, Mr. Nolan," said the doctor. "You are a professional. You understand. We are never as sure as we would like to be."

"Is he responding?"

"Oh, yes," said Dr. Erdman, interrupting himself with a strange, gay little laugh. "Your father responds, all right. He responds at considerable length. He is full of advice. I find him quite a delightful man."

"Yes," said Nolan.

The doctor was serious again when he continued.

"I understand you are bringing back the other son—your brother—from overseas. The Red Cross contacted me just yesterday. I think it is a good idea."

"The situation is that bad?" said Nolan.

"I cannot tell you it isn't," said the doctor. "Every episode is worse than the one before. We're seeing some pneumonia this time."

Nolan knew that already. He took in the stale air as shallowly as he could.

"It's always difficult to see a parent suffering," said the doctor. "But you mustn't give up on him."

"That's what I keep telling my sister," Nolan said.

"I know. It is the easiest thing in the world to say."

The doctor paused, went through some papers on his desk.

"I'm afraid I cannot report very much in the way of comfort about your father's prognosis," he said, and it sounded to Nolan like a speech he had been preparing for quite a while. "But there is something new, and that is why I asked you to come here for a visit. Dr. Owen, I think, has already mentioned to you the possibility that your father's condition is hereditary."

"He has."

"There is nothing conclusive as yet by any means," said the doctor, "but I felt I should tell you about some work recently published on the West Coast. A disease with symptoms very similar to your father's has been shown to be an autosomal dominant genetic condition. The gene need only be inherited from one parent. Any offspring, male or female, stands one chance in two of inheriting it and getting the disease."

Nolan sat back in his chair and looked over at the flowers on the sill leaning away from the glass.

"I'd like to be tested," said Nolan. "I'd like to know for sure."

"I'm sorry to say that there are no tests," said the doctor.

The doctor leaned forward across the desk.

"You don't feel any shortness of breath," he said.

"I do right now," said Nolan. The doctor smiled, and Nolan felt like a child.

"The devilish thing is that there is no way of knowing that a person is carrying the gene until the symptoms begin to appear. That can be at any time from puberty on. You are what age?"

"Twenty-nine."

"The oldest in the family."

"Yes."

"In your father's case, you see, the onset was quite late. He was very lucky. Sometimes the thing comes on at a much earlier stage. It is quite common to see it emerging in childhood. That is one peculiarity about the West Coast research. It shows a great variance in the onset but a period of deterioration that is remarkably constant in all cases."

"How long."

"Ten years to mortality."

"So there is no hope for him."

"I think it is possible that he will survive this crisis. We do not know precisely when the symptoms began. He apparently was not entirely open with Dr. Owen."

"What are the odds, doctor?"

"Of his having the disease? It is impossible to calculate them at this point without having a complete family history."

"If he does have the disease."

"Then I would say that there is a chance that he could survive a matter of months, perhaps longer. And the odds that you have inherited the condition would be fifty-fifty. That much I can say for certain."

Nolan turned the numbers over in his mind. They were the same from every angle.

"I'm worried about my sister," he said. "Maybe I'm just imagining it, but I've been noticing things. Clumsiness. Lack of coordination. She's been very tired."

"She has been caring for your father, I understand."

"Yes."

"That can be wearing. Perhaps you ought to have her come in one day to see me. Try not to alarm her. She is how old again?"

"Twenty-two."

The doctor nodded, wrote a note, and made a quarter turn in his chair.

"I came to this field quite by chance," he said, touching the leaf of one of his plants. "My research in retardation led me into it. Genetic change is the mechanism of progress, the instrument of evolution, if you will. Pure randomness drives it—the collision of a particle of radiation with a reproductive cell, a slight chemical error in the transmission of the chromosomal message. If the mutation is fortuitous—if, for example, it prepares the immune system against a hitherto lethal virus—the individual's offspring are strengthened. On the other hand, there are some mutations that are apparently transparent to survival, matters of pigmentation or slight variations in bone structure. But if the mutation is profoundly harmful, then ordinarily such events will result in the death of the carrier well before the age of reproduction. In the usual case, damaged genes do not perpetuate themselves.

"But in some relatively rare instances the mutation does not do its damage until after a succeeding generation has been born. The weakness is passed on. The suffering is multiplied. And there is no automatic process by which such failures eliminate themselves."

Nolan took this in without a word. He knew what was coming next.

"Of course," said the doctor, "in human beings there is the faculty of choice. I have heard it argued that this allows us to control our own evolution, to correct ourselves, to advance."

"There are no grandchildren yet," said Nolan.

"I know," said the doctor. "Please do not get me wrong. This is a very individual matter. I don't mean to presume. There is a Promethean quality to this whole field that can make one quite uncomfortable."

"You aren't telling me that I can't have children," said Nolan, just to get it on the record.

"That is not a medical judgment," said the doctor. "I can only give you the facts. You have to realize that in your father's case, circumstance has been very kind. This disease can be worse. Much worse."

"Life is full of risk," said Nolan.

"But some risks can be avoided."

"Promise me something, doctor."

"I will do whatever I can to reach some kind of firm conclusion."

"Please promise that you will keep this between us."

"I wouldn't think of troubling your father about it. But I will need some help in putting a family history together."

"Let me tell my sister what it's all about, then you can talk to her. But I don't want my wife to know about it."

"At some point, I think, you will have to discuss it."

"She wants to have children," said Nolan.

"I think I understand," said the doctor.

Nolan stood up and shook Dr. Erdman's hand. He was not ready to give up yet, but he was not ready to face her either. He had learned something in his work at the courthouse: you could always manage, if you took it one death at a time.

6

*B*efore returning to her class, Ruth stopped at the big window of the multipurpose room. It looked out over the playground, which was still too wet for outdoor recess. Beyond the yard, the housing development stretched out for miles. The landscape was not nearly so stark as when she had gone to school here. She remembered the dreams she'd had when the family first moved into the new house. There were no trees then to help you get your bearings. No flowers. No lawns. Just huge piles of mud left from the excavations. She had often dreamed of being lost. She would go from house to house, all of them the same, asking if her mommy and daddy lived there. But the funny thing was that even in the dream something always drew her to the right street, as if she could follow her father's scent, the pipe and cigarette smoke, the tonic he used on his hair. And when she got to the door, she knew it as surely as she knew her flesh.

Ruth reached into the pocket of her smock for a tissue. She wasn't weeping, but she wanted to be sure she'd give the children no sign of distress. It was important that she be rock-solid before them. The little ones needed that. When she withdrew her hand, coins spilled out onto the dark tile of the floor. Clumsy, accident-prone. It was not one of her better days. She leaned over and picked up the change, the shiny disks sliding away between her fingers. Finally she retrieved them all and stood again, taking a long breath. It was all right. Really. Nothing had changed.

The children were busy at their tables when she came through the door, a measured smile on her lips. Some of them turned and grinned. Bobby held up his drawing for her approval.

"Very, very good," she said.

"It's a starship," he said loudly.

"Of course," she said. "Anybody could see that."

The assistant principal stood up and took Ruth into the corner.

"Everything all right?" she said.

"I'll be fine."

"Is there anything I can . . ."

"He's the same," said Ruth. "I wish Frank had waited. I don't know why he had to interrupt class."

"If you want to go home, I can finish up."

"Not necessary," said Ruth, touching the other woman's hand. "It's only a few minutes. I don't want to alarm them. But thanks."

For the rest of the class period, Ruth went through the motions, praising and correcting them, catching the tired ones before they went over the edge. But she wasn't all there for them, and she hoped they would not notice how much she was torn.

Frank had been very brusk and precise on the telephone. I have three points to make. First, I talked to the doctor and he thinks Dad's condition might be hereditary, with even odds that he passed it on. Second, the doctor needs to talk to you, to get a genealogy. Maybe you should go and see him. Third, I don't want Laura to find out about this right now. Promise me you won't say a word.

He might have been laying out the provisions of a trust. But that didn't fool Ruth. She knew Frank's ways, what he gave and what he held back. She hung up the phone and held her hand out before her eyes, opening and closing it. She wished she could go straight home and get on the recorder and pour out her feelings, hoping that somebody might be there to listen someday, as healthy as an elk.

"All right," she announced a few minutes before the bell, "time for cleanup. Susie, I want you in charge of the dress-up corner. Sam, you handle the blocks. Tommy, I want you to help me organize the crayons. Does everyone have his picture to take home? Put them somewhere where you won't forget them."

They went about their chores with a minimum of complaint, and she was pleased that they did not exploit her fragility. Sometimes when she was short on patience, they sensed it and tested her. They picked up on everything so quickly at this age.

"How did I get such a wonderful group of children?" she asked.

They laughed and tried to answer.

"Because you're nice too," said Bobby.

"God gave us to you," said Sam.

"Mommy says it's easier for teachers," said Sandra, and Ruth had to smile.

Melinda Brock came up next to Ruth and hugged her around the waist.

"That's sweet, Mindy," said Ruth. She was not usually an affectionate child, and so Ruth had to stop there before her voice cracked with emotion. She did not want to frighten Mindy off.

The bell finally sounded, and the room became clamorous as the children prepared to go. In theory, each one was supposed to be able to get dressed on his own, but a six-year-old could not be expected to deal with snagged zippers or overshoes a size too small. Ruth shuttled among the children, meeting all the little crises. Soon the last one was gone and she was alone, sitting uncomfortably, knees to chest, on a tiny chair.

She couldn't be angry with Frank. Compared with Jake, he was awfully stiff and self-righteous at times. But he was always there when she needed him. And so she could hardly begrudge his calling her. There was no real emergency, but he must have felt that he needed her just as she had needed him the morning of their dad's latest spell.

When she had summoned Frank out of court to come help her, she hadn't known what else to do. Their dad was conscious, but he had soiled himself and was saying crazy things, like someone in a daze. Frank arrived quickly, took one look at him, and called an ambulance. Then he returned to the bedroom and explained to their father what he had done. When the paramedics came, they had to strap him to the litter. He was cursing Frank and pleading with Ruth. She did not think she would have had the strength alone.

But she didn't like the fact that Frank was hiding the truth from Laura. As different as Laura was from Ruth, they had always understood each other. The saddest thing was that Laura wanted so badly to have children. She said she felt an emptiness in her belly just waiting to be filled, and Ruth could appreciate that. Sometimes she felt pretty incomplete herself, especially now that her father was in the hospital and the house was silent. But Ruth had not really thought about having kids herself. The children in her class were enough for now. She was into nurture more than nature. Frankly, nature had gotten pretty scary all of a sudden.

She stood up from the miniature chair and went to the desk. Now that the kids were gone, she was no longer eager to go home. She could hear the noise from the gym down the hall, the boys and girls running back and forth chasing basketballs. It was a lively, lovely sound. She pulled out her lesson plans, which lately she had been letting slide.

A tiny scrape interrupted her, and she looked up. Mindy Brock stood across the desk in her slicker and rain hat, an odd look on her face, strangely knowing and unafraid.

"Hello there," said Ruth. "Did you forget something?"

Mindy looked away. The confidence vanished. She was usually so shy.

"I was getting kind of lonely," said Ruth. "I was hoping somebody might come by."

Mindy stood up straight and mustered her courage.

"Are you OK, Miss Nolan?" she asked.

"Why, of course, Mindy."

"I just wondered."

"I'm fine."

"That's good," said Mindy, and she finally smiled.

"Did I seem worried?"

"I don't know."

"You're a very sensitive girl. You feel things, don't you?"

"Sometimes."

"Well, it's good that you do. It's because you care about people," said Ruth. "Does your mommy know you stayed late?"

"No."

"I'll call her. Would you mind very much if I walked home with you?"

"No."

"Good. Wait here a minute."

Ruth got up and went quickly to the lounge, where she splashed cold water on her face before going to make the call. The whole business with her father had gotten her all turned around. And now to see it come between Laura and Frank. She wished she could talk to somebody about it, to explain it all and maybe get hold of it that way herself. Was that the emptiness Laura felt? No, Laura was not confused about who she was and what she wanted. You could tell that from her music. She knew.

7

*T*he car was running funny. Cold, wet, it needed a tune. At a stoplight the engine balked. Come on, Nolan mumbled, leaning forward into the steering wheel and pumping the gas.

If he swung onto the expressway he could gun it out to the Drive. And then it would be a straight, smooth shot to the apartment. But he sputtered on past the entrance ramp. After calling Ruth, he had gone back to the office to read through the file and his notes, and now there was still one more thing he had to do.

The night was chilly and damp. There wasn't much action on the streets. It was the wrong time and place to lose your power and have to go on foot. As he got near his destination, he slowed down and watched for numbers, squinting at the dull, peeling paint of the signs.

The engine held up as he turned into the alley. He drove slowly through the narrow, cluttered passage until his headlights reached an obstacle. There it sat, right in the middle, the rusted steel can where the Tatum girl had been laid to rest.

Nolan stopped the car and put it into park. He left the engine on, goosing it a few times to give it some momentum, and clicked the lights to high beam. It was not like the cops to leave the thing out there like a barricade. Maybe some kids had been curious after all the excitement was over. Or maybe somebody meant it to block the way, an ambush. Nolan looked behind him. The mist diffused the red glow of his taillights. He could see the street twenty-five yards behind him. Nothing there but shadows. He opened the door and climbed out from behind the wheel.

In the afternoon he had not had time to feel the presence of the place. But now it closed in around him. He pulled up the collar of his trenchcoat and drew the front flap over his tie. His feet scraped on the pavement. When he reached the front of the car, he stopped. There was a radio playing in the distance, flat mariachi trumpets and the strum of guitars.

The can was empty now. Near the top, where the light hit it in a perfect curve, he could see a few faint smears of red along the side where the body had rubbed against it. They seemed to bear the mark of a hand, like a child's fingerpainting. He took hold of the rim, the steel cold and slippery, then tipped it back against his body and rolled it off to the side.

Nolan looked upward along the line of the roofs. The sky had a sickly glow. There were no stars. Mrs. Zabrinski's windows would be right there beneath the chimney. They were dark.

He tried to imagine Williams coming up this alley, the child's body wrapped in blankets and slung over his shoulder. Was she dead already when he brought her here, or did she still have one more struggle left? He imagined her little hand grabbing at the rim, smearing her blood against the steel as he choked the last breath from her throat. Wrong hand. Wrong time. It didn't make sense.

Somebody coughed, and Nolan crouched down behind the can. At the other end of the alley, a man in a pea coat and knit cap stopped in the lights of the car.

"Hey!" he shouted. "You OK?"

"No problem," Nolan shouted back as he stood up again. "Police."

"Shit," said the man, then he coughed again and moved off out of sight.

It was all wrong. The times were out of line somehow. When the police looked in the garbage can, they found the body under a newspaper. It was the one the Zabrinski woman had thrown out the night before Williams was seen in the alley. She hadn't noticed the body, but that didn't mean anything. She was probably so drunk she wouldn't have noticed a locomotive coming down the alley at her. Of course, Williams could have put the little girl under the paper that next afternoon. But it was odd that he had picked up all the sections from that one day's paper and no others. No, Nolan was not satisfied. Alone now, his fingers touching the metal where her tiny body had lain, he still could not feel the deep, engulfing hollow that always told him that, yes, this was how death had come. The thing just did not fit together properly: this man, this girl, this place.

You had to be right about the dead. You had to pick up the pieces of evidence, turn them this way and that, see how they matched up, one with the other. You did not discover the truth step by step. The detective shows always got that wrong. It came to you in a rush, like inspiration. Until it hit you, you just groped around in the dark. Then something clicked and you knew. There was in a murder a perfect order that stretched all the way back to the beginning, killer and victim, propelling them toward the act. It was as slow and sure as the movement of glaciers, the extinction of species too weak to survive.

Frank returned to his car and closed the door. The warmth of the engine came up from under the dash. It was running smoothly again now, all the connections dried out and sparking just fine. He put the shift in gear and eased forward past the barrel. Then he turned into the street and headed toward the Drive.

The piano music was muffled behind the apartment door. Nolan stopped to listen. He did not recognize the piece. A neighbor's television mumbled and laughed down the hallway. The elevators thumped above and below. He pulled his keys from his pocket and softly turned the cylinder of the lock.

Once inside he pulled off his coat and dropped it. Then he squeezed out of his shoes and stepped carefully across the rug until he was just beyond her sight.

She was trying out a new idiom, and it pleased him. The song was a ballad, slow and pleading. The melody rose over blue, unclassical chords as mournful as a man calling rags and old iron. He knew that it was wrong to put a story to her music. She had told him that this marred the purity with particulars that she struggled to transcend. But still he heard her groping toward him now, the sounds of the streets, the things he found there.

He closed his eyes as the notes whelmed over him like the fulfillment of a prayer. But that was not the end. The chords fell away and in their place came a questioning series of turns, fleeting, treble, uncertain. They were like the questions he was not prepared to answer. He stepped back, thinking for a moment that he might rattle the front door and pretend to come in unawares. But then he stopped himself and moved quietly into the room.

She did not see him at first. He watched her over the length of the instrument, her body bent toward the keyboard, fingers lifted from it now, touching her brow. City lights spread behind her through the window like the score of an intricate, unplayable fugue.

"That was lovely," he said softly.

She looked up at him.

"You ruined my secret," she said. "It was going to be for your birthday."

He was flattered, but still he drew back. The song had found and touched him. And it troubled him that this was the only language they seemed to share anymore.

"It sounded finished to me," he said.

"I'm not satisfied yet. There are certain things in it I still haven't found."

"Would it be decent of me to ask to hear it through?" he asked.

"But your birthday."

"It would do me more good today."

"Has it been that bad?"

"Frustrating."

"The song may be different when it's finished."

"That's all right," he said.

She watched his eyes for a moment, then lowered her head and touched the keys.

The song opened with the prescient, skeptical little runs that had ended it. Then it rose in prayer, something that spoke of primitive churches, congregations wailing, swaying, speaking in tongues. He had always worried about their differences, she so distilled and abstract, he as gritty as a sidewalk after the snow has melted. And yet she could reach all the way across the distance and touch his raw world like a chord.

"I don't know how you could improve it," he said when the song was over.

She got up and moved to his side.

"You'll see," she said.

He sensed that she was holding back, too. He wished he knew a way to bracket off the secret and the questions and hide them somewhere out of sight.

"You want perfection," he said, "and I can't even imagine it."

"You could if you let yourself try."

"I guess it's my way of avoiding disappointment."

"You're too afraid to fail."

"Not when I hear your music," he said. He wanted to make sure they were talking about the same thing.

"There are always parts that could be better," she said, "sounds I can only hear inside."

"But it was beautiful," he said.

"You should have heard me earlier. There were a lot of false starts. I don't come naturally to the blues."

"I guess everyone feels them sometimes," he said.

She turned away from him.

"It made me angry last night when you snapped at me about your father," she said. "It wasn't right for you to say those things."

"I know," he said.

She moved past him without touching and went into another room. He did not follow. Instead, he returned to the hallway and picked up his coat and shoes. He carried them into their bedroom and then went to the bathroom and washed the filth of the day off his hands and face. He could feel his skin tightening as it dried, as if there were bands of rawhide around his skull.

He had first met her at the university, and she had seemed to be at ease there in a way he could never be. Naturally, he assumed that she had been born to privilege. It was easy to believe that, listening to her music.

One day during the last spring before their graduation, the two of them had gone out to the green for a picnic. He had told her all about his family and admitted the modesty of his plans.

"It isn't much of a dream," he said, "not for you."

"You haven't the foggiest idea where my dreams come from,"·she said. "You don't even know where I grew up."

"Horace, Pennsylvania," he said.

"I mean what it really was. You never asked."

"People can be as uncomfortable talking about good fortune as bad," he said.

"You're so foolish sometimes," she said. "I grew up near a factory. My father works in the mills. We never had very much. My God, Frank, I played the bells in my high school marching band. We wore terribly short skirts and white boots with pompoms on them. When it was cold, my legs turned blue."

"We've all done things we regret," he said.

She shook her head, smiling.

"I ought to be mad at you," she said. "We're like Alphonse and Gaston in love."

At that point Nolan spilled his wine all over the front of his sweater. Remembering back on it now, he thought it was the only thing that had kept him from proposing marriage on the spot. She was able to take the stain out later with white wine and salt.

He did not know how he finally forced himself to decide. The memory of his mother's flight kept intervening, the possibility that he could set himself up again for loss. But somehow Laura overcame the fear. One evening he took her to dinner at a fancy restaurant. He could see that it was all she could do to contain her certainty of what was to come, and that made it even harder to begin. After dessert they had one more drink and he finally asked her to be his wife. And she simply said, "Of course."

Later that night when they made love, it dazzled him the way she opened herself to him. He had never been able to let himself go so completely, then or after. And lately, with his father's illness eating away at him and the question of children dividing them like nothing they had ever known, she had become the same way again in their bed. It frightened him the way she thrust up against him, her fingers beating bold rhythms on his back. He drew away from her. From the very beginning she seemed to want something beyond what he could give.

Before the wedding they had made a trip to Horace, where he hoped he might find out what that something was. They stayed with her parents in the simple little apartment where Laura had grown up. Her father nodded and smiled when they arrived. Her mother wept. They sat down to celebrate with a cup of coffee and some schnapps in the kitchen.

Her mother had insisted on an engagement photograph for the local paper even though the wedding was only a couple of weeks away. These were things folks expected, she had said.

That night they made the rounds of the kin. Nolan met and forgot the names of countless aunts, uncles, cousins, and men her father played poker with at the lodge. Several ladies allowed as how Nolan seemed too nice to be a lawyer. Several others asked for advice about their wills. The drink of the day was rye. Nobody got drunk, though it was not for lack of trying.

One of her uncles drew Nolan aside and asked him what he thought about big families.

"I like you all very much," Nolan said.

"She deserves a brood of her own," the uncle said. "I know that up to now you've had to fire blanks. But now you gotta let 'er rip."

The next morning Nolan awakened to the smell of coffee and at first felt disoriented, there alone in her room, which seemed as if it had gone unchanged since the day she went off to college. Books, a record player, a music stand, a pair of ballet slippers hanging from the wall. And dozens of beautiful dolls. Not the plastic kind that are supposed to be cute because they wet the bed or say some unintelligible word. Ablaze in bright costumes from around the world, these dolls were like something out of a museum.

"Sleep well?" asked Laura's mother when Nolan emerged into the kitchen.

"Fine," he said. "But I feel bad about dislocating everybody."

"We wouldn't have a guest sleeping on the couch," she said. "Laura's used to it. She's always given up her room for guests. How do you like your eggs?"

"Whatever's quickest for you."

She shook her head gravely. "If you ask me," she said, "you're too easy to please. Laura's going to take advantage of you if you don't watch out."

"She says you always gave her whatever she wanted," he said. "I couldn't help noticing all those dolls."

"Had plenty of everything," said her father with a note of satisfaction as he sat down to his coffee.

"You must have worked very hard for her," Nolan said.

"Would of spoiled her even worse, if I could."

"It doesn't seem to have done any harm," said Nolan. "She's become quite an artist. You should be proud."

"Ain't pride," said her father, lighting a battered old pipe. "Ain't pride so much as it is a feeling of ease."

Then the door opened and Laura came inside. She put a package of groceries on the table. She was dressed in an old jacket that she must have had since high school. It was odd how comfortable she looked in it.

"You seem quite rested," she said to Nolan.

"I was watched over by a thousand eyes," he said.

They kissed, and it was chaste and awkward and very sweet.

"Sometimes this man of yours talks like a cop," said her father, "and sometimes he's as fancy as a preacher."

"He's a little of both, Daddy," said Laura. "You get used to it after a while."

When they finished their breakfast, they borrowed the car and left for an appointment at the hairdresser. On the way she gave him a tour of Horace. First she took him to her high school, a big Depression-era brownstone. They got out and walked the playing fields behind it. Nolan had a hard time imagining her here. Pep rallies. Ball games. Those awful mixers.

"When did you start writing music?" he asked.

"Nobody paid much attention until I got to college. Then it was all right."

"It must have been hard for you."

"It was a wonderful time," she said. And he did not believe it for an instant.

Laura led him back to the car and they drove down a street without trees. Storefronts squatted along the sidewalks. Behind them the tall stacks of the factories rose and pumped out the soot that colored the air. The car banged over some railroad tracks. An old caboose on a siding had been turned into a sandwich stand.

Finally she spoke up over the dull, pneumatic thumping of the mills.

"I told you about Horace," she said.

"I kind of like it."

"Don't be patronizing."

"It's always a little sad, coming home."

"Horace hasn't changed."

"And you have changed so much."

"You're impossible," she said. "Here. Take the next right."

He wheeled around the corner onto a commercial street. There were stoplights every block and taverns at the intersections. When he stopped in front of a grocery store, a promenade of women crossed in front of the car. Even though they dressed in formless housedresses or bulging toreador pants, their hair was done up for a ball.

"Look," he said, pointing at a lady whose gray ringlets were like a thousand hoops of silver. "There's a sight." From the neck down she was as plain as a grandmother, but her hair rose like a billowing cloud. "Which style are you going to choose?" he asked.

She laughed.

"Tony used to fix me that way. He had me looking like Marie Antoinette for the prom, but he knows that now I like it cut plain. It's up here on the left. You don't have to come in if you don't want."

"I wouldn't miss it."

Nolan parked along the opposite curb. They crossed the street in the middle of the block. The front window of the shop was decorated in begonia pink and green. Inside it was warm and humid, and the windows ran with sweat. The waiting room was separated from the rest of the shop by a translucent partition like the ones at City Hall. It rose to within a couple of feet of the low ceiling, and a lace valance hung at the top. A cigarette burned unattended in an ashtray next to the cash register. The smell was sugar and smoke.

Nolan took off his coat and parked himself in a molded plastic chair. He lifted the magazines on the table next to him, but they weren't meant for him. On the shelves stood a wide range of pastel nostrums and balms. He did not even know what they were for.

A tall, skinny woman in a white smock came from behind the partition. She wore nurse's shoes.

"You just wait there a little minute, Mrs. Simka," she said over her shoulder. "I'll be back with you in a sec."

Oblivious of Nolan and Laura, she went to the cash register, took a package of slim cigarettes from the ledge, slid one out, and ignited it with a brightly colored lighter. Without exhaling, she took another long drag.

"Tired," she said.

Nolan nodded.

"Big night ahead," she said. "Heavy date."

A radio atop the shelves played a tune he could not name. The beautician took one more puff and rested the smoldering cigarette in the tray, then disappeared back behind the partition.

"I don't know whether I'm going to make it today, Mrs. Simka," she confided. "I'm so tired." The voice gave way to a yawn. "Did I ever tell you about Eddie? He's so sweet. You know him, don't you? He used to go with Doris Rochester, but she was no good for him. Too snooty."

The song changed. A lot of violins began to play. Everyone in the place fell silent.

"Oh, I want that louder," said the beautician, racing in and reaching up high to turn the knob. "Can you hear that now, Tony? It's your favorite."

Nolan recognized the tune. It was what they used to call a slow one, and when you danced to it, the girls would always hold on tight and you could feel their curves through the cloth.

"Theme from *A Summer Place*," said Laura.

"God, I love that song," said the beautician.

"It brings back memories," said Laura.

"Good ones?" asked Nolan.

"I remember wanting something. I didn't really know what."

The beautician vanished again. He could still hear her voice above the music.

"I was at this wedding reception last night. It was real nice, Mrs. Simka. Tom Porcelli and his quartet did the music. They had a real big dance floor. Eddie is a good dancer. I wore my satin dress. Have you ever seen it? I had to lower the hem just a little, but luckily when I raised it a few years ago I left the material in. I'm afraid we got a little carried away with the punch."

She yawned again, loudly. A spray can hissed, and a wave of sweetness wafted over the partition.

"All done," said the beautician.

She emerged with a thick little woman in her mid-fifties who wore her hair in tight, girlish curls. The woman pulled out a ten-dollar bill and the beautician gave her change.

"Will I see you again Friday?" she asked.

"You know I always make time for you when you need me, Mrs. Simka," said the beautician.

As the lady padded out, the beautician sprawled in a chair and lighted up again.

"Tired," she announced and began to inspect her nails.

Nolan heard movement deep in the shop. Then a heavily made-up blonde in her thirties came from behind the partition followed by a big, dark man in a white uniform shirt open to the middle of his chest. His arms were aswirl with black hair that did not quite hide two tattoos—an anchor and a heart. He winked at Laura. She blushed.

The man's hands were so big that Nolan was surprised he could work the little keys of the register. He whispered something in the ear of the blonde. She chirped and pulled out some bills.

"Tony, you're just awful," she said.

Then Tony finally spoke aloud. Nolan expected the giant's voice to bellow, but instead it came out as a tiny countertenor.

"We'll see you again soon," he peeped.

"My God," Nolan whispered to Laura. She shot him a silencing look.

Tony rang up the money and deposited it in the register. Then he turned to Laura.

"Little Laura," he said. "Little Laura all grown up."

"I came all the way home just to have a haircut from you," she said.

"That's sweet," Tony squeaked.

"How's your wife?" Laura asked as they went behind the partition.

"Fine. Fine," he said. "She'll be so excited to hear that you're in town. Could you stop by the house?"

Nolan strained to hear their conversation and caught snatches from the back of the store. She was talking about the wedding, her voice as excited as a schoolgirl's. He heard her confide about their living together, and that made him wince. Then Tony said something equally confiding in return, but Nolan couldn't make it out.

They went on and on, and Nolan was jealous of the intimacy. When the two of them emerged, Tony bounded toward Nolan with his hand out.

"Congratulations," he said, his voice going even higher. "You're a lucky man. The most beautiful girl in Horace."

"Thank you," said Nolan.

"Why thank me?" Tony said. "I don't have to do much when the material is this good."

Laura promised she would stop by Tony's house before they left, and then she accepted a big kiss on the cheek that made her giggle.

Outside in the cold again, she seemed to walk more lightly.

"In a way," she said, "he's my closest friend in town."

"Seems like a nice fellow," said Nolan.

"Of all the people in Horace, he was the only one who saw through me. To him the music and the honors in school weren't everything. He thought of me as a lonely little girl, and I love him for that."

"I won't let you be lonely again," Nolan said, believing it.

And he still believed it, even now. The distance between them would narrow again in time. They would work out the thing about children. He would find out where he stood and explain himself. He would make everything all right somehow.

He went back into the living room where Laura was waiting.

"I'm sorry about last night," he said. "There's been a lot on my mind."

"Your father," she said.

"Other things too."

"Work?"

"Today I watched a dirty movie," he said.

"Did it do any good?" she asked, but she was smiling and he did not have to hide.

"Afterward they sent me out on a murder. A little girl. Beaten and strangled. Maybe you heard about it on the news."

"The one they found in a garbage can?" she said. "It sounded terrible."

"They think they killed the guy who did it."

"You don't sound so sure," she said.

She came up next to him and put her hand on his arm.

"It shouldn't affect me as much as it does," he said. "I'm sorry."

"It's all right, Frank. Really."

They kissed, still lightly. And then they sat down next to each other on the couch. They were close enough to touch, if it came to that. And he felt the need stirring in him again, the willingness to risk her abandon. But not yet. They had to build something stronger between them first, made of simple elements, smaller truths.

"How was your day?" he asked.

"It was wonderful," she said, and she put her hand on his. "I worked all morning on your song. Then Carol Johnson came by and brought the little one. They named him Jonathan, and he's so cute, so tiny and red and innocent. He got tired and began to cry. Then he went to sleep in Carol's arms. It was beautiful, really."

"Laura," he said.

"I know," she said. "I'm sorry. But it made me so envious."

He moved his hand away and took a long breath.

She watched him for a moment, then stood up and went to the kitchen door.

"Let me make you a drink," she said.

TWO

CODES

8

*E*ver since the day they blew Hansen away, Jake Nolan hadn't been sleeping right. Any little thing would wake him up—the whine of a mosquito, a shift in wind that brought the stink of the paddies to his nose, the tremor of the earth as the 105s on the other side of Landing Zone Condor fired off a mission. His eyes would pop open in the humid darkness of the hootch, and he would remember the dream, the long, coiling series of letters and figures that bound him, a choking cipher that would not let him breathe.

He would climb off his cot, soaking with sweat, and run the thing over and over again in his mind, but the answer would not come. The code was beating him. He could not get relief.

First it had been Hansen, his body lashed to a pulp on the road to Binh Tho. The shell must have landed right on top of him to do that kind of damage. Then Tompkins had bought it right here in the compound. He'd been taking a dump when the first rounds landed, and the fool just sat there riding it out as the gunners zeroed in.

Shit, they were getting hammered and they didn't even know who the bastards were. The grunts in the hills around the perimeter reported hearing strange sounds in the darkness, eerie, distant laughter. But the ambush patrols that went out every day at dusk returned empty-handed at first light. They could not find a target.

The only thing anybody had to go on was the radio traffic they had intercepted at the LZ, and it was encrypted in a strong new code. The scale of the transmissions suggested a major unit, but which one? And most important, where? They were like devils. They killed and then vanished into the air. The bastards never stayed where you could get them in your sights. But if Jake could just read the signals that said where they were heading and when, then the jets could streak in and give back what

Hansen and Tompkins had gotten, could light the motherfuckers up like Christmas candles.

Jake looked at his watch, dial aglow, and saw that it was nearly dawn. He went to the small table at the far end of the room and switched on the little light. He had rigged it with a cardboard shade so that it did not shine on Whitelaw when he needed it in the night. It cut a tight, bright circle on the tabletop, and Jake pulled a fresh sheet of paper out of the drawer and wrote out a portion of the text from memory.

If it hadn't been for his aptitude, Jake would have been out in the bush with the grunts where he belonged. He was a natural fighter, born to raise hell. But at the induction station they had put everyone through a long battery of tests and Jake had idled away at the questions, just to pass the time. They were mindbenders like the riddles his father used to challenge them with when they were kids. He had always been best at them. Frank was too methodical to see the trick, and Ruth . . . well, Ruth just didn't care.

It was only after he had taken the oath that they told him. You ain't gonna go into the infantry, boy, they said. Uncle Sam's got other plans.

The only way out would have been to sign up to become an officer. But Jake wasn't interested. That was Frank's game, taking charge. So after basic they put him through the crypto school and then taught him the strange Asian language, hour after hour with the headphones on, speaking the foreign words. And when they finally sent him across the pond it was in a critical specialty. They did not even issue him a rifle.

So now he was stuck at LZ Condor, watching the others get greased, random rounds coming in without warning, and the only way he could fight back was to shatter the cipher and discover the enemy's true name.

Jake stood up from the table and went to the doorway of the hootch. Rain was just beginning to fall outside. The drops tapped on the roof and soaked into the green sandbags of the bunkers. Dawn was coming up gray as he stood there watching the clouds roll in over the hills where the grunts were dug in for the night. Lightning flashed, and behind it came the roar of thunder. Jake stepped outside.

The raindrops wet down his T-shirt and washed away the sweat. He stretched his neck back and let the water splash on the tight skin of his face. When he opened his eyes, he saw Spurgeon Whitelaw in the door of the hootch wearing only his olive underwear and boots.

"Come in out of the rain, Jake," Whitelaw said.

Water was collecting in little pools around Jake's feet. The sky lighted up again with a ferocious crack. A tree toppled over just outside the wire. Jake began to laugh.

"Aw hell, boy," said Whitelaw as lamps began to pop on here and there in the compound. "It's too damned early for this."

Jake lifted his arms and stood there. On his face was a manic grin, and from his fists the two middle fingers poked upward toward the sky. He twisted back and forth in that posture, like an antenna in the wind.

"OK, asshole," said Whitelaw, "you can come in now and dry up."

A spot opened in the clouds as the thunder marched off toward the sea. A bright shaft of light angled down to the jungled hilltop where the mortars might have been. Jake brought down his arms and slumped where he stood. Then he moved past Whitelaw into the hootch and, dripping, sat down on his cot.

"Woke up again, huh?" said Whitelaw.

"Same old shit."

"Look, when you do finally crack it, what do you think you're gonna have?"

"I don't know, Spurgeon. Suppose you tell me."

"It ain't gonna be General Giap."

"You never know."

"Gonna be some sorry-assed gook on the Trail complaining about his corns or the endless self-criticism of Sergeant Dong."

"I want him," said Jake. "I want the motherfucker dead."

"You want lots of things, boy," said Whitelaw. "You want everything you can't get. You want that slant-eyed bitch, but I ain't seen too much action there either."

"You don't see everything, Spurgeon."

That lady was from a different dream. But the way to escape it was the same. Whenever he got deep into a cipher, so deep that he lost all sense of place and drift, only then did he forget the other messages that beset him, the persistent, uncoded orders of fire and flesh.

"Ain't it some kind of shit?" said Whitelaw. "In a nation of hoors you picked yourself a woman of virtue."

Jake rose from the cot and started to pull off the wet clothes.

"Well, don't give up on her, old buddy," said Whitelaw. "They all become hoors eventually."

Everyone seemed to have advice for him on this subject. But for Jake it was ordinarily the easiest thing in the world. He had learned early how to see from a woman's eyes what she wanted. And he discovered that he could usually give it to her, or at least part of it, the part that came and went.

"It's not the end of the world, Jake," his father had told him once, speaking man to man. "Now I'm not saying that it's no better than a kick in the head. But it isn't something that will carry you either. You might as well live for a sneeze."

Jake remembered the way his father had talked about these matters, so earnest and wise. But that was after Jake's mother had run off and died. It was funny, really, what with Jake banging away at everything that moved and his father unable even to hang on to his own damned wife. Funny as hell.

Jake wasn't interested in guidance, then or now. He figured he knew pretty much all there was to know about women, except maybe why they'd run out, and that didn't matter now. He didn't plan to hang around anyone long enough to risk finding out. He just took what he could and then moved on.

But that was before he met Luong.

She worked in a shop in Binh Tho, a little shack made of castoff boards and uncut sheets of beercan tin, and as poor as she was, she lighted up the room. She was small and had a gentle voice, but it was her eyes that bewitched him. He looked into those animal eyes and thought he knew the hunger there. But to his astonishment, she turned aside all his advances and declined all his gifts. Day after day he would go to her. She would welcome him as if he wanted nothing but what she sold. And they would talk. Sometimes they spoke her language, sometimes his. Whenever he took the conversation in a dangerous direction, she simply said, "You must go now." And he did.

"Can't ever figure the broads out anyway," said Whitelaw as Jake hung his wet clothes over the edge of his cot to dry. "Roundeyes or slopes, they're all the same. What they want and what they don't."

But Jake just could not leave a mystery alone. He had to get behind the cipher and find out what was there. And the first step was to correct for randomness. The best way to confuse a man was to throw a meaningless jumble of letters into the text. You found yourself trying to detect a pattern in the empty figures. Her smiles, the yearning looks. You had to determine what made sense and what didn't, like the mortar round that killed Tompkins as he squeezed the last shit from his bowels. You could waste a lot of energy tracking garble.

"Fuck it," said Jake.

"Hey," said Whitelaw, snapping his fingers before Jake's eyes. "You didn't even like Tompkins."

The sun was out when Jake left Whitelaw and headed for the operations center. The ground had already dried. He made his way across a wide field strung with antenna wire. The mountains rose in the distance, dark with jungles. Midway across the yard, the company clerk caught up with him at a run.

"Major wants you on the double," said the clerk.

"On the double," said Jake. "You gotta be kidding."

"You're going home, asshole. It's something to do with your old man."

"Is he all right?"

"Beats hell outa me," said the clerk.

Jake took off. It was a moment he had feared and rehearsed for so long that he could not believe it was upon him now.

"Please have a seat, Specialist Nolan," said the major.

"The prick said it was my father."

Jake remained standing. A powerful hand had hold of his chest, and it was squeezing.

"The Red Cross has informed us that your father is hospitalized in intensive care. Your family has asked that you be allowed to return home. The Red Cross concurs. I have cut orders for a thirty-day leave."

"Is he dead yet?"

"I'm sorry," said the major. "They didn't give us very much to go on. I did have . . . I had the impression he was dying."

"He's always been dying."

"I'm sorry."

When Jake returned to the hootch, Whitelaw was still there, fiddling with his footlocker.

"You look like you just lost your best buddy," he said.

"My father."

"Say again."

"I just lost my father."

"Oh, sweet Jesus," said Whitelaw.

"I'm going home."

"Anything I can do?"

"Not you," said Jake.

He walked to the main gate of the compound and used his friendship with the MPs as a pass. He hurried to Binh Tho, but Luong was not there in the store. The mama-san said she was in the next village and would return soon. So Jake went to the edge of town, found a stone highway marker, and sat down to wait.

They had never talked about their pasts. She preferred to describe the delicacy of a tropical flower or the way the clouds made mountains in the sky. He spoke of people at the LZ, the foolish things the officers did, his anger. But now, suddenly, he wanted to tell her about his father, all the eccentricities, the man's pure genius for loving children.

Jake's father could collect more helpers than any other parent in the neighborhood. He was always fixing things, or trying to. He'd rewire the toaster, explaining every shortcut and shunt to the kids crowding around him, and when he plugged it in, it incinerated the bread. Once he tried to fix the clutch on their car. When he was done, it would not go into reverse. To get the thing out of the driveway come morning, he had to recruit a crew of boys. They were always there when the time came.

One day Ruth was baby-sitting some little children in their front room as his father was trying to work on his taxes in the kitchen. The children were making a lot of noise. Jake watched his father scribbling at the table and thought this time he would finally lose his temper. But it didn't happen that way. He got up from the table calmly and went to the big upright FM radio in the livingroom. He turned it on and the music was Beethoven.

"Loud," he said, turning the volume up to catch the children's attention.

The children looked and giggled.

"Loud!" he said, notching the volume higher.

"Loud!" they answered in delight.

"LOUD!" he roared over the deafening music.

"LOUD!" the children screamed with all their little voices.

Then a grin spread over his stubbly face and he began to turn the volume back down.

"Softer," he said, hushing. "Softer."

And the children, of course, dropped their voices, too.

"Shshshshsh," he said. "Softer."

And they whispered it ever so quietly and moved closer to the radio so they could hear the sound.

"Very, very soft," he said.

And quite remarkably, they said "shshshshshsh" like two tiny leaking valves and sat raptly, seeing who could make the very least noise.

Jake looked up the highway. A few old mama-sans bobbed along under their yokes and trays. Not far away a boy walked with a water buffalo.

The stone marker was getting uncomfortable, so Jake slid down to the dust. He glanced at the worn words painted on the sign. "Phuoc Loc 8k." Eight klicks. Sometimes the rockets came in from near Phuoc Loc. And it was not far from here that they had blown Hansen away.

The sun was fire, and Jake had grown wings of sweat. He could not focus right. The glare made it like looking through a flame. Then he saw her, an apparition in the distance.

He stood up and walked toward her. She quickened her pace. When they met, he took some of the packages she was carrying and asked if they might talk, this time away from her shop, alone.

"My father has died," he said. He did not mean it as a lie.

"I am sorry," she said, but she did not lower her eyes.

"Look," he said as she led him to her hootch, "a man can live on. There are ways."

"Many different ways," she said. They spoke in her language now. "For you there is life after death."

"My father never believed in that."

They reached her hootch and she led him inside.

"For us there is a sort of life in the worship of our ancestors," she said. "We pray to them, but they do not answer. We pray to them because it gives them life."

"I want a son," he said softly in his own language. It shamed him that the words were so flat, so frail. "I want you to have my son."

He could not read her expression. He hurried on.

"It is not for the pleasure," he said. "I have known the pleasure with others, and that is not what matters to me now."

She turned and began to arrange her packages on the mat.

"It is for the future," he said. "I would have you chastely if I could."

She laughed.

"You do not believe me," he said.

"I do not believe it is possible to have a son chastely," she said.

"You do not think I am serious. I want you to marry me." Then he used her words again. "I love you," he said.

"It is only because I am here," she said, moving to a corner of the hootch and holding the distance there. "Because I am here and because I resist you."

"I would love you anywhere," he said. "I would love you even if you resisted me less."

"You must understand," she said. "It is from a kind of love that I refuse you—a kind of love and a kind of shame."

"It is because I am an American."

She turned toward him then, and her eyes were soft and pleading.

"I do not want you to hate me," she said and then she paused. "I will tell you what no one else here knows. Then you will understand and go away. You will never return to me."

She told it as if it were a very old tale. Once upon a time, she said, she had been a girl in a part of the country where there were no mountains. Her father had been very rich and had sent her to France to study. Each time she returned, the fighting had gotten worse. A loyal man and a landowner, her father had hated the guerrillas and what they stood for more than he hated the French or the Americans. She did not feel strongly herself, though, because Paris was a cosmopolitan city, and the school put the children of both sides into classrooms together and made no distinctions. The French were by that time very wise and progressive about these matters, having lost.

When her brother died in combat, Luong returned home to stay. Her father's holdings were on an island in a river. It was a fertile place, bathed in floodwaters before the planting season. There was plentiful rice. Silkworms lived in the mulberries. The breeze smelled of flowers. But what made their property beautiful also made it vulnerable to the guerrillas, and the government decided that the only way to protect such places was to move the people away.

It was almost harvest time when the government soldiers arrived to tell them. The peasants were gathered on a large, covered platform her father had built near their house. To the peasants, leaving the graves of their ancestors was a sin against the past. To her father, it meant ruin. He had grown too old to hope of rebuilding his wealth elsewhere. The soldiers said the trucks would come at dawn. Each person could bring only what he could carry. Meantime, the soldiers camped nearby for the night.

That evening she went to try to reason with them. The soldiers were led by a young and handsome officer. He was courteous at first, the way they said the Germans had been when they first occupied Paris. He explained that it was not a matter for his decision. Was there nothing she could offer them to make them go away? she asked. One of the soldiers began to laugh. He was stripped to the waist, and the red light of the cooking fire flared against his scarred, amber skin. The officer stood and spoke. He might be able to give them a few more days, he said. But that would require an inducement from a very pretty woman. She was not shocked. She had heard of such things many times before. She turned to leave.

The half-naked man leaped up and stopped her. You must not insult the lieutenant, he spat. The lieutenant is a powerful man. She replied: "He has shown his manliness." The officer approached and simply said, "Hold her."

He cut Luong's clothes away with his bayonet and raped her standing. The others watched and then each had his turn. After it was over, she lay bleeding near the fire, and she prayed that she would be shot. But the officer merely poked her in the belly with the toe of his boot and told her to go home.

She did not tell her father, for women are meant to bear the shame. In the morning they were loaded into the trucks. The officer put his hand on her breast as she climbed in. She did not have the strength to push him away.

Jake stopped her by putting his finger to her lips.

"With me you could recover," he said. "With me you could remember gentleness again."

But there was more to tell. She stepped back away from him and continued.

One of the men who had her that night had left her with a child. She wept when by her body's signs she knew it. Finally, she had to tell her father. He sat impassively as she revealed that even this last corner of his wealth had been plundered. The next day he took her to a hospital. It was there that the doctors discovered that in addition to the child she had conceived, she had received infected seed. It was a strain the local doctors did not know how to cure. They aborted the child, who would have been born to suffering and disfigurement. They also destroyed within her the means ever to bear children again.

The disease is dormant, she said, but never to be healed. The thing he wanted of her was impossible.

Jake remembered the lifers' warnings about "black syph," a venereal disease so terrible that if you got it, they wouldn't let you go home. He had never believed it before, any more than he had believed the stories they told about the VC women who put razor blades up inside them to dismember any dumb grunt foolish enough to let himself be seduced. But he did not think Luong was lying now. The calmness of her voice transfixed him, took away his power of speech.

"Please do not say anything," she said, and he knew that she must have taken his silence for disgrace. "Please go and do not come back. It is important that you know these things, but we must never speak of them again. I envy the woman who will bear your son."

A small wind lifted the dust as he walked back to the LZ. He sat all afternoon in the hootch alone, and the others respected his silence, thinking it was grief. By nightfall a new idea had grown in him. It spread and rooted itself. There would be no son. He returned to her hootch in the darkness.

"I want you," he said.

"You must not," she said. "You mock yourself, your father's death."

"For a moment you were my hope," he said, "and now it is different. But I need you still, the way a man can need the truth."

"I will not allow you to be hurt," she said.

"I will be safe," he said, and then he showed her the moist, ugly sheath he said would protect him.

"It would be so barren," she said.

"Then you agree."

He closed the door. She stood slowly in the light of the gas lantern. When she went to turn it off, he stopped her. She began to remove her clothes. The light played upon her high, infected breasts and the dark, corrupt, and futile mound beneath. When she was all revealed, she rolled out the sleeping mat. He began to undress himself, but she wanted to serve him this night. She slowly caressed him naked and then drew him down to her.

He turned off the lantern, and the darkness made the room infinite. They lay together on a horizonless plain. She moved with the pleasure of him but made no sound, for a woman is to be silent. He rose up in an unimaginable tension. Then he finally burst, releasing the anathema of his love within her and receiving, in a white rush of silence, all her joy and her aspersion.

When it was over and they breathed together in darkness, Jake felt the ground with his fingers to find and hide the protective sheath that lay somewhere near the mat, empty and unused.

9

*H*e made it easy on Laura by getting up before dawn and slipping out quietly. Still, when he touched her shoulder as he left the bed, he could tell that she was only pretending to be asleep. He could not blame her for turning away from him in the morning just as he had turned from her the night before.

It could have been just fine if he had let it be: the song she had written, all the ways she tried to reach him. She had been so careful and indirect. And yet he had felt as tightly strung as if he were on trial. He had gone out of his way to sharpen the edge that divided them, to cut her short. And all she had wanted was to make love.

Lord, she had even tried to tell him it would be safe, even though she had always found it awkward to talk about the measures she took. The mechanics put her off, the business of hydraulics and blockage. She made her preparations in secret so they both could pretend that there was no barrier between them. She used a diaphragm for fear of the risks of the pill, and long ago he had told her that it was all right for him if it was all right for her. He had told her he could not tell the difference. But, of course, he could.

She must have believed him about not being able to feel whether it was in or out. She must have thought he was afraid she would trick him by leaving the ugly rubber membrane in her drawer when her fertile time had come. It must have been terrible for her to feel the need to promise what she did, as if he thought her capable of a betrayal so deep. But that wasn't what he feared. Why couldn't he find the words to tell her that he trusted her?

It was himself that he did not trust, the feelings she summoned up in him when they lay together. He did not know whether once they began he would have the strength to keep from yielding to her need, because

maybe he wanted the same thing she did, and maybe it was wrong. And
so he had sat in strained silence before the television set and drunk wine
until his feelings grew dull. And when it was time and she gently touched
him with outstretched fingers, he turned away. He had to discipline
himself to lie as still as death because, though he could not see her or hear
a sound, he could tell by the movement of the bed that she was crying and
refusing to let it show.

So when he awakened in the darkness before dawn after a short and
fitful sleep and put his hand on her shoulder and she did not acknowledge
it, he understood.

The rain had grown heavy by the time he reached the courthouse. The air
was cold. It seeped through the window frames and swept down the halls.
Nolan sat at his desk warming his hands on a cup of coffee as the draft
stirred loose pages that strayed out of the file jackets on his desk. Nothing
but prostitutes. Somebody had picked up the Tatum papers already. They
didn't waste any time.

O'Neill stuck his head inside the cubicle.

"In early," he said.

"Couldn't sleep."

"Thinking about all those hookers, I imagine," said O'Neill. "Got to
put your nose back to the old rhinestone."

Nolan did not even give him the satisfaction of a frown. "What about
the little girl?" he said.

"I want Talley in court with you today. Let him go through the docket,
but watch him, OK? He's a little green."

"He can handle himself."

"Forget about the Tatum girl, Frank. I'm putting Sammy Czerny
on it."

"Czerny? For Chrissake, Terry."

"It's on a fast track. We're going to wrap it up quick. They've already
scheduled the inquests and the shooting board. It'll be over before you
know it."

"There are a few things I want to follow up on," said Nolan.

"Your brother's coming in when?"

"Tomorrow. But I'll have time."

"Inquests are tomorrow."

"Sammy's a water-carrier, Terry."

"Don't worry about it. You've got enough on your mind."

"Pricer's going to raise hell if we kiss this off."

"Mr. Pricer is satisfied," said O'Neill.

"How could he be?"

"He is a sophisticated man, Frank. He understands the risks."

"Risks?"

"The loss of privacy. The attention it would focus on his daughter. I guess she's taking this very badly."

"Maybe I'd better talk to him again."

"I wouldn't if I were you," said O'Neill. "He's made up his mind."

"I'm not afraid of him," said Nolan.

"He's a strong man, Frank. The cream always rises to the top."

Nolan leaned forward in his chair.

"So does the grease," he said.

O'Neill moved around the desk and laid his hand on Nolan's shoulder. "What did the doctor tell you?" he asked.

"More of the same."

"You need some time, Frank? Take some time."

"There's nothing to do right now," said Nolan. He looked down at his hands, and they were as numb as separate beings. "They say the disease might be hereditary. I could pass it on to my child."

"Laura's pregnant?" O'Neill did not even try to hide his delight. "You didn't tell me."

"She's not, Terry. But she wants to be."

"Nobody asked me, but if they did I'd tell them you'd make a hell of a father."

"I'm not sure."

"Laura isn't having second thoughts, is she?"

"I haven't told her about it," said Nolan. "Not until I know something for sure."

"Hell, Frank, you aren't breeding horses."

"You haven't seen him," said Nolan. "He's younger than you are and he's down for the count. The doctors say it can come on much earlier. And I'm worried about Ruth, the way she's been behaving. They're telling me that the only way to prevent this disease is to keep from having kids."

"What the hell do they know? Look, my old man died when I was in high school. I don't know what the hell it was. Don't want to know. And I'll tell you something. My kids are fine. And me?" He slapped himself on the belly. "I'm gonna live until I die. And the hell with it."

When O'Neill left, Nolan sat staring at the blank smoked glass that enclosed him. If it had only been the disease, then maybe it would be as

easy as O'Neill said. But it was more than that. The disease was just a
name to put on a whole universe of reasons, and they all came down to
this: he did not know whether he had the strength. The words the doctor
gave him—ataxia, autosomal dominant—they were only the summation
of a wrong. The age of ice and flood that he had prepared for as a child
was upon him, and there was no way to escape.

Yet there was another feeling, too; it tore at Nolan, testing all his
resolve. At times he wanted to believe in it as deeply as Laura did. And
if he had to put a word to this yearning, it would have been his father's
name.

Sam Nolan had been, for as long as his son could remember, the very
scourge of illusion. He faced things plainly and never flinched. When
Sam Nolan read about the time of ice, he did not shiver. Even in his
extremity, he found the breath to talk of grandchildren. He was a man
who was at home in the cold.

But not everyone had it in him to go Sam Nolan's way. Frank's mother
did not, and more than anything else, this was why she had left them. She
had tried to find comfort in religion, but Sam Nolan challenged every
promise she wanted to believe in, riddled the books she read, the prayers
she gave at the dinner table, the rituals she wanted her children to share.
It had been painful to watch, even though her daughter and sons had
already accepted their father's lessons and would have sided with him
comfortably against anyone else. Still she persisted, until one day she'd
had enough.

Frank remembered how it had happened. The night before she left she
had been weeping. He heard them arguing through his bedroom wall. His
father did not say much. Frank could not make out the words, but he was
frightened by the tone that had crept into her voice.

The next day when he got home from school she was gone. Ruth told
him about the way she had packed up her books, and he called around
after her. But she wasn't at the church, and none of her friends knew a
thing. When their father got home, he had an explanation. He said she
had left them for good. She wasn't coming back.

"It's me she's running away from," he said, as if this were a
consolation.

Ruth cried and Frank held himself in check. Their father told them not
to worry because they would be able to visit her soon, once the details
were all straightened out and she was settled. But they never saw her
again. On the second day of her trip her car ran head-on into a truck. At

the funeral they had not even opened the coffin, and Frank had to whisper his goodbye to her through the steel.

He could not be sure what had happened. The highway police said she had been in the oncoming lane. She must have been lost, because the road she was on led nowhere. Ruth made up her mind that their mother was on her way back home when it happened, that she had fallen asleep, driving all night so as not to lose another precious hour. From the way the police talked about it, Frank gathered that they thought she had aimed the car into the high headlights of the semi and held it steady there until the crash. He assumed that his father recognized this, too. But at least he did not feel obliged to correct Ruth's version. This time his father just let it go.

Nolan tapped his fingers on the stack of files. It gave way like the springs of an old bed. He leaned back in his chair and was suddenly very tired. He had always in the past been able to count on his stamina. He had always prided himself on being fit for the long pull. But now he no longer had any confidence in wind or time.

"Talley!" he shouted at a shadow passing near his cubicle.

"You OK?"

"I've got an idea."

"What's that?"

"Talley, today I'm gonna make you a prosecutor."

Nolan's open hand slapped the curling top cover on the stack of files.

"Whores?"

"You're gonna make them wish they'd been born boys."

And with that he lifted the stack and hefted it into Talley's arms.

"You'd better hurry," Nolan said. "You're already late."

"Give me a quick fill on the way up."

"No way, Talley," said Nolan. "You're on your own."

"What are you going to do?"

"I've got business with Sam Czerny," said Nolan.

"That case is over," said Talley.

"It is with Sammy on it."

"What are you trying to prove, Frank?"

"Maybe that I can still go the distance."

Czerny's office was in a high corner of the building, out of the way. You could tell as soon as you walked in exactly what the man was all about. On the wall behind him was his late father's picture, a committeeman the mayor had been forced to dump. The mayor's picture was up there, too, because when Sammy's father died without leaving him a patrimony, the mayor had stepped in to take care of him. The Boss understood that Sammy's talents ran to acceptance of what was given, so he put him in the Criminal Courts Building where he could draw a salary, do no harm, and maybe even once in a while come in handy for some odd job or another.

They kept him upstairs under the eaves, using him only when the thing was already in the bag and they wanted to make sure the bag got to its destination with no questions asked. When Nolan stepped inside the door, Czerny was sitting behind his empty desk working the crosswords in the morning tabloid. He stood up, beaming, and stuck out his hand. Nolan shook it as if he were a visitor from out of state.

"What's the occasion, Frank?" he said, surreptitiously slipping the puzzle into the drawer. "You been on vacation? I haven't seen you around."

"I'm here to ask you for some help."

"Jeez," said Czerny, "I'd be glad to give you a hand, but Terry O'Neill just put me on this case this morning. It's a murder. Fast track. Wait, you were on this one yourself, weren't you? I think Terry mentioned your name. A little girl named Tatum. You remember it?"

"Like it was yesterday, Sammy."

Czerny pulled out a stack of papers from another drawer, fiddled with them, and then looked up sheepishly.

"It was yesterday, I guess, wasn't it," he said. "I've been kind of busy, and I haven't had a chance to go through the file the way I should."

"I stopped by to see if anything came in overnight."

"Well," said Czerny, scrambling through the papers, "as I said, I'm just now beginning my review."

"Maybe I can give you a hand."

"Actually," said Czerny, slouching back in his chair, "I don't think there's too much for either of us to do. O'Neill said they killed the guy who did the murder. A couple of inquests and a shooting board. That's the extent of it. I guess I'm just there to watch."

"You see anything interesting in the case, Sammy?"

"It's been a long time since I had a real one."

"You looked at the file at all?"

"Glanced at it," Czerny said, and then he laughed. "Not carefully enough to remember that you were there."

"Anything strike you?"

"I don't know, Frank. It looks tight to me."

"But you did notice something."

"What's the use?"

"If nothing else, just for the exercise."

"I'm not sure."

"What did you see, Sammy?"

"Well," said Czerny, handing Nolan a single sheet. "That came in the morning."

"And?"

"The bum was a junkie," said Czerny.

Nolan looked at the words on the page, but he did not read them. He did not need to. He had seen tracks on Williams's arms as he lay dead on the floor.

"So he was," said Nolan. "So he was."

"It don't make sense," said Czerny, "a doper molesting a child."

"No it doesn't."

"But it probably didn't mean nothing."

"What does, Sammy? What the hell does?"

10

*R*uth had never kept a diary as a girl. She was not comfortable risking her privacy in a house full of curious men. But now when she sat before the microphone in her father's study, she found the feelings pouring out of her, confession and celebration, unashamed. Begun as history, the tapes had become a kind of therapy.

"I think it's time to make a proper introduction of Jake," she said, turning a curl at her temple on her finger as the little wheels spun silently before her. "He's on his way home, and that means we're in for quite a ride. Don't get me wrong. All of us are excited about seeing him again. And it ought to be a real tonic for Dad. He has always had a lot of faith that Jake would eventually make his peace. If you want to know a secret, I never believed that he was such a hard case to begin with. Oh, he kept you guessing, all right. Sometimes he'd make you wonder whether he had any kindness in him at all. But even Jake couldn't hide it all the time.

"He had his reasons, of course. It couldn't have been easy following Frank, all the expectations he created. So Jake simply flouted them. And even when you understood what he was doing, he could make life in this house absolutely miserable at times.

"Lord, he was a prize, all right. He was the one who brought all the bad words home first, the one who found out the whole sloppy truth about how babies are made. My mother caught him explaining it to me one day, demonstrating by pumping the finger of one hand through the circle he made with the fingers of his other. There was no mistaking what had my rapt attention, and I thought my mother might faint when she saw it.

"My father often found himself having to defend him against her. That always annoyed Jake. The Lone Ranger, my father called him. 'Who was that masked man?' he would say when Jake swept into the house and holed up somewhere alone."

Ruth paused. She wanted to go on, but she wondered whether she ought to. What would they think of her, years from now, when they came upon this record of her adolescent follies? If they were really Nolans, she suspected they might smile.

"Thanks to Jake," she said, smiling herself, "I had a rather advanced idea about some of the more clinical details, at least in the abstract. Sometimes when everyone was out of the house I would sneak into his room and pull out his men's magazines to compare myself with the ladies in the pictures. I won't kid you; I didn't stack up very well. I'd open the centerfold and put it next to the mirror, then step down and strike an awkward profile. No matter how far backward I leaned or how much I was able to push up my breasts with my palms, it was always a real disappointment. In those days the pictures didn't show the lower parts, and that was a shame because it might have been easier to find a flattering comparison down there where the differences are subtler, flower to flower.

"Not that I was promiscuous, you understand. Sure, I read the stories in the magazines and got a certain amount of guilty pleasure from them. But maybe I had enough of my mother in me to worry about getting pregnant. Until the pill came along, I was very strict with the boys. Drawing lines: this far and no farther. The most they got was what the camera got, no more. I only opened my knees to the mirror, and wondered, wondered, wondered.

"Of course, this came as something of a shock to some of the boys who asked me out. You see, Jake had left quite a reputation, and by the time I got to high school the name Nolan carried with it certain connotations that I had to overcome. When I was a freshman in high school, I used to hear the older ones talking about him in a tone that was equal parts loathing and longing: he would, I couldn't, I wish.

"But I always thought that down deep Jake was as confused as Mother was. In the cosmic sense. He wanted to believe in something beyond himself, too. He really did. But what, I can't really say. And maybe Jake couldn't either.

"I hope he's found it, though. You see, I've always counted on him to let me in on the important secrets. Just relax and enjoy it, kid. That's what I want him to tell me now."

11

*T*he solution to the cipher came to Jake in one great rush. He worked all night and into the morning tricking out the words. When he finished, he took the text to the Tactical Operations Center. The officer in charge understood the implications immediately and sent for the colonel. Meantime, Jake went to the huge laminated map that hung on the wall and found the grid squares that marked the area where the killer unit stalked.

"Aren't you supposed to be catching a chopper?" said the colonel.

"There," said Jake, his finger tapping on the clear plastic. "Right there."

"They move pretty fast," said the colonel.

"The last transmission was this morning," said Jake. "They don't operate in the light. We're working in real time here."

"It's all real, son."

"I know what I'm talking about," said Jake. "Waste the motherfuckers."

The colonel got on the horn, and Jake went to the hootch to gather up his things. He didn't have any more than he could fit in a little AWOL bag, so it didn't take long.

"Here comes the bird," said Spurgeon Whitelaw.

Jake could hear the thumping of the rotors in the distance. He went to the door.

"Stay out of trouble, boy," said Whitelaw. "Don't do anything I wouldn't do."

"That covers a lot of ground."

"We want your ass back here in one piece."

"Better worry about your own, Spurgeon."

"Count on it," said Whitelaw, and he grabbed himself around the tail and hung on tight.

Then the chopper touched down in the yard, kicking up great swirls of debris. Jake went outside.

"So long, Spurgeon!" he shouted.

Whitelaw gave him a thumbs up, then turned his back against the wind. Jake hunched down and ran into it, the grit blasting his face. When he climbed inside, it was like the eye of a storm. The crew chief motioned him into a sling chair and had him buckle up.

"Fuck it," said Jake. The crew chief smiled, and the chopper swayed as the pilot got it light on its skids. Then the big machine rose up over the TOC and headquarters building, over the wire. Suddenly Jake saw the jets streaking in from the east. Three of them. Phantoms. Going like a dream of hell. They dove toward the hillside. The jungles erupted in magnificent fire.

"Get some," whispered Jake.

He could see the places he had pinpointed. The jets dove again, right on. But by this time the chopper had put some distance between itself and the hills. It plodded toward the coast, where it would turn south toward Da Nang. And when the explosions came they were just little twinkles in the green.

"The bastards," Jake said, but he was not satisfied. The fire was too far away.

When he reached the World, he was tired and disoriented. But when they let him loose in Oakland and he found out the first plane back to Chicago did not leave until after midnight, he hopped into a taxi and told the man he was looking for action.

"Professional or amateur?" asked the hack.

"I'm not interested in a whore."

"Suit yourself, pal. I got just the place for you. You can have anything you want. Broads, dope, guys. Whatever. Let me give you a tip, though. The hippy chicks'll put out like crazy for you if you just say your lines."

"What's that supposed to mean?"

"Tell them about peace. It'll knock 'em over, coming from a stud in uniform."

But Jake wasn't out to get laid. He wasn't exactly sure what he wanted. He just needed to finish something he had started, something cut short. The hard cipher of his father dying. Finding the enemy and lighting him up.

Something. And when the driver pulled up at a joint called the Stoned Balloon, he had a strong feeling that he had found what he was looking for.

It was a dump, with old wooden tables and a banged-up bar. The music was loud and the lights as nervous as flares on the perimeter. Oh yes, he thought. This is the place.

He had one beer, then another. The bartender did not look like the kind who'd be interested in war stories. He was a big man with a bushy beard and a single earring that winked in the light. But he didn't give Jake any lip, and when Jake made a crack about the jewel, the man just moved on down the bar.

It was beginning to look as though Jake was going to be disappointed when suddenly a woman appeared on the stool beside him and started giving him the eye. She was either drunk or spaced out on something strong, and she wore a blue T-shirt that showed the tips of her breasts.

"What do you think *you're* looking at?" she said.

"Your chest," he said.

"Don't get any ideas."

"They tell me that the way to score is to say how sorry I am about the war."

"You're a smart one."

Jake gestured with the glass and the bartender came over.

"Trouble is," Jake went on, "I kind of get a kick out of it, you know? The war, I mean. Seeing the arms and legs fly."

"Outasight," said the woman, trying to make it look like disgust.

"We don't want no trouble," said the sweet bartender.

"I'm basically a peaceable guy," said Jake, as he pushed a bill across the slick counter and left the change. "One for the lady, too."

"I don't take drinks from killers," she said.

Jake had to laugh out loud.

"I only regret," he said, "that I have but one cock to stick to the dinks."

And as he watched the woman take this in and then turn to show her distress to the rest of the room, he was only really sorry for what Luong would think if she knew. He imagined her eyes pleading with him not to take the thing to the end, but it was too late now. He had a need, that's all. And despite her, or because of the emptiness they had finally shared, he was pleased when a fair Lancelot in shoulder-length hair and a work shirt interceded.

"What did you say to her?" asked Lancelot.

He was not too big and not all that steady on his pins. Jake looked up at him from the stool, then he turned back to his beer.

"I asked you a question."

"She yours?" Jake said.

"Maybe," said Lancelot.

"Nice tits."

He turned away from the guy again and felt a hand on his shoulder. It was not enough to hold him, just a way of moving things forward.

"Fuck off, little hero," said Jake, because there was no use in dragging these things out.

Lancelot swung. Jake blocked it easily. He saw an opening, straight to the guy's jaw. But then something happened. Jake checked his punch and let it drift into Lancelot's shoulder. The woman screamed. Lancelot took a second shot, and Jake hardly moved. It clipped his cheek and opened a gusher inside his mouth. He spat blood onto the floor.

Then somebody grabbed him from the back, and Lancelot got in two brave, inconclusive swings before someone took charge of him, too.

"I told you no trouble," said the bartender. "Out of here or I'll call the cops."

Jake did not have to waste his own energy leaving. The patrons of the Stoned Balloon joined together to give him the bum's rush.

When he was on the airplane, nursing his cuts and bruises and testing the stiffness of his ankle, he wondered why he had let Lancelot off so easily. Luong would have had an explanation. The hands of dead ancestors stayed your hands. But the only ancestor who counted was still alive, as far as Jake knew. No, he had simply not been satisfied until he had taken his hits. Then the anger had subsided, the need replaced by a pain you could touch with your fingers. Luong, I am sorry. The ancestors can get you all fucked up sometimes.

But it wasn't only his father. It was Luong herself, what they had done together. He expected the symptoms of her disease to show up in him anytime now. You are a fool, Jake, she would have said. You made me hurt you when all I wanted was to give you comfort. But wait, Luong, wait. We made a communion. We reached the rotten center of things. She would simply have shaken her head and grieved.

And then there was Frank, the great Galahad. Jake did not look forward to meeting him at the airport. Not with a bruise blooming on his cheek and the drip about to come on any minute. You're a mess, Frank would say. Or at least he'd think it. Frank always had an opinion.

When they were boys they shared a room. Frank kept his side neat: bed made to bounce a quarter on, shoes and slippers squared away under the bureau, Scout merit badges on a carefully hung sash. On Jake's side, the walls were draped with ghoulish posters, photos of the Bomb going off. His clothes were heaped in piles, his drawers half-opened. Stuff that had collected in his pockets cluttered every surface—loose change, paper clips, wrappers, buttons, and pebbles picked up off the street. It annoyed Frank. Jake could always count on that.

"I'll clean up for you just this once, Jake."

"You'd better not."

"Cooties grow in this junk."

"Cooties are my friends."

He often let Jake have the last word, but it was never as satisfying as it should have been because Frank would simply walk away. He was like a ceramic figure on the shelf, so damned perfect, as cold and brittle as ice.

Jake remembered the time his brother came back from college for the high school homecoming. Ruth was only a freshman then, just beginning to get pretty, filling out. Older boys hovered around the house day and night. Somebody was always calling her on the phone.

Her best friend was an upperclassman named Sue who wore a hearing aid and spoke oddly. They spent hours together every day, going over homework, telling secrets, doing each other's hair. Some of the boys Ruth dated agreed to take Sue along to the movies or the drive-in for a Coke and fries. Jake would see them from time to time waiting in line at a theater or lolling in the halls at school, the boys trying to disregard Sue's presence and Ruth drawing her firmly in.

When everyone started lining up dates for the homecoming dance, Ruth took Jake aside and asked him if he was going to go.

"You kidding?" he said.

"Why not?"

"Got better ideas."

"I thought maybe you might ask Sue. She kind of likes you, you know."

"Give me a break."

"She'd be good for you. Better than those others."

"They know what I want."

"Do you?"

After a few days Ruth gave up on him and called long-distance to the university. Their father said he could squeeze out the money for the plane if Frank wanted to come home. And to everyone's surprise, Frank agreed.

During the last few days before he arrived, Ruth could talk of nothing else. The preparations were an agony. She dragged their father out to buy a new dress and help Sue choose hers. She went through the house, cleaning it, rearranging the furniture, making sure everything was different from the way it ought to be. One day Jake came home to find that she had gone over his side of the room, folding up clothes, hiding his cycle paraphernalia in the closet, cleaning ashtrays, polishing wood. In one drawer she had even lined up all the cigarette packs in a neat little row. He took them out again and scattered them around.

The morning she and her father went to the airport to pick Frank up, she prevailed upon Jake to get Sue's corsage. The parade and game were that afternoon, the dance in the evening, so nobody else had any time to stop by the florist. Jake said he had things to do, too. But his father pressed him, and he finally gave in.

She had picked out an orchid, just the right shade of purple to complement Sue's dress. It would be so beautiful, she said, but make sure the florist gives you the right one. She handed him a little swatch of dress material just to make sure. And he stuffed it in his hip pocket along with his dirty handkerchief.

After they had left, Jake put on his leathers and hauled his cycle out of the garage. The engine roared as Jake raced around the back roads before finally settling down to the errand. When he reached the shop he pulled the chopper back on its stand and began to tighten a greasy bolt.

"Hey, Jake."

Jake turned and saw Chicken Karlson in boots and a black jacket, bounding across the street.

"Hear you're getting it off Judy these days," said the Chicken.

"That so?"

"You giving her flowers? That how you get her to come across?"

"It's for my sister."

"Flowers for your sister. What a good boy."

"Fuck off, Chicken," said Jake, rising off his haunches. The Chicken backed away.

"Maybe you're going to homecoming," he taunted, from a careful distance. "Maybe you're pussy-whipped."

"We're cruising tonight," said Jake.

"What time?"

"I told her I'd pick her up at eight."

"Meet you at the Dog 'n' Suds," said Chicken. "Maybe a little of Judy's hots will turn up the fire in my bitch."

"Don't count on it," said Jake as the Chicken strutted away.

The florist's shop was steamy and sweet. The glass-doored case was stacked with little boxes tied with ribbons.

"Lessee," said the balding old guy who ran the place. "Nolan. Nolan. Nolan." He tapped each box in turn until he came to the right one. "You're Frank Nolan."

"Jake. I'm picking it up for my brother."

The little man untied the ribbon, opened the box, and showed Jake the frail little flower.

"That's all right," said Jake, and he pulled out his money. The swatch of cloth came out with the bills, and he wadded it back into his pants.

"I have a few left," said the little man, "if you want one for your girl, too."

"She doesn't go in for flowers."

"You might be surprised."

Jake leaned his two grimy fists on the glass of the counter.

"Just give me the change," he said.

The florist shrugged and broke the bill.

The damned box was too big to fit in the saddlebags without crushing it, so Jake had to drive home slowly, holding the thing by the ribbon. He stayed on the back streets, just so he would not be seen.

If Frank wanted to do this great deed for humanity, well, Jake didn't care. But it was still a loser's game. He imagined Sue all trussed up in her fancy dress, awkwardly trying to jiggle to music she could not hear, and it was sad as hell because at some point she would have to realize that the Cinderella shot ended at midnight and that was it.

The car was still gone when he got back to the house. He parked his chopper on the front lawn and went inside with the package. He pitched the box onto the kitchen table, where it bounced once and landed upside down. He drew himself a glass of water. The house was silent. He looked at his watch. The parade would just about be beginning downtown. The whole neighborhood must have been down there watching it. Not a car on the street.

Jake looked at the box. He put down his glass, dried his hands on his shirt, and set the package right. The ribbon came open easily, and he smoothed it out before pulling open the flap of the box. The orchid crouched like a gaudy insect in one corner. Jake pulled it out and turned it between his fingers. The petals fell back into place. There didn't seem to be any damage. He brought it to his nose and sniffed, then he laid it back in its place and tied the ribbon in a careful bow. He drank a little more water, straightened out the ribbon some more, and then put the box away in the refrigerator. He didn't give a shit what happened once it was out of his hands.

That night they cruised to hell and gone. Judy held him tightly around the waist. He ran some punk from the Catholic school, wiped him out on the marked-off quarter on the old farm road. Chicken was full of admiration. But Chicken's girl was on the rag about something. They drank some whiskey, and Judy got smashed, even though she hardly had enough to talk about. Chicken's girl drank much more, but it didn't do any good. It was her idea to ride over to the dance and see what the wimps were up to.

The doorway of the gymnasium was hung with red and white crepe. Somebody had scrawled the score of the game in shaving cream on one of the windows. Jake had to help Judy off the back of the bike, she was acting so tipsy. The band twanged away in the distance.

"Wanna try to get in?" said the Chicken. "Nobody's checking."

"Let's go around back and have a look first," said Jake.

They stumbled down the sidewalk bordering the boxy swimming-pool building. In the shadows, Jake tripped over a beer can. He kicked it up against the wall.

"Somebody's been a naughty little pecker," said Judy, giggling like an idiot. The Chicken winked.

Jake maneuvered her to the back entrance, where they both leaned up against the big windows and peered into the dusky gym. The band was playing a slow one, and all the little adults, dressed up in their Sunday suits and awkward high heels, swayed back and forth, rubbing one another up in the closest approximation of the act that most of them ever dared. Jake held his hands at his temples like blinders in order to get a better look. The cold wind kicked up against the wall, and Judy put her hands in his back pockets. She couldn't keep them still.

When he finally found his brother in the crowd, he was dancing with the deaf girl. As they passed other couples, Frank would smile at people he knew. For a moment Jake wanted to burst in and rescue Sue from the ignominy of it, the whole pathetic scene.

The couple circled slowly. Frank's herringbone back came into view. He nodded to somebody, and Jake wanted to deck him for his smugness. But then suddenly he saw her face. Sue danced with her neck nuzzled on his woolen shoulder, her gauzy breasts pressed lightly against him, her eyes neither open nor closed. The flower was pretty against the fabric. And on her lips Jake saw an expression so happy, so gay that it pierced him like the wind.

12

*F*rank heaved and groaned and pushed toward the light. His head felt as if someone were squeezing his temples. He did not know which surprised him most, what he was doing or how much it hurt. The muscles of his belly strained as he hauled himself up with a moan. That made nine. He wanted fifteen.

He had taken the membership in the health club for Laura's benefit. She liked to come here and swim in the afternoon to reward herself and relax. Reward, hell. To Frank, it was a torture chamber. And the pool was an icy pit. The track turned through narrow corridors like a nightmare of flight and pursuit. And in the exercise room, the body-building machines could have been designed by Torquemada.

Ten sit-ups were enough. He pushed himself up off the floor, and when the spots before his eyes subsided, he bent over to touch his toes. He did not get as far as he had expected. The sinews along the backs of his legs stopped him short, tight as cables. Lord, this had been a stupid thing to try.

Laura would be pleased if she knew what he was doing. She was always trying to get him to join her when she made a trip to the pool. But he was a weak swimmer. Too heavy in the head. Don't float right, he said. Chlorine kicks up my sinuses. He was in perfectly terrible shape.

He did a few push-ups, the ache spreading across his shoulders and down his arms. Heart attack, he thought, his chest heaving. Stroke. He collapsed on the floor.

Well, he'd better start getting into condition. At his age, it was now or never. But that had not been his thought when he had dug out his old gym clothes and sneakers and driven to the club. He had simply seen that there were a few hours before Jake's flight was due and felt an overwhelming impulse to work himself hard.

104

It wasn't just to test his strength. He had awakened tightly strung, and he needed to give his nerves an outlet. But now all his anxious reserves of energy were failing. He was already worn out and he had not yet run a step.

He could hear others pounding away on the track, and they sounded as if they were moving at a pretty good clip. In the exercise room itself, a big man was pumping iron; a wide leather belt studded with silver nailheads girdled his waist. A thin woman did yoga on the mats. Her face was rapturous as she went through the movements, as if she were making love to the Invisible Man. And another, younger woman was working out on each machine in turn to the creak of pulley and clang of weights. He watched her mount a device that was supposed to tone up your thighs. She put her feet in the stirrups, lay back, and spread her legs. She did not seem to mind that he was looking. It was as clinical as a doctor's office. Frank turned away.

The track was so short you had to go fifteen laps to make a mile. When he was younger, he had been a pretty good runner. Not so hot in sprints, but capable of holding his own in the longer races. He had run cross-country as well as track, and it had always pleased him to feel his legs stretching out beneath him, his stride cushioned by the spongy grass. He had bounded over the countryside and felt like something not entirely tame.

But Frank did not even think of stretching out today. He took short, choppy steps and paced his breath. There was some pain, of course, as the muscles pulled and twisted. But that was to be expected. You had to work through the discomfort and into that purified, numb state in which the momentum carried you along as steadily as an engine in overdrive. He glanced at the clock as he passed it, not to measure his speed but only to double-check that he had time to make it to the airport to meet Jake's plane. In the army they made sure a man stayed in shape.

The pain didn't let up, and the air in Frank's lungs was afire. He had gone less than half a mile, and he was already exhausted. He wanted to stop, but he wouldn't let himself. He had to be able to make at least a mile. Frank let his arms go slack and shook out the tightness as he shuffled around a curve. A group of older men passed him, and he heard them talking. One of them laughed. Another said hello. Frank barely had the wind to grunt an acknowledgment.

But he would not quit. No gain without pain. It had been a mistake to let himself get so miserably run-down. The only way to stay even was to press ahead.

Work. Work. Work. Work. Every step was a rabbit punch, knocking the wind out of him. The woman who had been exercising on the machines ran past, and for a few steps he tried to hold a steady interval behind her shapely rear. But then he let himself fall back again.

With only two laps left to go, Frank tried to put on a little speed. His legs were willing, and he knew he could run through the cramp in his side. Kick. Work it all out. Jake. Jake. Jake.

The girl had lapped him and was even with him now. He gave it everything he had, but his wind just wasn't up to it. He heaved and gasped; he could not breathe out the exhausted air. The girl pulled away from him again, and he slowed down to a walk. Head down, coughing, he walked the last hundred yards and told himself that it was close enough.

The rush hour was just beginning when Frank pulled onto the expressway to O'Hare. His arms and legs were limp from his workout. He knew that tomorrow he would be mighty stiff.

The traffic slowed down as it neared the airport. A big jet roared overhead, low enough so that he could see its markings. He turned into the parking garage and spiraled up the ramp until he found an empty space.

When he reached the terminal, he picked up a paper and looked through it quickly. Not a word about the Tatum murders. The story was already forgotten, except for the sad black agate of the paid death notice that said services were to be private and donations to Children's Memorial were preferred in lieu of flowers.

The huge sign near the ticket counters showed that Jake's flight was on schedule. Frank noted the gate and lined up at the metal detectors. He had to go through twice because of the change and keys in his pockets. When he finally passed inspection, he looked at his watch and saw that there wasn't enough time to make a telephone call.

The jumbo jet was just taxiing up when Frank arrived at the gate. It took a while before the door opened and the passengers started to emerge. First came some businessman carrying leather suitbags and attaché cases. Then a family with four little kids. A group of nuns. A man with a guitar. Then came Jake.

He looked tired. His green uniform was rumpled, his shoulders hunched over. Beneath the stubble of an overnight beard, his jaw seemed swollen. He looked right past where Frank was waiting, and the crowd carried him out into the corridor.

"Over here!" said Frank.

Jake stopped. The line split in two and surged around him. Frank jostled forward.

"Well, I made it," said Jake.

"Damned decent of you," said Frank, clapping his arm around his brother's shoulder and leading him to a spot away from the traffic. "You have a good flight?"

"It went up and it came down."

"You can't do better than that. Here, let me take your bag."

"It's OK. I can carry it."

"You must be tired," said Frank.

Seeing his brother again made everything seem grave and final, but Frank tried not to show his feelings. The only way to handle a moment like this was to leave the important things unsaid.

But Jake never much cared for protocol. He took Frank's elbow and said, "Is he still . . . ?"

Frank pulled back a step. "Hanging in there," he said.

"I'm going to have to stop somewhere and clean up before I see him."

"There's plenty of time, I'm afraid," said Frank. "They don't want us there during the day. They're doing some tests. We'll surprise him tonight."

"He doesn't know I'm coming?"

"Ruth and I weren't sure it was a good idea."

"You could have told him after I called."

"It was pretty late, Jake."

"Did you really think I'd let you down?"

"He's fighting," said Frank. Nothing more.

The flight crew was last off the jet. They filed past, and one of the stewardesses gave Jake a look.

"How bad is it, Frank?"

"I won't try to kid you. It isn't very good."

"He's a tough one," said Jake, but his eyes contradicted him.

"This is different. I want you to be ready for that."

Frank hung back for a moment as Jake moved into the stream of people headed for the terminal. He was walking with a limp, so it was easy for Frank to catch up.

"You all right?"

"War injury."

"What happened? You should have written, Jake."

"Defending the family honor," said Jake. "Last night in a San Francisco bar."

"You shouldn't toy with people," said Frank.

"Let's not get started on each other."

"He's proud of you."

"I didn't do so well," said Jake. "I didn't even land a decent punch."

"All right," said Frank. "Forget it."

As they walked down the concourse in silence, Frank moved painfully. His limbs were heavy. They must have looked like two of the wounded, and Frank wished they could feel the comradeship just this once, the bond of blood. But it was hard. They had always had trouble that way.

You've been smoking in our room again, Jake.
Who says?
It stinks in here.
You stink.
Don't be a jerk.
Fuck you.
Mother will hear you.
Fuck her too.
Jake, stop it!
Fuck her. Fuck her. Fuck her.

They could be such incredible fools sometimes, both of them. Frank caught himself limping too, and he had to laugh.

"What's so funny?"

"I was just thinking about the way we used to get into it as kids," said Frank.

"We were regular assholes," said Jake.

When they reached the main building, Frank led the way toward a bank of phones. "Look," he said, "I've got to make a call."

"I'll hit the latrine."

"This won't take long," said Frank.

He found a free phone and dialed Dr. Tomanelli's private line.

"County morgue."

"Hello, Tony. It's Frank Nolan."

"I heard about your dad. How's he doing?"

"About the same."

"They know what it is?"

"A respiratory problem. Some form of ataxia, the thing I asked you about the other day."

"Christ, Frank. I wouldn't have given you the brushoff if I'd known."

"I could have told you. I don't know why I didn't."

"If there's anything I can do."

"I'm calling about the Tatum inquest."

"Pretty cut and dried," said Dr. Tomanelli. "I called the girl a murder, of course. The Williams shooting was justifiable homicide. Everybody seemed pleased."

"Did you establish a time of death on the girl?"

"I don't see how she could have been dead less than twelve hours when they found the body. Probably longer."

"Anybody pick up on that?"

"Czerny didn't even stir."

"How about the sexual abuse?"

"No evidence of it. But still, the girl had been through hell."

"Do you figure it, Tony?"

"Off the record?"

"Sure. Sure."

"I got my part right," said the pathologist. "Murder and justifiable homicide. But the way they're telling the story doesn't make much sense. Times are all screwed up."

"Bootleg me a copy of your results, Tony."

"What for?"

"Scientific curiosity. Just say I admire your work."

When Frank hung up, he noticed his brother standing off a distance waiting for him.

"It wasn't private, Jake."

"It wasn't any of my business."

"Maybe we can change that."

"We going to start jerking each other around again already?" said Jake.

"I'm serious. How'd you like to give me a hand on a case I've been working?"

Jake shrugged.

"I've got some stops to make," Frank said. "I thought you might want to come along."

"In this shit?" Jake touched the sleeve of his uniform as if it were something diseased.

"You can change when we get to our first stop. I brought along some clothes. They ought to be about the right size."

"What kind of case is this?"

"A murder. Everybody's got it all wrong."

"Except you, of course."

"Jake, you never change."

"Neither do you."

"I change so much that when I get up in the morning, I don't know who I'm going to shave."

"You're so full of shit your breath stinks," said Jake.

Frank smiled.

"So's your old man," he said. Then he stopped smiling.

"So's yours," said Jake.

13

*F*rank did not stay on the expressway long. He took a turnoff and headed south through the ethnic neighborhoods. The drizzle in the air had begun to turn to ice. A mist spun off the streets onto the windshield. The wipers left a smear.

When Frank stopped at a light, a fire truck turned the corner in front of them, sirens shining, then an ambulance. All the cars pulled over to let the emergency vehicles pass. Frank gunned his engine and ran the red.

"Hold on tight," he said.

"What the hell are you doing?" said Jake.

"Reach into the glove compartment and give me the dome light."

Jake fumbled until he got it out, maps and papers spilling into his lap. Frank put it on the dash and gave Jake the cord.

"Plug it into the lighter," he said.

They tailgated the ambulance, racing down the left lane past the traffic. A police cruiser pulled out in front of the fire engine and added its siren to the commotion. The dome light on the dash slashed back and forth, reflecting off the glass.

Frank leaned into the steering wheel, gripping it tightly as he weaved in and out among the cars. When he cut around a corner, Jake banged up against the door.

"Take it easy, Frank," he said.

By now they were deep into the black neighborhoods. The buildings were run-down, some of them only burned-out shells. Frank could see smoke billowing up into the sky ahead of them. There were already a dozen trucks pouring water onto the blaze. A snorkel poked up high into the air.

"Got to be at least a three-bagger," said Frank, slowing down now.

The fire was in an apartment building, and it was threatening to spread down the block. The temperature was still dropping, and icicles formed where the water poured off the roof. The front wall shone with a frigid glaze. Flames flared against the ice.

"What are you trying to prove?" said Jake.

Frank did not answer him.

He pulled onto a side street and switched off the dome light. The parked cars, a collection of wrecks and shiny customized cruisers, made the passage narrow. From time to time they passed pedestrians, who followed the car with their eyes, as if Frank and Jake were visitors from another world.

"Where the hell are we going?" Jake asked.

"To see a friend. We're almost there."

"Funny neighborhood for a friend."

The building where Frank pulled over was better than most, but there was only so much anyone could do. The window frames were freshly painted, and someone had put sand on the walks to take care of the slick spots. There was a marked-out place for a flower garden against the front wall, and shrubs almost hid the bars on the cellar windows. Still there was no way to hide the desolate alley that ran next to the apartment or compensate for the barren lack of trees.

The inner door in the vestibule was locked, but all Frank needed to do was to say his name into the mouthpiece by the mailbox, and the buzzer squawked them in. The stairway was clean except for some children's toys on the landing. They stopped at the second floor at the door marked "Superintendent." The woman opened it and gave Frank a hug and a kiss on the cheek.

"Sam didn't tell me you were coming," she said. "I'd have cleaned up this mess of toys."

"Diana, meet my brother, Jake. Jake, this is Diana Harrison."

"Can I make you some breakfast?"

"We can't stay long," said Frank. "I'll tell you what, though. My brother would like to get out of the uniform if you've got a room he could use."

"He looks kinda cute in it," she said, winking, "just like Sam did when he came home. The pants give them such tight little fannies. Sam! Get on out of that kitchen. Frank Nolan's here, and his brother back from Nam."

Frank was alone in the living room when Harrison came through the door.

"Where'd she go to?" he said.

"She's showing my brother a room where he can change."

"He back for good now?"

"Just for a little while."

"The dude didn't reenlist, did he? You told me he was a tough kid, but you didn't say he was crazy."

"My father is pretty sick. We brought him home on a leave."

"Sorry to hear that. Real sorry."

"I'm afraid I'm here on business, Sam."

Just then the kids burst into the room and leaped onto the couch where Frank was sitting. They bounced up and down and hugged him. He tickled them and ran his fingers through their hair. Then Diana returned and rescued him.

"Don't be making pests of yourselves now," she said.

"Better take them somewhere, honey," said Harrison. "The man says he's here on business."

"Oh no, Sam," she said. "Lord help us."

Jake returned wearing jeans, sweatshirt, and the letter jacket Frank had brought along for him.

"How do I look?" he said. But no one answered. The Harrisons were as grim as suspects in a show-up. Diana sent the children to their room, and Frank knew he'd better get on with it.

"Monroe Williams," he said. Diana turned her face away.

"I heard what happened," said Harrison.

"You figure it?"

"Ain't something you figure, one way or another. You just say a prayer and thank the Man it wasn't you."

"You ever talk to him about kidnapping?"

"He was a hustler, Frank, just a scared little man."

"Did he like young girls?" Frank asked, then something came over him. Suddenly he was angry, and his voice grew mean. "Little white girls?" He heard his brother suck in a breath. "Was that his thing, Sam? Pale little dollies?"

"Come on, man," said Harrison.

"Look," said Frank. "I need it straight."

Harrison stiffened and put his hand on his wife's arm. Frank thought she might begin to weep, and he was ready for it.

"He wasn't that way," said Harrison. "He stayed in his place. He was on the needle, Frank."

"He ever talk to you about it?"

"What are you, my parole officer?"

"You know who I am."

Harrison waited, stood up, sat down again, rubbed at his jaw.

"He came by the counter one day," he finally said. "He was strung out and sniffing like a dog. He asked me about action. Had I heard of any? The poor, sick motherfucker."

"Sam," said Diana. He pulled away from her touch.

"I mean, shit," he said, "there he was, tapped out, no place to go but back to the joint. And there I was in my apron, flipping burgers on the grill."

Harrison turned his back.

"Look," said Frank. "I've got to ask about this. I've got to know."

"With you it's always gotta this, gotta that."

"It's the law, Sam. It's not a matter of what you want."

"I should of kicked his ass out the door," said Harrison. "But I didn't do it. I gave him a little cash from the register so he could get himself well. What the hell else is a man supposed to do?"

"I'm not saying what you should have done or shouldn't have," said Frank.

"OK, Frank. Sure."

"Do you see Williams as a guy who could maul a little girl and stuff her in a garbage can?"

"He was a joke on the block, man," said Harrison. "I mean, he couldn't even watch two dudes punching it out without looking away. He was soft. You knew the man."

"Yeah. I knew him."

"Then why'd they blow him away, Frank? He was just a sick little shit in over his head."

"They gave him a chance."

"It isn't right."

"I didn't say it was."

"I was scared to tell you about seeing the dude," said Harrison. "Somebody could call it consorting with a felon and yank my parole."

"What do they want from you?" said Frank, and he finally allowed himself a smile. "Around here, everybody's a felon."

The traffic became heavy as they approached the Loop. But so far it showed no signs of slowing down. Frank looked over at Jake, who was gazing at the towering mass of buildings up ahead.

"You miss it?"

"What's that?" said Jake.

"The city."

"Not much."

"It can get pretty rough."

"Look," said Jake. "It's all right with me that you're a cop."

"I'm not a cop."

"That you act like one then."

Frank looked back to the road just in time to see a pothole. He swerved but did not use the brake. Jake put his hand on the dash to steady himself.

"What's the hurry?" he said.

"Maybe I should take you back to the apartment."

"Don't worry about me," said Jake.

But Frank was worried. He had thought it would be all right if he could just go about his business. But it wasn't working. He didn't know why they always behaved this way when they were together, like little boys measuring their shadows against one another at dusk.

Look how tall I am.

Big deal.

Bigger than you, Jake.

It all depends on where you stand.

Shadows and sun, the last light dying behind them. And instead of mourning it together, they bickered over whose darkness stretched out farthest on the cold, bare earth.

The streets were crowded, but there was a space in front of the building where Nicholas Tatum had his office.

"This is it," Frank said, stopping next to the no-parking sign and then putting an official business notice in the window that made it all right.

The building had to be a hundred years old. The brick was blackened, and rusty air conditioners stuck out of some of the windows. On the ground level, the storefronts housed a shoe stand, a natural-food store, and a novelty shop where junior could buy a dribble glass or a pornographic magazine. The lobby was in bad shape. The fancy brass fixtures had all tarnished, and the marble veneer on the walls had cracked in many places.

Frank went to the tenant listing and ran his finger past an electrolysis salon, an optometrist, a film lab, a telephone answering service, and a used-book dealer before he came to the firm he was looking for. He led Jake into the elevator, which crawled slowly up the shaft.

When it reached seven, there was a sign directing them to the left down a dingy corridor. At the end of it stood a smoked-glass door marked in simple black letters "Paxton Apparel, Inc." Frank tried the knob. It was open.

The waiting room was tiny. The receptionist was busy pruning a forlorn little plant on her desk and talking on the telephone. Frank cleared his throat, and when she looked up, she did not make him feel welcome.

"Can I help you?" she said, putting one hand over the mouthpiece of the phone.

"We're here to see Mr. Tatum."

"Is he expecting you?"

"No," said Frank, and he fished in his breast pocket until he found his credentials.

"Oh," she said. Then she made a quarter turn away and whispered into the phone, "I have to call you back, Betsy. Some men are here."

Frank looked over at his brother and tried to catch his eye, but it was no use.

"Is this about his daughter?" said the receptionist.

"Yes."

"I hope you aren't going to upset him," she said. "It's all so terrible."

"I'll try not to, ma'am."

"He's a fine man. This shouldn't have happened to him."

The waiting-room walls were hung with photographs of handsome young men in suits that would have looked cheap on anyone else. The furniture was made of a serviceable plastic, and the reading material was trade-related.

When Tatum appeared, Frank could see why the receptionist wanted to protect him. He was groomed as well as the models in the pictures, and his face was so fresh and boyish that the care lines around his eyes stood out like wounds.

"What can I do for you?" he said.

"Well, first you could sell us a decent suit of clothes for my brother here," said Frank, flicking his thumb toward Jake, who was not amused.

"I'm afraid we don't keep any stock," said Tatum. "But I could special-order and get it to you within a week."

"Just kidding," said Frank.

"Oh," said Tatum. "Right."

"She told you why we're here."

"Yes, sir."

"I'm Frank Nolan from the state's attorney's office," he said, extending his hand. Tatum rubbed his fingers against the fabric of his pants. His grip was moist but firm. "This is my brother Jake. I've got him on special duty with me."

"You want to ask some more questions," said Tatum.

"There are just a few things I need to clear up."

"You already talked to Linda, I understand."

"I tried, yes."

"She worried that she hadn't been as helpful as she should have been. I hope you understand."

"Look," said Frank, "is there somewhere we can go?"

"I'm sorry. Of course," said Tatum. "It's just that I thought they said the investigation was over."

"Some loose ends is all," said Frank.

"My brother is a very neat and orderly man," said Jake.

"As you can see," said Frank, "it doesn't run in families."

Tatum looked from one to the other, and it was clear he did not know how they fit together or where he was supposed to stand.

"We can go into my office," he said, "if you don't mind the clutter."

"That would be fine."

Tatum led the way to the inner offices, which were even shabbier than the waiting room. The hallway could have used a coat of paint, and the asphalt tile was coming up in places.

"We do most of our selling on the road," Tatum explained. "This place just serves as our base of operations. It's not too impressive, but it doesn't have to be."

He opened the door of his office and showed them in. It wasn't large, but somebody had taken a fair amount of care with it. The desk was old, but well appointed. On it stood a pair of lamps, a monogrammed desk set, and a couple of pewter mugs filled with pens and sharpened pencils.

"I can offer you some instant coffee," said Tatum, turning in his chair and lifting a glass pot from a hotplate on the shelf behind him. Frank shook his head and Jake raised a hand to wave the offer away.

"I wasn't sure you'd be back at work," said Frank.

Tatum poured himself a cup, steadying his right hand with his left as he did. Next to the pot there were framed photographs of his wife and daughter. He did not look at them.

"It's easy to get buried in this business," he said. "I figured I might as well keep myself occupied."

He stacked up a pile of order forms and correspondence and put them in a wooden tray.

"I guess there's a lot of pressure in sales," said Frank.

"Keeps me busy."

"Out of town a lot?"

Tatum seemed wary, but he did not hesitate.

"At this time of year," he said. "It's the season. But I don't imagine you mean in general. You're talking about the day she disappeared."

"I was going to get to that," said Frank. He looked over at Jake, who was fiddling with the zipper of the old jacket.

"Des Moines," said Tatum, "on the way to St. Louis and points between. I don't know if I'll ever be able to face that territory again."

"Linda's father was here at least," said Frank.

"Yes, at least that."

Frank thought he detected a slight edge of resentment.

"He's around a lot, is he?"

But Tatum was not interested in getting on the couch. "He's there when we need him," he said.

"He told me he helps you out," said Frank. "Financially, I mean."

Tatum held his head high, but you could see that it was a strain.

"He's very generous," he said.

"Business kind of slow?"

"I don't see where this is leading," said Tatum.

"Frank," said Jake. "Get to it, for Chrissake."

"My brother's been on an airplane all night," Frank explained. "He's usually a lot bigger pain in the ass, but he's kind of tired."

"What is it you want to know exactly?" said Tatum.

Frank put it bluntly.

"Establishing your whereabouts."

"An alibi."

"That's one word for it."

"She was my daughter," Tatum said. "I mean, what the hell can you be thinking of?"

"For the record, Mr. Tatum."

Tatum sat back in his chair.

"I was on a swing through Iowa and Missouri. My territory covers nine states. I had left the day that—"

"That would be a Sunday," said Frank, jotting down a note.

"I guess so," said Tatum. "I've kind of lost track of time."

"And you didn't let Linda know where you were," said Frank.

"She had a general idea," said Tatum. "She could always have called Karen. The woman at the front desk. She keeps tabs on me. But no, you're right. I didn't check in with her that night. I got to the motel late. I didn't want to wake everybody up. It was a terrible mistake."

"The way I understand it," said Frank, "she was out much of the night searching. You might not have reached anybody if you had called."

"Might. Might not. I've gone over it again and again."

"I understand, Mr. Tatum. It's difficult, I know. But could you tell me when you actually heard?"

"I phoned when I checked into the room in St. Louis," he said. "Here, I've got the bill somewhere."

He opened the drawer of the desk, and the documents were right on top. He handed them over, a yellow expense report that was already neatly filled out, the Des Moines and St. Louis hotel bills, some restaurant receipts and gas-card slips. On the St. Louis statement there was a charge for the dining room, a movie, one long-distance call. The number was printed on the form.

"This looks complete," said Frank. "I wonder if you could make a copy."

"Sure," said Tatum. He rang for the receptionist and had her make two sets, one for each brother.

"Now tell me about Williams," said Frank when she had gone.

"You tell me."

Tatum did not show as much anger as he might have. But everyone reacted differently.

"When did you first meet him?"

"Meet him?"

"There's got to be a connection somewhere," said Frank. "See, that's what's bothering me. These things almost never happen completely at random."

"I never saw the man in my life," said Tatum.

"Don't get me wrong, Mr. Tatum. I'm thinking of some passing contact. Maybe he was a messenger who made deliveries here. Or a guy who parked your car."

Frank handed him a photograph from the mugbook and caught Jake leaning over to glance at it. The face was flat and impassive under the stark booking-room lights.

"Try, Mr. Tatum," said Frank. "Try to recall."

Tatum held the smudged photograph at the edges. He did not look at it long.

"Never," he said.

"You're sure."

"It's always possible he was around somewhere, I guess, but not that I noticed."

Frank took the mug shot back and put it away.

"We think he was into drugs," he said.

"I can't figure it," said Tatum. "What did a man like that have against my little girl?"

"One more thing," Frank said. "I understand that your daughter had a habit of running away."

"Did my father-in-law tell you that?"

"He seemed sensitive about it when I asked him."

"I wouldn't call it running away," said Tatum. "Sometimes she went out without asking. The way kids do. There was a park down the street that she liked to play in. You know, swings, a slide, that sort of thing. We warned her about it. What could happen. God, you can't just lock them up, can you?"

He picked up a paper clip and twisted it into a spiral. Then he saw Frank watching and tossed it away.

"Linda was usually so careful," he said.

"She's having a hard time of it, isn't she," said Frank.

"It's horrible for her. She's not a strong woman," said Tatum, spreading his fingers along the edge of the desk. "She'd been going to doctors, but I don't know how much they helped. And now this."

"Her father blames her?"

Tatum kept his eyes on Jake, who had slumped down in his chair and was no help at all.

"The doctors were his idea," said Tatum. "I didn't resist it."

"What do they say?"

"Anxiety. Depression. They have a lot of words. But I didn't really understand it. I mean, we were doing just fine. This might not look like much," he said, opening his hands to the little office and then touching the stack of forms, "but it's an opportunity for me. I've been hustling. Making it work. Everything was looking up."

Frank stood at his chair. Jake leaped up as if he had just been reprieved. He was halfway out the door when Frank put the last question.

"Did you and your wife have happy childhoods, Mr. Tatum?"

Tatum was slow to respond.

"I can't speak for Linda," he said. "I know she had everything she asked for. But as for me, I guess I was like every kid. I didn't have a lot."

"You don't need all that much, I guess," said Frank.

"I'm afraid I don't see your point," said Tatum.

And then Frank spoke for his brother's benefit.

"It's what gets you through the hard places," he said. "What you've had as a kid."

With that, Jake excused himself and disappeared down the hall. Frank hung back to shake Tatum's hand again and offer whatever encouragement he could. He left his card in case Tatum remembered something later. Then he stopped off and picked up the copies of the hotel bills and receipts from the receptionist.

Jake was holding an elevator for him.

"I don't get you sometimes, Frank," he said.

"How's that?"

"What's the guy's childhood got to do with anything?"

Jake's question hung in the silence as Frank stepped to the back of the old elevator, which shuddered as he leaned against the wall.

14

A flock of birds burst upward from the station platform as the commuter train strained to a start. They wheeled and spiraled black against the gray sky until the last car cleared, then they settled back down amid the litter eddying in the wind. Laura shivered as the red light of the train retreated in silence.

When it had disappeared, she left the platform and crossed over into a sprawling housing development. It was curious the way the homes had aged. They had been built to identical plans, but they had grown apart like twins. Time had made distinctions, giving them each a special look, the lines of joys and sorrows.

She was glad Frank had suggested she come down on the train by herself today. He needed time with Jake. And he had said he might even be able to do some work on the case of the murdered little girl. He was awfully wrought up over it. Maybe that was just his way of taking his mind off his father. If it was, she was glad for it. She hadn't been able to help him much herself.

It was as if he was afraid that if he let her share his pain it would create a debt he could only repay by giving her what she most wanted. She did not know how to tell him that she herself wasn't sure what that was, couldn't be until she knew he wanted it, too.

Sometimes the yearning came over her like a fever and she shuddered. Would a baby make the music go away? She had a powerful need to create. To make and then to let go. But she did not know whether having children would sustain or sate it, whether she had the energy to do both or would someday have to choose.

Frank's father had no such doubts about her. He made that clear the very first time they met. Laura and Frank had stopped at his house on the last leg of their trip from the coast, parking the rented truck full of secondhand furniture and paperback books in the driveway. Frank's father had not been able to go to the wedding because of his illness, and his awkward apology was the only time Laura ever saw him at a loss for words. He got over it quickly.

"Looks like you found yourself a breeder, Frank," he said. And before she had a chance to protest, he took her by the arm and led her to the living room. "Well, lady, I've had the piano tuned. I expect you to play for your supper. But first I want you to tell me how you fell for my son. Don't you think he kind of favors me?"

It didn't take her long to realize that he was courting her.

She played for him that night, Chopin and Beethoven, then some compositions of her own.

"Lady," he said, "I don't mean to be crude, but you are awfully pretty, even if you do play a mean piano."

That settled it. She was his.

Sam Nolan was a man of universal tastes. Everywhere in the house there were great heaps of books. He could not remember his next-door neighbor's name, but he had instant recall when it came to the location of Emerson's essays under a pile of five-year-old *New Yorker* magazines in the spare bedroom. In addition to the books, there were gizmos all over the place: compasses and quadrants, telescopes, balances, calipers, rock specimens, a microscope. He moved from instrument to instrument in the evening, working out strange hypotheses that came to him in such a profusion that he did not have time to explain them all.

But the disease made him husband his strength. His coordination was poor. He banged into things and had to struggle mightily simply to adjust his telescope with any precision. His speech slurred. The disease had attacked the muscles of his hands, and he was forced to give up playing the cello. She bought a transcription of some of the Bach suites and played it for him. He seemed transported. Bach had always been special for her, too, his amazing balance of form and invention. She explained to Frank's father that form was the only way she could defend against the sentiment that always threatened to overrun her music like flowering weeds.

"No matter how much you talk about it," he said, "you can't ruin Bach for me."

"I guess I can get pretty analytical at times," she said.

"Bach was prolific with kids, too," he said. "He lived a long and fruitful life."

"He didn't have to bear or breast-feed them," said Laura. "He didn't have to get them off to school in the morning. Mrs. Bach did."

"Oh, no. Not you, lady," he huffed. "I thought you were beyond emancipation."

Laura could not help but laugh.

And she smiled again now as she turned a corner into the wind. A small grocery store was up ahead. The cold had numbed her nose and made her eyes water. She decided to stop to get something to take to Ruth.

The store smelled fresh and mealy. It reminded her of the little shop back home in the shadow of the mills where she and her folks had bought pastry and the paper every Sunday after church. She wandered down the narrow aisles crammed with boxes and cans. Pulling off her gloves, she worked her long fingers free of stiffness, doing Hanon exercises in the air. The doughnuts did not look fresh, so she bought a package of sweet, sticky buns instead.

"Pretty cold out there still?" asked the lady at the counter.

"Not too bad if you keep moving," said Laura.

"How is he?" the lady asked.

"Pardon?"

"Sam Nolan. You're the daughter-in-law, aren't you?"

"How did you know?"

"From the pictures he was always showing off."

"He's still in the hospital."

"Poor man," the lady said.

"I'll tell him you were asking after him."

"Such a terrible disease. And him so young. I hear he's slipping."

"I have to be going," Laura said.

She gathered up her change and hurried outside, buttoning her coat. There had been certain indications lately that Frank's father was preparing for the end. Ruth had said that for several weeks before he collapsed he had been doing some mysterious work in his study. She could hear him talking to himself in there sometimes, but whenever she got close to the door, he chased her away. Then one day he insisted that Ruth drive him to the bank. He had a little package with him and some papers in a file jacket. He descended into the vault alone, and when he returned his hands were empty.

"It was a will," said Ruth. "I know it."

"Don't bury him yet," said Frank.

The wind picked up and rasped at her face. There was a threat of snow in the air. She pulled out a scarf and tied it in a babushka around her head.

No, he still had some life in him. She knew that he did. She remembered one night not so long ago when she and Frank had stayed over a few days for his birthday. Ruth was out and Frank was late getting home from work.

"Lady, come here, will you?" Frank's father had said.

"I'm deep in a book," she had replied.

"This is better."

He was on the back patio. The night was warm, more like spring than fall. His voice was muffled.

"You really ought to save your energy," she said as she got out of her chair and went to the back door.

"Shows how much you know, lady," he said. "You can't save energy. It runs down. That's thermodynamics."

He had on his usual baggy gray work pants, plaid shirt, and clashing necktie. "Adaptability," he had explained once when she asked him about the way he dressed. "A man wants to work in the garden, he doesn't have to fret about dirtying his knees. He goes to the bank, his neck is already duly noosed."

Laura went out onto the patio with him, and as her eyes got used to the dark she saw that he was at work with his telescope.

"What do you have there?" she asked.

"Lady," he said, "there are two ways of looking at the firmament. You can look to find something new or you can look to find something old worth remembering. When I poke my nose into the sky what I have in mind is the latter. I have this machine trained on something I thought you ought to see. Go ahead. Have a peek. Don't be afraid. It's not pointed at the neighbor's window."

She approached the large, complicated mechanism carefully for fear she would knock it out of kilter. She sat down on a folding chair and moved her eye to the lens.

And what she saw was beautiful: abstract, brilliant, a haloed point of light.

"Is this the way they all look?" she said. "No wonder you like to come out here at night."

"You're a religious person, aren't you?" he said. "Don't worry. I don't hold it against you. But here's the point. What you're looking at is a nova, an exploding star. Imagine an event a thousand times brighter— a supernova. An explosion that sends phosphorescent gases billions of miles into space. The supernova event was probably what was seen as the star of Bethlehem. I just thought you should know."

"I pray for peace."

"Makes as much sense as praying for anything else," he said. "Someday the sun will explode, too. Maybe it will be seen somewhere. And who knows where that will lead."

"A second coming."

"At least history repeating itself," he said. "Don't you ever look up at the stars, lady?"

"Sometimes out on a walk," she said. "City lights make it hard."

"It's history you're seeing up in the sky," he said. "Events millions of miles away and centuries ago. Everything since creation is still present out there somewhere. It's a kind of immortality, I guess, or as close to it as man can get."

"You don't believe in God."

"Not the way churches talk about it. No. But let me tell you this. They say you must fear God. And I'm afraid, all right, looking up into the emptiness. They say you must love God. And sometimes I get as dizzy as a schoolboy sick with infatuation when I think of the very idea of being alive under that sky. They say you must have faith in God. And I can tell you here and now that I keep faith with the mystery of it. I can attest the most heaven-bent sense of wonder, and if that isn't enough, then I don't know what is.

"Lady, look," he whispered, holding out his hand. "Isn't that something."

The moon spread silver across his palm.

"It makes a mark," he said, pointing down at the silhouette of his hand on the bricks. "Even in the night."

As she walked on, she pulled her collar higher and watched her shape stretching out before her as the sun came out from behind the clouds. The air barely stirred the branches of the tall old trees. Everything else was still, the indifferent silence that must have first driven men to song.

It reminded her of the cathedrals they had visited in England, great stone monuments enclosing the emptiness, shaping it to the mysterious proportions of the cross. The one she loved most was not noted in their guidebooks. It had no special architectural or historical significance. They had stopped there early one morning. Frank had wanted to reach Cornwall before the holiday traffic, but because they were making such good time they decided to stretch their legs.

They entered the church by the main door. Laura dropped some coins into the wooden poor box and moved up the long center aisle. The stone supporting the vaulted roof was discolored. The names on the marble burial markers were written in an obscure script. Light from stained-glass windows cast bright patterns on the worn floor, the figures warped and elided by the pews. She saw the pipes of the great organ, tarnished but still majestic, rising above the choir. It was an instrument to make the stone of wall and heart vibrate in sympathy or terror.

Then into the cavernous hush came a tiny, whistling fugue, small as a drunkard's tune. She looked to the organ console, but no one was there. The counterpoint twisted on and then ended. Someone laughed, and the echo came from many directions.

"Over here," said a voice. "I hope I didn't frighten you."

Off in a far corner a small, red-faced man in a white collar and black clerical robe stood and waved to them.

"We don't want to disturb you," said Laura as they moved toward him.

"No trouble, really," said the organist. "Heavens no. We don't usually attract visitors."

The instrument was a small, self-contained pump organ not much grander than a harmonium.

"It doesn't look like much," said the organist, "but it is very old. I sneak in from time to time amorning to have a go at it. Quite a pretty little sound, I think."

"Is it original to the church?"

"Oh my, no," said the organist. "It's German, actually. Some of the boys from the local regiment picked it up during the war. It traveled very well, don't you think?"

"Please go ahead and play," said Laura.

He sat down and began pumping furiously with his legs. His fingers snapped at the stops and then began picking out an allegro theme. He touched the keys lightly, and the pumping sounded beneath the melody like the beating of a pulse.

Laura and Frank watched for a while as the organist improvised, his head thrown back. Then they started slowly for the door. As they reached it, the lines of the fugue untangled and resolved. Laura stopped, and the echo faded into the high spaces above her. Then there was silence again.

She remembered the silence as she walked now alone in the cold. Today the only sound was a dog barking in the distance. It spoke, then paused, as if waiting for an answer. Hearing none, it barked again.

15

Jake wasn't exactly sure where they were. The bars along the street had folding steel gates crosshatching the windows, and every wall was papered with fight bills and posters of the Maharishi in repose. The drizzle had stopped, but the sun was cold behind the clouds.

"You hungry?" asked Frank.

"Not especially."

"There's a joint up the way. I thought we'd stop."

Jake's stomach was operating by a different clock. It seemed impossible that only a day or two ago he had broken the cipher and brought the jets screaming in. Any time now he expected the drip to start burning in his groin. He was tired and annoyed. All he wanted to do was to see his old man, but here he was trapped in a car with this person who claimed to be his brother.

"Let's just go to the hospital," said Jake. "They'd have to let us in."

"They have rules."

"It's his life, isn't it?"

"I wish it were that easy."

Frank turned into a parking lot next to a police station. At the far end stood a ramshackle hot dog stand.

"Is this the place?" said Jake.

"It won't kill you."

Frank climbed out of the car, and Jake slid down in the seat, bundling his arms around himself against the chill. Over the dash he watched his brother at the carryout counter, stamping his feet and rubbing his hands, the breath bursting from his lips like smoke.

Two uniformed cops lined up behind him and started a conversation. The counterman gave Frank a white bag, and Frank gestured toward the car.

"Here you go," he said when he got back in behind the wheel. He lifted out a Coke and a greasy envelope full of fries. "I bought an extra dog if you want one."

"Not right now."

The two cops got their food and shuffled toward the car. Frank unlocked the rear door to let them in.

"Who's your new partner?"

"My brother Jake," said Frank. "Back from the army."

"No shit?" said the cop.

"This is John Jefferson and Bob Fitzpatrick," said Frank. "They work out of the dump next door."

"Can you turn up the heater some, Frank?" said Fitzpatrick. "It's colder in here than a whore in the morning."

Frank started the engine and slid the plastic controls on the dash all the way over.

"Where were you stationed?" asked Jefferson.

"I Corps. South of Hue," said Jake.

"They stuck me in the Delta," said Fitzpatrick through a mouthful of dog. "I guess it's all the same."

Jake chewed a few soggy fries and then washed them down.

"They say you're still nosing around in that shooting, Frankie," said Fitzpatrick. "That can't be right, can it?"

"Keeps me busy," said Frank.

"Some guys say you'd be better off taking up the martial arts or something," said Fitzpatrick. "They think that when you make trouble you get trouble."

"You don't say," said Frank.

"Shooting board gave our guy an easy pass," said Jefferson.

"I've got no quarrel with the shooting," said Frank.

"Don't take a law degree to know when a case is closed," said Jefferson.

"I've seen guys in your office dry up when they can't get cooperation," said Fitzpatrick.

"To get along, go along," said Frank.

"There you go, counselor," said Fitzpatrick. "See, Frankie, we have ways of telling the good guys from the bad guys."

"How's that?" said Frank.

"It ain't so hard to figure out where you stand."

Frank turned around in his seat.

"We're on the same side on this one," he said. "I guarantee it."

"We just know how it looks, Frankie," said Fitzpatrick.

"I'm telling you how it is," said Frank.

"We'd better split," said Jefferson.

As they piled out of the car, Frank shouted, "Watch me. Just watch me."

They had their backs to him now, and Fitzpatrick batted down the words with the flat of his hand.

"Nice fellas," said Jake.

"They're buddies of the shooter," said Frank. "They think I'm trying to do a number on him." He tossed the trash out the window toward a can, then pulled out of the lot. "Hell, I would've shot the sonofabitch myself."

Chicago Avenue was pretty run-down near the station house, but as they went east it began to change. Up ahead, Jake could see the high rises on Michigan and beyond them the open sky above the lake. They passed the cathedral, then Frank made a left and within a few blocks it was like entering another city, older, preserved against time.

"Why are you pushing it?" Jake asked.

"I get something in my mind and I can't let it go," Frank said. "We're the same that way."

"Come on, Frank. We're night and day."

"Two sides of the coin," said Frank. "I always thought you might make a good cop."

"Me?"

"It's a thought."

The side street was narrow, and the buildings along it were grand. You didn't see any drunks on the steps here, and the only people on the sidewalk were black ladies in unform, walking other people's dogs.

"Look in the glove compartment," said Frank, pulling into a space and turning off the key. "There's an envelope."

Jake found it and pulled it out. Frank took it from him and slipped it into the breast pocket of his suit jacket. Then he led Jake up the walk to an ornate Victorian building. Inside the vestibule they were met by a big man in his fifties. If it hadn't been for the blue-and-gold uniform, you could have mistaken him for the owner of the place. His shirt was starched and white, his tie just so. His gray hair was neatly tapered in the back the old-fashioned way. Jake was not surprised when the man challenged his presence. Tradesmen, said the quiet little sign on the wall, were to go to the rear.

But then Frank told him who they were, and the man pulled at his collar button and said, "Sumbitch. More coppers."

"Gets a little warm, does it?" said Frank.

"Ain't the Sout' Pole."

"Meet Ralph Celcik, Jake," said Frank. "He doesn't call himself that anymore, though. Now he's Ray Crone. A changed man, right, Ralph?"

"I been straight," said the man. "That was a long time ago. Look, I already told the coppers everyt'ing I know."

"I read your statement, Ralph," said Frank. "Funny, it didn't say anything about your rather colorful past."

"How did you get my sheet?"

"Just a lucky break. They had you filed both ways in my office. I guess the uniforms didn't know about your alias."

"I'm an old man," said the doorman. "I got steady work for six, seven years here. They don't know not'ing about before."

"I don't suppose they do," said Frank.

"I told the coppers the trut'."

"Ah, the truth," said Frank. "The truth is that the little girl was roughed up pretty badly. It was definitely not a case of taking a spill on a bike."

"I don't know not'ing about it," said the doorman, his eyes going to the floor.

"You don't?" said Frank. "I'm surprised you didn't savor all the grisly details, Ralph." The tone was raw, but there was no passion in his face, which only made it worse.

"Come on, Frank," said Jake. "Lighten up a little."

"I like that," said Frank. "Good cop, bad cop. You know the routine, don't you, Ralphie? My partner here wants to be on your side. Go ahead. Amuse him."

"I'll tell you anyt'ing you want."

"Kid me, Ralph," said Frank. "Tell me a story."

The doorman looked up and took a breath.

"The Tatums are good people," he said. "They always treated me right."

"But they didn't know who they were dealing with, did they, Ralph?"

"I didn't have not'ing to do with this t'ing. You got to believe that. I'm an old man now."

"But you liked the little girl, didn't you?"

"Sure, she was a good kid," said the doorman. "I said hello to her. That's all."

"The day she was killed, did Mrs. Tatum ask you if you'd seen her?"

"She didn't say a t'ing to me."

"But she must've seemed upset."

"I saw her leave. But I didn't t'ink anyt'ing about it. They come and go all the time."

Frank went to the glass door and looked outside. Then he put his hand against the wall and rubbed his fingers on the plush.

"You aren't very much help then, are you?" he said.

The doorman took a step forward and touched Frank's elbow. Frank pulled away.

"If I were you, I'd start reassessing my position, Ralph," he said. "This thing isn't over yet."

The doorman shook his head.

"Of all places in the city, it had to happen here," he said.

"That's just what I was thinking," said Frank. He reached into his pocket and pulled out the envelope. Then he withdrew a photograph from it and handed it to the doorman. Jake could not see what it showed.

"Do you recognize that man?"

"I seen his pictures in the papers," said the doorman. "He's the one the coppers killed."

"Have you ever seen him around here?"

"I'm not real sure."

"Come on, Ralph. Think."

"Maybe once," said the doorman. "There was a guy that looked kind of like him asking one day if Mr. Tatum was home."

"You're not bullshitting me, are you, Ralph?"

"I said I don't remember real good. But there was a *schwartze* who came around once. The Tatums were all out, so I sent him away. I don't know," he said, holding the photograph at arm's length now. "I can't remember so well the faces."

"When would this have been?"

"Month ago maybe," said the doorman. "Maybe two."

"Why didn't you tell that to the police when they talked to you?"

The doorman looked at Jake, but Jake couldn't help him.

"I was scared to say anyt'ing," said the man. "I thought if I didn't know not'ing, they'd just forget about me."

"You almost got away with it," said Frank.

He took the photograph back and put it in the envelope. Then he pulled out another one.

"Maybe you'd be interested in this other snapshot," he said.

When the doorman looked down at the photo, his face contorted. But he did not take his eyes off it.

"I didn't know it was like this," he said.

"Didn't you, Ralph? She'd been beaten. Remember that, Mr. Ray Crone. She'd been beaten to death, and I've got my eye on you."

He grabbed the photograph out of the doorman's hand and burst out the door. Jake hesitated a moment, but he didn't have anything to say to the man. When he got inside the car, Frank handed him the envelope.

"Go ahead," he said. "You might as well take a look."

The first photo was of the dead man in the morgue. It was curled up, and the light reflected off it, giving the body the look of a mannequin. The skin was gray, the eyes open wide.

The next picture showed a pretty little girl with blond hair and blue eyes and a mole on her right cheek that did not mar her looks.

"That's the victim," said Frank.

Jake pulled the last photo from behind the others, and he was stunned. The face was a horrible, pulpy wound. The eyes were nothing but deep bruises, and where the mole had been there was a raw red burn.

"A person doesn't do that for ransom," said Frank.

"My God," said Jake.

"Ralph Celcik was put away for manslaughter fifteen years ago," said Frank. He turned to Jake, and his face was hard. "He got drunk and hit his pretty young wife with a baseball bat until she was dead. Then he beat his daughter. You still think I should lighten up?"

"I didn't know," said Jake.

"Now you do."

As Frank pulled away from the curb, Jake watched his eyes, glad they were directed outward toward the street, because these were eyes that could tear into you like shrapnel.

Jake remembered the first time he had seen his brother flare up this way. It had been a long time ago, when they were boys. They had gone out walking in the woods a few blocks from the house. It wasn't much of a forest, but to them it had seemed like a wilderness. They were pioneers there, building forts and bridges over the creek with rocks and fallen limbs.

The leaves had begun to drop to the ground, and a light rain during the night left them sparkling in reds and yellows like a brightly colored carpet.

Frank cut two branches off a sapling and stripped them. They used the staffs to prod the ground before them, looking for sinkholes and traps. They walked past the climbing trees, past their lookouts, past the camouflaged fort behind a row of bushes. They crossed the creek, which was little more than a dribble in the mud. They leaped from rock to rock. The woods broke the west wind, and the sun was surprisingly warm through the high branches. Jake stopped to take off his jacket and tie it around his waist. When he was finished, he had to run to catch up with his brother.

Suddenly, his foot sank into the leaves and he toppled over. A frightened rabbit jumped away from him and went hopping into a field of high grass. The fall knocked the wind out of Jake, and as he recovered his breath, he heard something rustling in the underbrush.

"Stay away from it!" Frank yelled, racing back to where Jake had fallen. "It might be a snake."

But Jake stood up and began poking the ground with his stick.

"I'm not afraid of any old snake."

He moved the leaves aside with the toe of his shoe until he uncovered the rabbit's nest. Inside it were two tiny, newborn bunnies, and they were trembling.

"Look here," said Jake. He reached over to touch them. At first, they cowered away. But then they got used to it and rubbed up against Jake's fingers. "I've never seen them so small."

"You shouldn't have touched them," Frank said.

"They like it."

"Put them down, Jake."

"Make me."

"The older rabbits will never come back now," Frank said. He dropped down onto a stump. "You've put your smell on them. And now they're gonna die."

"Get out."

"It's so."

"Is not."

"I read it in a book."

"Maybe we can wash it off them."

"Won't work. Forget about it."

Jake stood up. He did not know whether to believe his brother or whether it was just Frank's way of making him feel bad.

"You go ahead and start back toward home," Frank said.

"What're you gonna do?"

"Never mind," said Frank. "Just go on."

Jake began to slouch away, feeling confused and guilty. He hadn't gone twenty steps before he heard a dull thudding behind him. He turned and saw his brother pounding the tiny bunnies with a rock. And on

Frank's cold face was a terrible look, like flames licking out of a wall of ice.

They rode in silence back into the West Side. Whole blocks had fallen into ruin. The wire fence along the expressway reminded him of a defensive perimeter. When they pulled off onto a narrow side street, Jake turned to make sure his door was locked.

"There it is," said Frank.

"What?"

"The Lone Star Hotel. Harrison gave me the address."

He turned into an alley and parked flush against the wall. Jake had to climb out Frank's side and jog to catch up with him.

The door of the Lone Star had a piece of folded cardboard where the window should have been. It was from a soap carton. It said, "Cheer."

Inside, the wiring hung down from the ceiling and the plaster was dark and broken. At a folding table in the corner sat a man of uncertain years. His fat hand lay on a tin box that must have been where he put the bums' nickels and dimes. He stood up as they crossed the sticky floor.

"What's the hassle?" the man said.

"We've been looking for suitable lodging," said Frank.

"Gotta be cops, right?"

"State's attorney's office," Frank said, proving it with his credentials.

"What you want?" said the man.

"We're just looking for a friend," said Frank.

"You ain't got no friends here. Nobody do."

"Name is Jones. Sylvester Jones. Little guy. Maybe thirty-five years old. Maybe twice that. Strung out."

"What's in it for me?" the man said, showing his yellowed teeth in what he probably thought was a smile.

"That warm feeling you get inside when you do your civic duty," said Frank.

"Fuck off, Jack. You can't muscle me."

"You've read the gospels, haven't you?" said Frank. "Where it says if you don't help the Man, the Man helps himself. Believe it. God's truth."

"Show me the warrant. Lay the paper on me, then maybe we'll have something to talk about. Or either we could discuss a fair price."

"Now here's a man who appreciates the value of his rights," Frank said to Jake, sweet as sin. But then he turned back to the man and the look was in his face again.

"Don't fuck with me, pal," he said, grabbing the man by the shirt.

"What you gonna do about it?"

Frank let go and took a step toward the door to the inner hall.

"No harm in asking questions, is there?" he said. "We'll just knock on every door. And let me tell you, we're going to knock real hard and identify ourselves as the law. We tend to speak pretty loudly, you know? And pretty soon the whole joint's going to think it's some kind of a raid. And anybody who flushes his stash isn't going to be very happy to hear that it happened because of your touching loyalty to poor Sylvester Jones."

The man showed his teeth again, and this time it was the small, pathetic smile of a person who knows his place.

"Second door on the right," he said. "Jones don't mean nothin' to me."

The corridor smelled worse than the lobby, and it was too dark to see what you were stepping into. Frank stopped and knocked on a door with a number scratched into the wood. Somebody coughed inside. Frank took it as an invitation and opened the door.

The room was nothing more than a narrow closet with a rickety cot in it. The windows were covered with yellowed newspapers. Jones lay doubled up, sniffing and clutching his belly.

"Sorry to disturb you," said Frank. The man did not stir. "I'm looking for information about a friend of yours. Monroe Williams."

Still no response. Jake moved a step closer, because for a moment he thought the man might be dying.

"I am the law," Frank said. "Do you understand that? I am the law."

The junkie slowly shook his head. Frank reached into his pocket, and Jake wondered whether he really thought the badge would matter. But Frank pulled out a ten-dollar bill and held it between two fingers.

"Here's a dime that can make you well," he said.

Jones got up on his elbows and painfully slid himself back until his shoulders rested against the wall.

"What I gotta do for it?" he said.

"Your name is Sylvester Jones, right?" said Frank.

"My name gotta come into it?"

"I just need to be sure who I'm dealing with."

"That's me."

"Let's try again with Williams. You knew the man."

"Sure. He lived next door here until he got rich and then got blown away."

"When did he move out?"

"Couple of months before he went down."

"Run out of money, did he?"

"Came into some."

"Where?"

"He don't talk about particulars, and I don't ask. He was dumb as a motherfucking stone, but he weren't no fool."

"What did he tell you?"

"Had a hustle going, that's all."

"He was a dealer?" asked Frank.

"Everybody deals if he can."

"So he was on a roll."

"You'd of thought he was on Easy Street, the way he was throwing the money around."

"Where did Williams score?"

"Look," said Jones, finally managing to sit up on the edge of the cot. "He scored here, he scored there, just like anybody else. But that's as far as I go. My life ain't worth much, but it's still worth more than a fucking dime."

"Where did Williams go when he was making a sale?"

"He never did say exactly," said Jones, rubbing at his stained trousers. "But this wasn't no case of glassine bags in the bus-station john. He wasn't working the street corner. Put the coke here. Pick up the money there. Nobody sees nobody. All a matter of trust. Like I said, the dude was dumber than shit. Now how about that dime?"

Frank held it out in front of him, just beyond his reach. The man struggled to stand up, and as he wobbled, pushing off from the cot with one frail hand, Frank grabbed him by the collar and yanked him sharply to his feet.

"Hey," said the junkie. "What you roughin' me up fo'?"

"You aren't leveling, Sylvester," said Frank. "Who was Williams working with?"

"He was a loner. Shit, man. Who'd want to go out on a limb with a fuckin' loser like that?"

Frank reached down and shook the junkie by the shoulders.

"You better start getting straight with me," he shouted.

The commotion set off some furious scuffling in the dark corner behind the cot. Jake looked over and saw a rat darting across the floor.

"I've got to get out of here," he said.

"Don't go soft on me, little brother," said Frank. "I'm just trying to reason with the man."

Something scurried under the bed, and Jake jumped backward, banging into the rickety partition that separated the bums' cells. Frank did not move, but his face lighted up with a hateful smile.

"A rat won't hurt you," said Frank. "A rat will leave you alone."

Jake backed out the door. Frank gave a sharp little laugh, but Jake did not care. He knew all about rats, their taste for blood and offal. He had been with them in their natural habitat among the dead, and so he did not need his brother's instruction. He just didn't want any part of them right now, that was all.

16

Laura reached the hospital first. The others were following in Ruth's car so that later Laura and Frank could go straight back to the city. In the morning she had to begin intensive rehearsals for her recital. Lately it had been hard to concentrate on the music. The notes were there, but some essential part of her was missing, drained into a silence she did not know how to fill.

The night before, she had gone with Frank to a reception downtown. They hadn't been able to attend the performance itself, but the violinist in the quartet was a friend of Laura's and it was her debut. So they left the hospital a little earlier than usual and sped to the hotel where the party was being held.

The crowd was just beginning to drift in when they arrived. They stopped at the door, and she looked around for her friend. Frank spotted the bar and asked Laura what she wanted. She said something strong.

Before she was able to find the violinist, Laura got cornered by several men, including one in a startling green jacket and luminous tie who said he was a designer. When Laura asked him what he designed, he said space.

All of them pretended to be familiar with her playing, and she pretended to be flattered. When Frank returned with a glass of whiskey, he was followed by a trim and brittle young woman who said right off that she had recently been divorced.

"Have you tried it?" she asked Laura.

"I'm really very happy," Laura said.

"It's like being born again," said the woman. "There were no children, of course."

"Of course," said Frank.

"Thank God for modern medicine," she said, "and the wheel of

Ortho-Novum. It's a liberation. No more wheel of fortune. Love should always be choice.''

The other men enthusiastically concurred.

The woman wore a provocative white silk gown that clung to her rounded parts, and she smoked a slim cigar in a pearl holder that did not look cheap. Laura glanced down toward the ground and saw her own shoes spotted with mud, the plain, drab lines of her skirt. The woman asked for a light and four flames sprang up.

But thank heaven Frank's was not among them. He seemed to be looking for goldfish in his scotch. The woman lazed back against a marble pillar and rested a hand on her breast. When Frank finally came up out of his drink, Laura did not know what to expect.

"Ma'am," he said, drawing out the word like a country lawyer, "I kind of like kids. They don't know anything about sex but the mystery of it. And whenever they want to be held, they just say so."

The woman clearly liked this speech. She stood up and took a step toward Frank, and Laura was on the verge of asserting her own superior claim.

"I want to be held," said the woman.

"We aren't kids anymore," said Frank.

Without warning, the woman flung the contents of her glass at him. It splashed off his shoulder and spotted the front of his shirt.

"Here," he said, "let me get you another." He sniffed at the wet spot on his sleeve. "Gin and tonic, isn't it?"

Laura should have loved him for it. And she did. She did. But only afterward, as she lay awake in bed later that night. Only when it was too late to tell him.

The hospital was stark and cold. The door slid open before Laura with a hiss. She walked past the reception desk, where a volunteer sat reading a paperback romance. No matter how many times Laura had come here, she still hated the feeling of the place. The directory on the wall was a catalog of all God's darkness. The halls were as hushed as mourning.

The elevator took forever to arrive. A little dial over the doors twisted downward from the third floor, where they had the intensive care unit, then went right past the lobby to the basement. That was where they kept the morgue. Laura had seen it one evening when she was wandering around looking for a coffee machine.

She watched the dial hovering on B and had a horrid thought. But then she got hold of herself. They would have called if anything had happened. They would not have moved the body before the family arrived.

The dial began to inch back upward, and then the doors opened. A nurse and a middle-aged couple were inside. Laura pushed the button for three and stared into the lobby as the doors slowly closed.

When she reached the intensive care unit, she checked in with the nurse, who assured her that his condition was guarded but unchanged. Laura went to the room and found him sleeping there, the big machine breathing beside the bed. She took off her coat and shuddered. All they had covering him was a thin sheet. She reached over his chest and touched the button clamped to the pillow. A chime outside the room began to sound.

"Couldn't you put a blanket on him?" she asked when a nurse arrived. "He looks so cold."

The nurse checked a chart hanging next to the door.

"Doctor ordered it this way," she said.

"Why?"

"I'm sure he knows what's best," said the nurse.

Their voices awakened him, and he stirred against the wires and tubes that bound him like an old, wasted Gulliver. A smile came over him, and he reached for her hand. She squeezed gently when he took it. His skin felt clammy, and the touch was weak. He looked past her to the door.

"They'll be here in a few minutes," she said. "They came in a separate car."

She forced herself to be cheerful. Frank's father would pick up on any show of pity. He pointed to the notepad and pencil on the table. She handed it to him, and he began to write. It was difficult for him. There was tape on his hand, an IV stuck into a vein. He could not sit up, so he could not really see what he was doing. Finally he held up the scrawl.

"Lady," it said, "you have a nice, easy touch, for a piano player."

"Thank you," she said. "And you have nice penmanship, for a writer."

He put the pad down and began to work again.

"You ought to know, though," he wrote, "that your hands give you away."

"You can't bluff me," she said. "Don't forget. My hands are actors. They'll never tell you what I really feel."

He wrote again, quickly this time.

"Such a clever lady."

Even though the tubes distorted his expression, he could still smile. And she could, too. Not even forcing herself. Simply because he was who he was, even now.

Just then a heavyset nurse tilted into the room.

"Well, Mr. Nolan," she said. "What a good-looking visitor you have. Is this your daughter?"

"Daughter-in-law," said Laura.

"Isn't that nice," said the nurse. "You know, Mr. Nolan is one of our problem patients. Very uncommunicative."

Frank's father grabbed the notepad again and began to write furiously. When he was finished, he thrust it toward the nurse. She puzzled over it.

"I can't read this scribble," she said.

Laura took the paper from her.

"It says, 'I am not accustomed to discussing my bowels and bladder with every blimp blown in on the breeze.' "

"Aren't we naughty tonight," said the nurse. "I'll be back in a few minutes to bathe you, Mr. Nolan. That'll make you feel a little better."

Frank's father scowled as she left the room.

"She kind of likes you," said Laura.

He closed his eyes with a look of great suffering indulged.

"You need someone to guard the door," she said.

But he was not listening now. His eyes went right past her.

"Hello, old man," said a voice behind her. It was Jake.

His father tried to rise up on the pillows, but he could not manage it. Jake came up to the bed, and she saw him take a deep breath before he seized his father's hand.

"I was just passing through," said Jake.

His father relaxed back into the pillows and picked up his pencil again.

"Kind of you," he wrote.

"Figured that as long as I had a chance to get a word in edgewise, I damned well better take advantage of it."

His father got that crooked smile again, paused, then wrote another line.

"Guilt got pretty bad, I suppose."

It stopped Jake, but not for long.

"That's Frank's game," he said. "You know me. I just come and go."

His father looked at him then, and it was as if he were trying to find a better way of communion. It was something best left private, so Laura turned her head away. When she looked back, he had written something else on the notepad.

"You OK?" it said.

"Sure," said Jake. "The bastards haven't laid a glove on me. You know what they say. 'Yea, though I walk through the valley of the shadow of death I will fear no evil . . .' "

His father looked puzzled. But then Jake went on.

" '. . . 'cause I'm the meanest motherfucker in the valley.' "

His father shook with laughter.

"I guess you'll survive," he wrote.

Then the nurse came back in and asked them all to please step outside to the waiting room because there were some chores that had to be done.

"I just got here," said Jake. "I've been traveling for two days to see this sorry old man."

"He's just like his father, isn't he?" said the nurse.

"How long will it be?" asked Frank.

"Maybe an hour. Maybe a little less."

"Couldn't we just stay for a few more minutes?" asked Frank.

"I suppose," said the nurse.

But by then Frank's father's eyes had almost closed. Jake sat down next to him, touching his shoulder.

"It's good to see you again, old man," he said. His father's eyes opened wide for a moment and then shut.

"He's awfully tired," said Laura. "He was sleeping when I got here."

Jake stood up and looked down on his father resting there. He slowly took his hand away.

"Maybe we should go and get something to eat," said Frank. "He'll have more energy when we come back."

Jake did not move. Frank went over next to him.

"It'll be better later," Frank said.

"The guilt, he says," said Jake. "He's something else, isn't he."

They found a place nearby, and it reminded Laura of the diner in Horace where her father took them on her mother's birthday or their wedding anniversary, when it wasn't right to cook.

None of them was very hungry, but they all ordered something to look at. Frank and Jake had a drink; it did not seem to do any good.

As they waited for the dinner to come, they tried to agree on whether their father seemed better or not. Jake had not seen him for quite a while, so he found it hard to believe that they thought his color was encouraging.

"Who are we kidding?" he said.

"He's getting excellent care," said Ruth.

"You know how Dr. Owen is," said Frank. "He's not the kind to let you down."

Ruth was obviously getting nervous about where this was leading, so she started to fill Jake in on all the people she thought he might remember.

"I heard from Sue Lasser just the other day," she said. "She just got married. To an accountant, no less. She seemed happy."

"I thought she was hot for Frank at one time," said Jake.

"You didn't tell me about that," said Laura, as coyly as she could.

"Deaf girl," said Jake. "Frank took pity on her."

"Ease up, Jake," said Frank.

"She's really very nice," said Ruth before it got worse.

Frank took a pull of his drink, and Laura excused herself to go to the ladies' room. It was usually this way with the two brothers together. Even when Jake had come home on his last leave before being sent overseas, there had been a tension between them that Laura did not know how to relieve.

With Jake alone, it had always been better. The last time he visited, he had even persuaded her to take a spin with him on his motorcycle. He was easy on her at first, gliding down the city streets, working smoothly through the gears. But when they reached the outskirts, he let the big machine loose. She tightened her hold on him and put her face to his back against the wind. He passed car after car, engine roaring, wheels sailing over the bumps. On the curves, they leaned over so far she thought they might fall. And on the straightaways, Jake pushed the machine hard. She was scared. But there was something else, too. She heard him singing, and she sang along, their voices lost in the wind.

Fence posts snapped past. It made her dizzy to look at them, so she closed her eyes. When they were near home again, Jake finally slowed down. She loosened her grip on him just a little. To her enormous surprise, she found herself laughing.

When Frank came home that night, she told him about their adventure. He looked at her as if she had confessed a crime.

"You ought to get yourself a cycle," said Jake. "I'll sell you mine if you give me a good price."

"We're too old for that," said Frank.

"It was fun," said Laura. "Exciting."

"You might be surprised at your woman," said Jake.

"Oh, for God's sake," said Frank. And then he left them standing there, conspirators.

Laura went to the mirror in the ladies' room and looked at the makeup around her eyes. It had not run.

When she joined them again, the dinners had arrived. They all picked at their food, and it gave them an excuse for silence. Eventually Frank paid the check and led them back outside.

Ruth and Frank walked ahead. Jake hung back with Laura, moving slowly, his hands stuffed in his pockets.

"Hi," Laura said to him.

"I guess maybe I'm just worn out," said Jake.

"It's hard for everyone," she said, and this seemed so utterly inadequate, being true.

When they arrived at the nurses' station outside the intensive care unit, the woman asked them to wait there for a minute. She went to the telephone and made a call. A man in white quickly emerged from a side door and asked them to follow him. He led the way into some kind of stockroom, filled with bedding and boxes.

"We tried to phone you," he said. Ruth moaned.

"We were just with him," said Frank.

"Sometimes it happens very quickly at the end," said the doctor.

Laura went to Frank and took hold of his arm. He did not move.

"I'm very sorry," the doctor said.

"What happened?" Frank asked softly.

"We couldn't breathe for him anymore," said the doctor.

"You turned off the machine!" Jake shouted.

The doctor turned to Frank.

"We did no such thing, of course," he said.

"I understand," said Frank.

"Your father was a fascinating man," said the doctor. "I had a chance to get to know him. I was glad that I did."

Jake had moved away from the others. Laura took a step toward him, but then what the doctor had said finally registered. She stopped. Her breath caught in her throat.

"You know that this case has been somewhat unusual," the doctor said to Frank. "I am terribly sorry to trouble you at this sad time, but it is something that cannot wait. Because of the complexity of your father's illness, it would be most helpful to perform an autopsy."

Laura swooned at the thought of the knife. She pictured it descending slowly, touching the bed-whitened skin. She waited for it to cut, but then it began all over again: the gloved hand, the glinting knife denting the flesh.

"My God," she said, "can't you just leave him alone?"

"It is a very routine procedure, Mrs. Nolan," the doctor said. "He was a scientifically minded person. I'm sure he would have agreed."

"We have to let them," said Frank.

And only then did the tears come. The doctor moved away. She was seized by great, wracking heaves. Frank held her, but it did not help. She wept for the simple, helpless indifference of the dead.

"You may see him if you like," said the doctor.

They went to the room where he lay. The nurses had put up a screen so that he could not be seen from the doorway. Behind it in the cold fluorescence of the hospital light, he rested at last unencumbered by tubes and needles and the crushing need to breathe. He seemed so tiny. Laura remembered the old pictures of him, big arms, mighty chest, stronger than his sons. Death had deprived him of the last things that had remained large within him, even in his frailty. And now all she saw was the flesh, as if for the first time, shrunken beyond pain.

Ruth went to her knees beside the bed.

"He would never have asked a single thing from You," she prayed. "But if You are there, be kind to him now."

Frank touched his father's hand, held it. He said nothing. Then he turned to leave.

Jake stayed at the head of the bed as the three of them went to the door. He leaned down and whispered something. Laura was on the other side of the screen now, and she saw Jake's shadow cast upon it, bending low.

THREE

TESTAMENT

17

*F*rank sat with his back to the door, his feet propped up on the gray window ledge, staring out into the dark yard below. Nearly all the stiffness was gone from his legs now. He hadn't worked out since the day Jake came home. Even with the arrangements and the funeral, he'd had time. It had just seemed pointless.

The spotlights beyond the wall of the jail shone through the smudged pane as lonely as stars. On the desk lay the papers he had collected on the Tatum case, the bootlegged copies of the police sheets, the coroner's report, the notes he had put together on Tatum and his wife, the transcript of the perfunctory shooting board. The offices were empty now. The old clock with his father's name on it chimed softly, and he counted the strokes. Laura should have been starting her performance about now.

"What are you doing here?"

Frank turned and saw O'Neill framed in the light from the corridor.

"Working," Frank said and clasped his hands behind his head.

O'Neill came into the cubicle and pulled up a chair.

"Forgot my damned wallet in my desk and had to come all the way back here to get it," he said. "What's your excuse?"

"Talley's coming by later. We have to talk to a guy."

"That Tatum business again," said O'Neill. "I don't know why you don't just give it up, Frank."

"It's my time."

"You want to tell me about it?" said O'Neill. "I mean, what you've got, where you're going with it?"

"I've got a doorman with a record. A doper who was spooked by the sight of blood. A bereaved granddad who gives me the willies."

He did not mention the doubts he had about Williams, the inconsistencies in the time of death, all the futile hunches that just hadn't panned

149

out. They didn't add up to anything that could stand the test of law.

"In case you didn't know it," said O'Neill, "Pricer isn't pleased that you're dragging this thing out."

"Has he been on your ass about it?"

"On the ass of the guy who's on the ass of the guy who's on my ass."

"Some daisy chain," said Nolan.

"I hear you've been having trouble with the cops."

"Nothing I can't handle."

"A thing like that can spill over, you know. It isn't just you alone."

"Look, that part of it's going to go away, one way or another. They're not going to hear a peep from me about the shooting. It's Pricer I can't figure. What he's trying to hide."

"Maybe he's just used to getting his way when he makes up his mind," said O'Neill. "I hear there are some guys who don't take a lot of shit from the people who work for them."

"That so?" said Nolan. "Must get pretty dull for them."

"It isn't like he's exactly proud of his daughter and her husband. I mean, what is this guy, some kind of rag peddler or something? And the girl, I understand she's a mess. Maybe he's just a guy who sees the blood running thin."

"Can you hold him off for a while?" said Nolan.

O'Neill didn't answer, and that was all right. He was silent so rarely that when he was, it meant something; the absence of criticism was almost as good as praise. Nolan looked back into the yard and hoped his boss would just take it as a mood and let it go at that. But O'Neill did not leave.

"Hey, didn't I read somewhere that Laura was putting on a show tonight?"

"A solo recital," said Nolan.

"Then what the hell are you doing here? Shouldn't you be with her?"

"She understands."

"I worry about you sometimes."

"We'll work it out."

"See, Frank, that's what I don't understand. I mean, what is there to work out? Just take what comes by."

"You're a regular stoic."

"My old man's been dead longer is all."

"When I get this case behind me I'll take a little time. Go away with her."

"Maybe you don't have anything to worry about. You look pretty healthy to me."

"The doctors give even odds."

"Want to know what I think?"

"When did you get your medical degree, Terry?"

"I think there's something waiting to get everybody."

O'Neill pushed himself up from the chair.

"Yeah, well, this is a little different," said Nolan.

"I've got some cheese and lunchmeat in the icebox in my office," said O'Neill, "if you feel like eating something. I think there may be a couple of beers, too."

"Thanks, Terry."

"Loosen up, Frank. I hate to see you this way."

"You don't have to look," said Nolan, but by then O'Neill was already gone.

The trouble was, the Tatum case had become linked in some deep way with his father's death, and he could not shake it loose. He pulled the photographs from the bottom drawer and switched on the desk lamp. The little girl lay on the slab. He stared at her broken body, the horrible bruises. And it was as if it were his own child lying there dead, the sum of all his grief and loss.

He swiveled around in his chair and propped his feet back on the sill. A dog wandered around down below, lifting his leg again and again. The place just cried out to be pissed on.

It hadn't always been that way. He remembered the Polish festivals his father used to take them to in the neighborhoods where the accordion bands played the same songs over and over and no one was ashamed to dance. The people sang in a language he did not understand, but he liked the sound of it, thick and round like the golabkis they sold at the street stands. Big old matriarchs stood at the center of a galaxy of kin and laughed like maidens. He remembered the smell of kielbasa—it had seemed so exotic then—and the bitter taste of the specially brewed beer. Just a sip, his father would say, to give you the sense of the thing.

But that neighborhood had died long ago. Now the only trade on the street was in dope and flesh, and nobody danced for joy. The little children were furtive; they stayed together in knots against the danger. Any punks who went looking for trouble didn't have any trouble finding it. And when the trouble was bad enough, maybe they would come face to face with Frank Nolan, and he would demand that they be tried as adults. Nobody was a child anymore.

The lights burst on, and Nolan wheeled around in his chair.

"You asleep?" It was Talley.

"Just thinking," said Nolan.

"You didn't even go home, did you."

Nolan pulled up his tie and hauled on his suit jacket.

"You ever drink Polish beer?" he asked.

"My wife and I found a good Eastern European restaurant," Talley said. "I'll take you there sometime. They've got more brands than you've ever heard of."

"It isn't the same," Nolan said, going past him to the door. "Look, tell me about this guy you've got lined up for us."

"Friend of a friend," said Talley. "My friend's a narc. The gentleman he offered up is into coke and the entertainment business and God knows what all. But it seems he has something to say about the Tatum case."

"How much is it going to cost us?"

"Not a cent," said Talley.

"Long as he talks, the white hats give him a pass."

"Something along those lines," said Talley. "I may have to duck out in the middle. O'Neill's got me on the blue-movie detail tonight."

"Well, we might as well get on with it," said Nolan. He yanked his trenchcoat off the hanger. The bent metal wire clanged against the wall. "You going to have kids, Talley?"

"Haven't really thought about it."

They took the stairs rather than wake the payroller who worked the elevators at night. Nolan moved quickly, and Talley kept up with him.

"Why wait?" Nolan asked.

"We're not ready yet," said Talley.

"You aren't getting any younger."

"Hey," said Talley, "you aren't so young yourself."

They let themselves out the side door, and when they reached the car, Talley got in on the driver's side.

The streets were brightly lighted. The mayor had put up huge mercury vapor lamps that cast everything in a sickly pallor. The idea was to make it hard on the criminals. Maybe it did, but you couldn't tell from the statistics. As far as Nolan was concerned, it just made it easier for the bad guys to aim.

As they approached the entertainment district, the traffic became heavy These were the streets you saw on the travel posters. Discos, nightclubs, high-priced ladies in fur. The Outfit had a piece of the action here. It was the kind of neighborhood where drying your hands in the men's room made you feel like a co-conspirator.

"You know this guy to see him?" Nolan asked as Talley parked the car in an alley.

"Got his description."

"I don't suppose he wants us asking after him."

"He's nervous. But no sweat. He's got a booth lined up for us at one of the dives, the Top of the Bottom. Right over there. We're supposed to wait for him."

They made their way against the crowds to the little basement hangout. It was still empty this early, before the swells finished their expense-account dinners. Inside it was dark and had the muzzy smell of spilled beer and cigarette butts. Nolan led the way to a booth and they sat down. The table was so small he had to sit sideways to keep his knees from bumping Talley's.

The only other customer in the place was a middle-aged woman at the bar. She had stringy hair and eyes so heavily made up you might have thought she had a shiner. She seemed to be holding a conversation with the bartender, but when he walked away she just kept on talking to the air.

"Two beers," said Nolan when the girl came for their order. "In bottles."

"You want 'em opened?" said the girl.

"Couldn't hurt."

"Anything you like, honey."

They hadn't even finished the first round when a man came through the door and went straight to the bar. He ordered something and watched the two of them in the mirror behind the bottles. He wore a Borsalino hat and a three-piece pink suit. Even in the dim light the fabric seemed to glow.

"Got to be our man," said Nolan.

"Our guy's white," said Talley. "Vanek is his name."

"Never heard of him."

"He's not real big-time, Frank."

"Do I have a button off or something?" said Nolan. "Is my tie screwed up? That guy just can't keep his eyes off me."

Just then the man picked up his drink and sauntered over to their table.

"I do believe," he said through a grin, "that you are looking for somebody."

"For Chrissake," said Nolan.

"We're not interested," said Talley.

The man just laughed.

"We don't like pimps," said Nolan. "See, we're cops."

"Not so loud, my man," said the dude. "Mr. Vanek don't like people knowing who's in on the trade."

"He was supposed to come here himself," said Talley. "That was the arrangement."

"Way I get it there weren't no deal at all," said the dude. "This one depends on what you have to offer."

"We don't bargain with the help," said Nolan.

The man sucked the drink from his glass.

"Heavy," he said. "I'll take you to him. But stay back a ways. I don't want to be seen with the heat."

When they hit the door, he strutted out ahead of them—neon flickering around him, hookers making way, his platform shoes tapping on the concrete—like Bojangles gone to hell. He led them several blocks through the crowds and then onto a side street heading toward the lake. At that point, the whole charade became absurd. Here was this phosphorescent dude, shuffling down the sidewalk, snapping his fingers like a fool. And twenty yards behind came Nolan and Talley, wearing broken-down wingtips and plainclothes by Mr. Fuzz. A blind man would have known who was who.

The setup was not at all promising. Nolan had not liked it when Talley had made the suggestion, and now he liked it even less. He hated dealing with the likes of Vanek, even when it was a way to break open a case. And this time the offer of information was so vague that he could not imagine it leading to anything. He had only agreed to the meeting because he was desperate for any lead and because Talley was trying so hard to help. The investigation was hopelessly stalled. Nolan's energy was running out.

Bojangles led them to a fairly decent address and waited at the door. The lobby was empty.

"What's the apartment number?" said Frank.

"I'll go up with you," said Bojangles. "My man wants to make sure it isn't a trap."

"Delusions of grandeur," said Talley.

"Speak English, man," said Bojangles.

The elevator's interior was paneled with wood, and when they reached their floor the door opened on a vestibule decorated with plants and flowers. Frank touched one and found that it was real.

Bojangles led them down a corridor and gestured for them to stop just short of the end. He stood with his back to the wall and slowly brought the palm of his hand up to cover the peephole in one of the doors. Suddenly, the doorknob rattled and the door swung open. Two big men came tumbling out, their hands reaching inside their coats. Then they saw Bojangles.

"What you be doin' that shit for?" said one of them.

"Testing your reaction time, my man," said Bojangles.

He went to the door across the hall and knocked twice, then once, then twice again. A young woman opened it. She wore blue jeans and a T-shirt that had "Tickle" written on it. One of the heavies from across the hall joined them going in.

"Where's Vanek?" Talley asked. "We're getting a little impatient here."

Just then the bathroom door opened to the gagging sound of the toilet flushing. A middle-aged man with a crewcut emerged. He wore a white shirt, school tie, and dumpy blue suit.

"Is this him?" said Nolan.

"I think it is," said Talley.

"Vanek," said Nolan, "you don't exactly look like what you are."

The man sat down in a big stuffed chair.

"In my business you have to be a freak. And in the circles in which I travel, that," he said, pointing to Bojangles, "is ordinary. But this"—his hand sweeping down his tie—"this is positively bizarre."

Nolan moved up directly in front of him, tempting his sidekicks to make a move. They did, but Vanek waved them back.

"I didn't appreciate the muscle you had waiting for us in the hall," Nolan said. "They were going for their pieces. That was not very polite."

"You must forgive my precautions."

All Nolan's anger and frustration rose up in his throat as he stared at the smug figure before him. He wasn't any closer to figuring out the murder than he was the day the little girl's body was discovered, and here he was doing business with a small-time drug dealer who was trying to save his skin by peddling another kind of junk.

"I ought to take you down," said Nolan.

One of the heavies leaped forward and began waving his pistol around as if it were a sparkler and this were the Fourth of July. Vanek let him do it for a while, and then he said, "I think I can handle these gentlemen by myself. You may take a break," He turned to the woman sprawled on the couch. "You, too, Fawn."

"Shit," she spat. "You always haul me up short."

"Get out," said Vanek, quite softly, considering his expression. But when they had left, he began to fidget, his hands working on each other like mating birds.

"If my guys turn on me, I'm a dead man," he said, but he did not put any more weight on that possibility than Nolan would have. "They don't know the terms of our arrangement. I'm sure you understand."

"I don't follow," said Talley.

"He doesn't want the help to know he's an informer," said Nolan. "He tells them he's paying us off."

"It is never quite so explicit," said Vanek, lighting up a cigarette. "It is just an impression I leave."

"Well, you'd better leave a hell of an impression on me, friend," said Nolan.

"I'm sure you won't be disappointed," said Vanek, "but first I think we should discuss the ground rules."

"You don't come across, we burn you," said Nolan. "Just that simple."

"That goes without saying," said Vanek, a pathetic expression souring on his lips. "I'm talking about testimony. What I tell you here does not get linked with my name. I do not testify. That is the deal."

They were all the same. The less confidence you had in them, the more they insisted on confidentiality.

"We're not talking about testimony," said Nolan.

Talley stepped in to make it firm.

"I think we are on the same wavelength," he said. "We will be operating under the agreement you have with Detective Ross."

"Beautiful," said Vanek.

"What do you know about the Tatum case?" said Nolan.

"Let's get this up front right away," said Vanek. "I'm as far away from this one as a man can be and still vote in city elections. Whoever got that little girl is scum, OK?"

"I didn't come here for a lesson in moral distinctions from a pusher," said Nolan.

"I don't talk about my own business, as a rule," said Vanek.

"Then what do you talk about?"

"What I hear about the guy you blew away, for example. That Williams guy."

"Give."

"He was a punk," said Vanek. "A bad actor. He didn't know enough to stay out of other people's business."

Nolan walked to the other side of the room. Vanek fumbled with another cigarette and ticked the first one flat into the tray with a flick of his finger. His face shone, and it was not an inner glow.

"Is this what you got us down here for?" Nolan demanded.

"Give me a chance, all right? I haven't gotten to it yet."

"Gotten to what?"

"The book on Williams."

"I know all about him," said Nolan. "I put the sonofabitch in the can."

"Not for long enough, I guess," Vanek observed, and Nolan did not appreciate his immunized smile. "When he came out of slam he went on the needle."

"Your kind of guy," said Nolan.

"No friend of mine. They way I hear it, the punk was out freelancing."

"He was selling," said Nolan. "So I heard."

"But did you hear where?"

"Why don't you surprise me," said Nolan.

"He was in the neighborhood here. Had some pretty good clients, too, I understand. Custom delivery. Premium price."

"You mean he was muscling into your territory."

"Muscle," said Vanek, and he let out a high, snorting laugh. "That's a good one."

"Who did he sell to exactly?"

"Maybe you ought to find out."

"Maybe you ought to tell me."

"Like I said, I didn't know the man myself. But I'll tell you this. Sometimes the high-class buyers aren't real careful about who they trade with."

"They aren't biologists," said Nolan. "They don't make distinctions among all the varieties of slime."

Vanek put out his cigarette. But he didn't take offense.

"You weren't out to get him, were you?" said Talley. "You didn't try to run him out of your game."

"Figure it out for yourself," said the man. "If I was on his ass, do you think I would have gotten you over here to talk about it?"

"To cover yourself, maybe."

"It never came to that," said Vanek. "Like I said, I heard certain things and wondered whether I was going to have to do something about it. But before I knew it, I read in the papers that the cops had taken him out."

"Is that what you wanted to tell us?" said Nolan. "That we blew away your competition?"

"I don't know how to thank you," said Vanek.

Nolan stood up and turned toward the door, Vanek's laughter clawing at his back. When he reached the hallway, he pounded on the door where Bojangles and the heavies were staked out. It opened a crack.

"If I were you I'd be a little more careful about who I worked for," he said. "Your man's a fucking snitch." Then he turned and walked away.

18

Which doctor are you, anyway? The black-haired one who told us that night that Dad was dead? Oh, the specialist. I remember. Sure, the cute one with the wire-rimmed glasses and the long, sensitive fingers. Has anybody ever told you that you kind of look like Jimmy Stewart when he was young? Maybe we ought to be talking in the flesh. I mean, who knows where the conversation might lead?

OK. OK. It's always business first with doctors. I'm not exactly sure I understand what you're after, though. I thought Dad's medical history had been worked up pretty well already, what with the autopsy and all. I'm not sure what I can add.

But if you want something about the family, you've come to the right place. My brothers don't give much of a damn about history. Maybe the reason I do is that it was something Dad and I could always talk about, even toward the end. It gave him solace to talk about all the dead Nolans before him. Don't ask me why.

From what Frank told me, I gather that you want to trace a genetic link. I guess that's the reason I keep catching Frank watching me for signs. When I bobble a dish at the sink, he's there staring. When I bump the table, his eyes are fixed. I'll tell you something, Doc. It's really gotten on my nerves.

But in a way, I'd like to believe that there is some physical fact that explains some of what has happened to us over the generations. Father, forgive me. It sure would take some of our forebears off the hook.

How far back shall we begin? The farther back, the less reliable the story. But no matter. For you, I'll do the whole show.

Let's start with Josiah Nolan. We meet him in the middle of the eighteenth century when he landed in Virginia as an indentured servant from Ireland. Back beyond that, it gets a little hazy. There's a black Irish streak in us that makes me think we have some Spanish sailors, beached in the sinking of the Armada, way back there in the line. Maybe even some Moors. Anyway, we ain't thoroughbreds.

Dad and I visited Ireland once. Dad wanted to see Joyce's Dublin, the home of Yeats and Swift. I was more interested in the boys of Trinity. But it turns out that there's a regular industry in discovering Americans' roots, so we tried to look old Josiah up. I'm afraid we never found him. He wasn't listed in the records of the crossings. Maybe he went under an assumed name. Maybe he left in disgrace. I'd like to think it was because of love.

Even though we didn't get anywhere with Josiah, you could still feel the family's presence there. It was uncanny. Everywhere I looked I saw people who might as well have been my relatives. There was one woman on a bus in County Cork who could have been my grandma reincarnated, from the pictures I've seen. Her skin was so fair it was transparent, like a flame, and her hair as white as ice.

Nobody has any pictures of Josiah, of course. But I can guess how he looked. He was probably on the smaller side, like all of us. I bet his eyes were wide and deep. And his eyebrows would have joined, cowlwise, in the middle. I'll give him my own nose, delicate of bone, all the time poking into things it shouldn't. What's more, he must have had that stoical expression you find in men who are ready to give up everything and launch themselves into the unknown.

You don't know what I'm talking about, do you? Well, just go into Pilsen someday or any of the other Hispanic neighborhoods. You'll see him sitting there, old and ravaged, on a doorstep. He's surely much younger than he looks. He has brought his people to a better place, stooping under the weight of them. He is about to die, and if he's an illegal, his family will have to lie about him even as they put him in the ground. Did I tell you how we found Josiah's grave marker? It was there where the notes in the family Bible said it would be. The wind had worn away the inscription. All you could see was his name and dates. Died at thirty-four. Don't know why. Could guess, though, now. Couldn't you?

Well, maybe thirty-four seems pretty young, but he'd had a hell of a life. Made a home for himself. Sired quite a few kids. Some of them died young. That runs throughout the family annals. But some survived, and all in all there was nothing to be sad about. The kids did quite well for themselves, actually, moving west beyond the first mountains and building a farm there. I've been to the place where they lighted. It's subdivided now, of course, but up in the mountains there are lookouts where you can see the whole valley, and if you kind of narrow your angle of vision and gaze into the distance, you can see nothing but beautiful green farms all the way to the other mountains.

Josiah's daughter married a preacher, bore him three daughters, and lived for seventy-five years. The family Bible doesn't follow her family or her sister's beyond the next generation. Josiah's only surviving son carried our name, and in the Bible it lists his dates as 1767-1802 and says, "God save him from the devil." I certainly hope so, because I have always had good feelings about Peter Nolan's short, heedless years.

Do you ever think that maybe the time of a life—the actual numbering of the days—doesn't really make a difference? Being the first one out, that's the tragedy, whenever it happens. Do you remember, when you were a kid, riding on the Ferris wheel? You got on, and there were all the others waiting in line behind you for a place. Then the wheel lifted, taking you high up over their heads, and you were filled with joy and fear. The wheel turned and turned, stopping now and then to let another person from the line climb aboard. Finally, the operator with his greasy shirt and rancid cigar stopped the machine as your car clanged to the bottom. "Your ride is over, sweetie," he would say through his tobacco-stained teeth. And you'd get out from behind the safety bar and climb down on the rickety platform and look back up at all the people who had been waiting with you in line, now waving and laughing as they went around. I think that is what it must be like to die.

OK. OK. Back to Peter Nolan. He reared seven children. All I know about the other Nolans of that generation is the names. You know, Doc, if old Josiah brought this disease over with his blood, you're going to have one hell of a time chasing down everyone who's got it. I mean, there must be thousands of Josiah's descendants around, each of them rutting like crazy. I know you stamped out polio, but it'll take a lot more than you think to stop the Nolans. We'll all talk sensibly. Rational as can be. Ending disease, yes indeed. But someone somewhere is going to sneak out and have some fun.

Me married? No. I'm old enough to know better. But I thought you'd never ask. The way I figure it, unless you're going to have kids, there's no advantage in tying yourself down. None of my friends have kids, anyway.

Whatever the disease may be, you don't have to worry about me. And I'd guess the same would be true of Jake. As for Frank, he'll be just as reasonable about this as you are. I mean, there's no chance that Frank would make a mistake in the heat of the moment. Not Frank. See, he believes from what you have told him that the whole human race would be better off without his genes. He is very big on cosmic responsibilities, just like Dad. I don't know how Laura stands it.

Don't get impatient with me, Doc. Where was I? Ah, yes. Peter Nolan. He had seven children before his untimely death. All but two of them perished in the cholera epidemic of 1819. One survivor was a boy, Walter, and the other a girl, Sally. The records don't show much about them, but Dad had his opinion. I don't know whether it was a secret passed down to him or whether he was just letting his imagination run. All we know for sure is that they both moved out of the Shenandoah Valley in 1825. Next we hear of Walter he's already settled in this state and married someone of obscure lineage who is listed in all the documents as Sarah. Dad thought Sarah was Sally and that they had headed west in shame.

It makes some sense, doesn't it? You can imagine the first thrill, the tickle and guilt as the young boy discovered how he could make his sister purr. The young girl awakening to what the wet caresses she gave her brother were named by law and the prophets. And this while everyone else was dying around them. You can just see them, can't you? Walking hand in hand like Hansel and Gretel to some enchanted bower. And on the soft pine needles they found their pleasure.

Maybe the incest had something to do with the flaw in our genes. I mean, you hear about that sort of thing—madness, hemophilia, and so forth. Kings and show dogs. But by the objective record, the family doesn't seem to have been that much worse off after them than it was before.

Sally died early, but not before she had some babies. One of the older sons was my great-great-grandfather, Thomas Nolan. He's the one who first moved off the farm and into the city. Thomas was the only steady child in the bunch. Two died in childhood. The rest became, as far as I know, hustlers and no-accounts of one sort or another. One signed up to be a soldier, like Jake. He died at the Battle of Bull Run. Folks said he had been looking to meet a miniéball all along.

It may have been their mother dying—especially the way she died—that messed the children up. She lost all physical control. It was as if something had short-circuited the line connecting her brain with her body. She talked like a drunk—you could hear a little of that in Dad toward the end—and she could not walk or even button her blouse.

Well, as I said, at least one of Walter and Sally's sons did well for himself in the city. He went into the livestock market and grain exchange, starting as an order runner and working up to be a broker. He married a frail young woman who seems to have brought to the family the rare and beautiful smile you can see today in Jake and Frank. She made Thomas very happy, but she had trouble bearing him children. Several were stillborn. Only one survived. That was Samuel, my great-grandfather.

Samuel begat four kids and took his father's place on the exchange when Thomas became too sick to go on. They all lived under the same roof in a house on the near South Side. It was an elegant neighborhood in those days. You can still see the place today; it's cut up into tenements.

Here's where I begin to have more confidence in the story. I can remember reading my grandpa's letters about his grandfather, Thomas, the way the man used to be carried around the house in a rocking chair by hired men, how he barked at them, nasty as a lush. But they indulged him until the very end, because he held on to his money and didn't open his hand until the family pried the fingers loose upon his death.

From here on out, Doc, I can draw you a fairly accurate family tree if that will help. There may be some gaps, but not many. For now, though, I'll just concentrate on the direct line.

My grandfather was the only person of his generation who had medical problems young. His brothers and sisters lived to a nice old age. Grandpa was already married and Dad was born before the first symptoms set in. And even then they didn't think much of it. But the matter came to a head when Dad's sister was born dead. Grandma couldn't accept it. She insisted that they go to a doctor to see what was wrong. The doctor listened to the slurred speech, took notice of Grandpa's awkwardness of movement. He put it all together and pronounced his verdict. He told Grandpa that he was suffering from syphilis and that it had affected his brain.

As you might guess, this news did not exactly draw the couple together. Grandpa insisted that he had not been messing around on the side. And Grandma said that she surely had not either. Nobody doubted the doctor's word, of course. They never do.

Can you imagine what a thing like that would do to a marriage today? But the vows were stronger in those days. So both Grandma and Grandpa, in Christian solidarity and obedience, and in the certainty that the other had inflicted the wages of immorality upon their dead child and themselves, stayed together and took the cure. It was not painless. It had something to do with mercury, I believe. Of course, it did nothing for Grandpa's symptoms, and it didn't exactly do wonders for dinner-table conversations either. Grandma, out of caution and a sense of duty to punish on earth what Grandpa, like Dad after him, did not believe would be punished elsewhere, moved into a separate bedroom and locked her knees to her husband forever. And that is how my father became an only child.

When they lost their fortune in the Great Crash, Grandma was satisfied that this was explained by his peccancy alone. They had to move out of the mansion into a dingy little apartment with only one room. Grandpa worked for the WPA. Grandma read the Good Book and turned it against her man. His only revenge was that they had made a deal, a love pact, back when they were courting. Since they disagreed so fundamentally on matters of faith, they had decided that he would handle the spiritual education of the sons and she would get the daughters. So by locking Grandpa out of her body, Grandma also ensured that she would be theologically outnumbered in the household, two to one.

I wonder if Dad had any idea what was in store for him. I guess maybe he didn't really think about it any more than we did until you forced us to. He probably had other explanations. I know I did. We had seen his condition begin to deteriorate after Mother died. He blamed himself for her leaving, of course. And we thought the symptoms were signs of the strain. They were so subtle at first that if you didn't know he had been a deft cabinetmaker and something of a virtuoso on the cello, you might not have noticed them at all.

But seeing him in the hospital, all wired up, machines doing his breathing for him. . . . Doctor, do you have to kill a man that particular way?

I'm sorry. It's just so pitiful, and all I really wanted to say to him over and over was how much I loved him but I didn't dare because he would have known that it was a way of telling him he was dying and neither of us wanted to admit that.

So we pretended that nothing had changed. And in some ways, nothing had. I remember one time he couldn't find a belt to wear, so he went uptown with his pants stapled to his shirt. "Same principle as suspenders," he said. Do you understand how we felt about him? The lousy clothes, the breakup of his marriage, the illness. He overcame everything. He was a hero, despite it all, and pretty soon you forgot about everything but his strength. How could anything ever conquer him?

He must have known what was going to happen to him once he saw that we had brought Jake back home. He was conscious then, but they couldn't get him to breathe on his own, and he was smart enough to realize what that meant. Do you know, Doc, that even with hoses down his throat and tubes in his arms, with only a few more hours to live and knowing it, Dad was smiling that morning, making fun of himself? Doing his Popeye face for me with his teeth out. He even let Mother's sister into the room to see him. And though she had never forgiven him, she didn't know what to do but cry. He wrote her a little note in that awful scribble of his. It just said, "I've never been quite as miserable as I have seemed." And in those words he summed up the whole of his life as he went into blackness with more joy than she or any of us could ever feel. Do I have to go on, Doc? I don't always sob like this. But the honest fact is that despite everything that I had learned from him I hoped there was a God to be kind to him, and at the same time I hated Dad for being so strong as to make us love him most at the moment of his dying.

Can you give me a minute, Doc? I'm going to throw some water on my face and blow my nose. Hold on.

Hello? I'm back. Sorry I lost control. You know, I want to be as steady as he was, but sometimes I get so damned afraid.

Well, anyway, I hope this little tale was of some use to you, Doc. It did me no good at all. But maybe we ought to get together over dinner and talk about it some more. You could come over afterward and look at the family album. It might be kind of pleasant, actually.

19

"I know I owe you one," said the lieutenant, whispering it across the desk. "But why this one, Frank?"

Nolan looked past him into the darkness outside the window. A fire was burning out west somewhere. It turned the low sky yellow against the darkness, like a match lighting up a face.

"You still have the tape, don't you?" he said.

"We keep them sixty days. Longer when we receive a formal request. I'll need it in writing."

"Don't jerk me around, Ed."

"Look, you've gotten me out of jams more than once. But this time you want to put me into one, and I just don't know."

"It's only between us."

Nolan didn't have any clear idea what he might find on the tape, but after he blew the questioning of Vanek, it was the last lead he had, unless you counted Ralph Celcik. And there wasn't even enough evidence to search his room.

"Look behind you," said the lieutenant, gesturing to the big windows that opened out on the communications center. Dozens of police officers worked at consoles fitted with phones, switch panels, and big lighted maps of the districts, marked out in beats. "You gonna tell me nobody noticed you coming in? You gonna tell me they don't know what you've been working on?"

"Nobody's going to get hurt."

"That's not the word on the street, Frank. Word is you're trying to create a mess."

"Word's wrong," said Nolan. But he knew what was circulating. When he stepped inside police headquarters he could hear the whispers everywhere he went. The desk sergeant at the First District downstairs didn't even say hello. A uniform in the elevator gave a knowing look to his partner when Frank got on. And the communications center seemed to fall into a hush as he walked through.

"I just don't see your angle," said the lieutenant.

"No angle at all, Ed. Straight on. I'm investigating a murder."

"Tell me about it."

"It hasn't got anything to do with the shooting. Williams had hostages. That part stands on its own. It went down like a textbook. But the kid's death was something else again."

"What makes you think Williams wasn't the man?"

"Hunches. That's all."

"How's the tape going to help?"

"Can't tell until I hear it."

"Sounds like you're trying to build a house out of smoke."

"Humor me, Ed."

"It could be my ass."

"Have you listened to it?"

"I pulled it out as soon as you called. There's nothing there, Frank. The woman is hysterical. She says a few words. Then click, she hangs up."

"Then what's the risk of playing it for me?"

"I know you, Frank. You don't give up."

"Can't you tell? I'm at the end of my string."

"Just promise me one thing," said the lieutenant. "Get me on as a bailiff if this thing blows up in my face."

"Hell, I'll get you made a judge."

The lieutenant spun in his chair and hit the button on a recorder that sat on a table behind the desk. His back stretched the blue cloth of his shirt as he hunched over the machine, fiddling with the controls. The speaker popped. A high-pitched hiss followed, then a voice.

"Police department," it said.

Nolan pulled out a notebook.

"Police department. May I help you?"

"Do you have Prince Albert in a can?" said a child's voice. Muffled giggles.

"We let him out, sonny," said the officer on the tape. "But we'll put you in the can when this call gets traced." The line went dead.

The lieutenant turned back to Nolan.

"It's coming up now," he said. "We get a hundred of those bullshit calls every watch. Drunks, dares, every damned thing. What did Nelly

Fox bat his best season? How much should you pay off á building inspector? Some people just call up to have somebody to talk to.''

The dispatcher's voice came on again, weary and flat.

"Police department."

"You've got to help!" shrieked a woman. "Right away!"

"What seems to be the—"

The woman's voice cut the dispatcher off.

"He's killed a little girl," she shouted.

"Where, ma'am? Give me a location."

There was a long pause. Then the woman screamed again.

"In the alley behind Rayburn at Slader Street. Come quick."

"Calm down, now. Did you see someone?"

"He carried her body."

"May I have your name, ma'am?"

Silence.

"A squad is on the way. Now please tell me your name."

But there was no response. The receiver clicked.

"That's it," said the lieutenant, flicking off the machine.

"The woman's voice seemed strange," said Frank. "Like she was far away."

"Bad connection. Probably a pay phone."

"But there wasn't any background noise. No cars going by."

"Could have been inside a store."

"But someone would have heard her scream."

"Maybe she was in a booth."

"It sounded like she was talking through a handkerchief or something."

"People do funny things. They don't want to get involved."

"There was something wrong with the rhythm, too."

"She wasn't reading a poem, Frank."

"Out of phase with the questions the dispatcher was asking."

The lieutenant pulled out a big notebook and flipped through its pages. When he found the one he was looking for he ran his finger down it.

"That day alone," he said, turning the book toward Nolan, "we got this many calls. This number here is the anonymous ones. People are scared shitless as a rule. They think if they give their names maybe we'll jump all over them. With all deference, Frank, they aren't so sure a guy like you won't try to put them away."

"I know what you mean. People are afraid of their shadows. They fret when I ask to hear a tape. Every damned thing."

The lieutenant stood up and walked to the door.

"Now we're even," he said.

"Thanks, Ed."

"Keep me out of it. That's all I ask."

"You got it," said Nolan, hauling on his coat.

"I was sorry to hear about your old man."

"I appreciate that."

"I wanted to make the wake. I just couldn't get away."

"It's all right. There were plenty of people there. We got your flowers."

"Everybody chipped in."

"Card was signed 'Friends in the Force.' I figured it was you."

"No names," said the lieutenant.

"I understand," said Nolan.

20

*E*ven when Laura lifted her hands from the keyboard, Jake was still not sure the piece was finished. There was no resolution, no sense of an ending. Then she looked toward the audience, and the applause whelmed over her. Jake stood and cheered. He thought for an instant that he caught her eye, and he clapped his hands above his head.

The last selection had been by Schönberg, abstract and elliptical. It had not moved him as the other pieces had: Bach and Beethoven and Debussy, the music of his childhood. But still he had been dazzled by her mastery, the feeling she had found in it, a twilight of hope in the fractured rows of tones.

She was on her feet now, too, taking her bows. Jake waited until she had left the stage to slip into the aisle in the shadows under the balcony. Then she was back again for an encore. He stayed at the door as she settled herself and began to play. It was the Prelude from *Le Tombeau de Couperin*. It had always been one of his father's favorites.

He quietly opened the door and entered the empty lobby. An usher stood leaning against the wall. Jake asked him directions to the stage.

"I'm with Laura Nolan," Jake said, and he did not know how he could ever verify such an incredible assertion.

But the usher did not demand proof. He just led Jake to a door off to the side of the hallway. It opened onto a narrow, grimy corridor. A stack of programs lay in a corner bound in twine. The air was close and musty, and the sound of the piano was as distant as a dream.

He followed the corridor to where it opened onto a dank practice room full of risers and stacked chairs. The light was dim, and music stands cast the shadows of men hunched against the cold.

"Looking for something?" said a voice. A man in gray work clothes emerged from behind a pillar.

"Is there somewhere I could take a leak?" asked Jake.

"You took a wrong turn, son," said the man, stepping into the light.

"I'm with the pianist. I'm supposed to meet her here."

"She's mighty good," said the man. "Good crowd, too. I was a little worried. Feels like snow."

"The toilet," said Jake. His bladder was burning now, false pressure crying out for relief.

"Right down that hall on your left," said the man.

The door was marked with a peeling decal. Inside, a bucket on wheels stood near a utility tub. A dirty gray mop lay in the bottom of the bucket like something that had once been alive. Jake went to the urinal.

The burning sensation was there as he emptied himself, but it was bearable. The shot Dr. Owen had given him in the morning seemed to be taking effect. And even on the worst days before he went to see the doctor, it had not been so very bad. Luong's disease was more tenacious than it was painful. And to Jake's surprise, Luong had been wrong. There was a cure.

"You mustn't neglect this, Jake," the doctor had said. "It could make you sterile, or worse."

"Tell me the truth, Doc," Jake had asked. "Will it make my pecker fall off?"

"It would serve you right if it did," said Dr. Owen. "You seem to be willing to put your member in places I would not put the tip of my umbrella."

The shot, he said, would minimize the symptoms for a time, but to get rid of the infection Jake would have to take medicine for a month and abstain from sexual intercourse.

"You know," said the doctor, "it will only exacerbate the ataxia if you let yourself get run-down."

"Ataxia?" said Jake. It was not like Dr Owen to talk in a foreign language.

"The disease that killed your father," said the doctor. "Haven't you been told?"

"I was only with him that once. I couldn't have caught it then, could I?"

"It's a hereditary condition, Jake," said the doctor. "Frank should have explained it to you."

"You mean I have it already?"

"The odds are fifty-fifty. But you seem to be in pretty good shape. No signs of it yet. I want to be candid with you. It could happen anytime. In your father's case, the onset was really very late."

"He wasn't so old."

"It all depends," said Dr. Owen, twisting his glasses off his face. "Sometimes it strikes early. We aren't sure why."

"Frank knows all this?" said Jake.

"He's been under quite a strain," said the doctor. "Now, I want you to bring this girl in as soon as possible. I presume you know who it was."

"What about the other thing?" said Jake. "What am I supposed to do about that?"

"Let's take care of the condition we can do something about," said the doctor.

The Ravel was coming to a close as Jake finished, zipped his pants, and washed his hands at a corroded old sink, splashing cold water on his face. The paper towels were rough against his skin. He wadded them up and tossed them into the trash barrel.

He had tried all day to call Frank, but his brother was always too busy to talk. Jake felt angry and betrayed. He fixed on Frank's deception as if that were the real disease. And it was like a confirmation of a fact that he had known all along, drawn to it the way he had been drawn to Luong, in a hopeless embrace.

Yes, that was it. He wanted to embrace the truth as tightly as his father always had. He wanted to force his brother to say the words and admit his terrible deceit.

Laura was just coming off the stage when Jake emerged. He drew a breath. Then another. She was radiant and she reached out and hugged him, kissed his cheek. The audience did not relent. She left him to take another bow.

A crowd was beginning to form backstage, and Jake felt himself being edged to the rear of it. The admirers gave Laura flowers and flattery. Touched her hands. Jake stood aside, but Laura looked past all the well-wishers until she found him there in a corner.

"Stay with me," she said.

"It's your moment."

"I saw you in the audience," she said. "I wasn't sure that you would come."

She held on to him as she accepted the praise of people she knew and people she didn't. He felt foolish and out of place. His clothes were shabby; he wasn't even wearing a tie. When she introduced him to someone, he did not know what to say.

He sensed an unease in her, too. Was it because she was part of the lie? If so, she had put on quite a front. Before he had talked to Dr. Owen, Jake had not had the slightest hint that she had been hiding anything from him. It did not surprise him that Frank and Ruth had been able to carry it off. But Laura. Laura was different.

When the last of the well-wishers had finally gone and the janitor had come up and passed on his compliments, Laura released Jake's arm.

"Will the soldier take the lady for a drink?" she said.

"Sure," he said.

They retrieved her coat from her small dressing room and left through the dark and empty hall.

"It's so lonely here when the people are gone," she said. "All those memories. Symphonies. Concertos. Sonatas. The children's voices, too, from when this place was part of a school. Do you suppose the vibrations make tiny changes in the structure of the molecules of wood and fabric? Single atoms excited, altered, resonating with every note."

"You sound like my father," said Jake.

"He had so many magical ideas," she said.

Outside the wind was cold. She moved up close to him for warmth.

It was no problem getting a table at the restaurant. The maître d' knew Laura and didn't give Jake a second glance. The place was not at all full.

"It must be because of the weather," she said. "Usually after a concert there's quite a crowd."

She waved to a group at a table across the room and then sloughed off her coat and ordered wine and soda. Jake asked for bourbon on the rocks.

"You must be tired," he said.

"It's supposed to look effortless," she said, pretending to be stung by criticism. But he had worse to say to her. He was not going to let her charm him out of it.

"Keeping everything bottled up," he said.

Laura seemed to pick up on that at first, then she let it go.

"With Schönberg," she said, "you have to hold back."

"For a person like you, that must take a lot of practice."

"I'm always tempted by my emotions," she said, and it was suddenly very cold, as if she knew they were talking about the same thing.

"I guess Frank is an example for you," he said. "His famous self-control."

"You aren't so different," she said, "if either of you would bother to look."

"We both know how to hurt people," he said, and the icy self-pity he heard in it made the anger burn all the more.

"That's just wrong, Jake," she said. "You can be every bit as sensitive to people as your father was, when you let yourself be. Maybe it's time for you to find a good woman."

She was teasing him, as coy as a schoolgirl. It disgusted him that she thought he was so easy to fool.

"I get what I want," he said.

This did not shock her. She went right on.

"You could start a family," she said. "I bet you'd be a good father. You probably don't think so, but a woman always knows."

She was taunting him. He hadn't thought her capable of such cruelty.

"What about you?" he said.

"I'm spoken for," she said, so sweetly that he could hardly bear to keep his eyes on her.

"I mean a family," he said. "Kids."

It stopped her. He was sure that she would not be so brazen as to bring the deception all the way home.

"We're still young," she said. "There's time."

Jake stood up at the table.

"I think maybe I'd better go," he said.

"Something is troubling you, Jake. Please don't leave. Tell me what it is."

"I didn't want you to lie, that's all," he said.

"Does the truth always have to be ugly?"

"I'll tell you the truth," he said, sitting down again and pressing his hand hard upon the circle of his glass. "I'm sick. I found a woman and she gave me a venereal disease. I'm unclean."

"Oh, Jake," she said. "Did you go to a doctor? You shouldn't let a thing like that go untreated."

He listened closely now, the way a hunter does, to locate and destroy.

"What difference does it make?" he said. "It's only a matter of time before I suffocate just like my father did."

"You're still a young man," she said. "You shouldn't talk that way."

He watched her face. He had her in his sights.

"Stop the bullshit, Laura," he said. "I know all about the thing that killed him. The doctor told me today about the way it runs in families. I might have it already. Any of us might."

"You must be wrong," she said.

"His father gave it to him, and his father, and his father before him. What the hell did you start talking about kids for? Jesus, I mean, what were you thinking about?"

"Jake," she said. "Please stop."

"You all knew about it and didn't tell me a thing. It's my life and you kept me in the dark."

"It isn't true," she said. She was weeping. She looked at him, and he began to feel the shame of his anger.

"Ask Frank," he said. "Ask the great man."

"He never told me."

"I thought you knew," he said.

She gathered up her coat and threw some money on the table.

"You don't think at all, Jake," she said. "Neither of you do."

21

*L*aura had left the hall light burning and set out a bottle of wine. A note said, "I'll be home as soon as I can." The mail was stacked in the center of a low table, a bulky package on top. Nolan picked it up. It was from their attorney. He shook it and felt something sliding back and forth inside.

It was nearly eleven o'clock. The concert had to be over by now. She must have gone to a reception. Nolan balanced a glass precariously on the mail, picked up the bottle and corkscrew in the other hand, and carried them into his study.

The package was done up in heavy wrapping paper and strong tape. It did not come open easily. He had to rip it apart with his penknife. Inside was a tape cassette wrapped in a short typewritten note, which he had managed in his struggle to cut into two equal strips. He put the whole mess down, pulled the bottle cork, and had a little wine. Then he laid the coiling pieces of paper side by side on the desk and lined them up until the words matched up across.

The letter said that his father had made the tape shortly before his last trip to the hospital. He had left orders that after his passing the lawyer was to deliver it to his eldest son. The lawyer reminded Nolan that there was already a proper will. An oral codicil, even one physically embodied in a coded magnetic tape, could not supersede, modify, or in any way interfere with or interpret the original testamentary document. The lawyer should have known better than to worry about that. This family never fought over money.

Nolan turned his head to read the last sentence where the strips curled around each other under the heel of his hand. It seemed to be an expression of sorrow at his father's death and hope for an early settlement of the estate. He pushed the note aside.

176

Then he took the tape to the machine and snapped it into place. But he did not turn it on. Not yet. Somehow he knew that his father would have expected him to hesitate, would have savored the drama of it.

Nolan returned to his chair and looked over to the corner of the desk where a framed wedding announcement held up one side of a row of books. Laura's mother had embellished it with little needlepoint fleurs-de-lis, glue-on swirls of pink and green, tiny spangles that caught the light. A Woolworth Book of Kells.

He rubbed the serrated edge of the picture frame, then put it down in front of him. There was no excuse for keeping the truth from Laura any longer. The doctors were as sure as they ever would be. He could not spare her. The dream of having children was out. He felt a sense of loss, but for him it was submerged in other feelings. For her it would be everything.

But there was only one way to prevent the disease from going on and on, generation to generation. You had to break the chain. You had to remember the suffering. This was his father's legacy.

Nolan spun the glass between his fingers and watched the red liquid swirl up the sides. His flesh was suddenly mysterious to him—fat, sinew, bone, and nail. And yet he held in his own hands the whole weight of the future. This was man's gift to evolution, Dr. Erdman had said, the possibility of choice. The very weakness in the cells called for uncommon strength. He stood up and waited for the feeling to pass. His arms hung heavy. He lifted them and grasped the back of the chair, squeezing until the metal frame bit into his palm. Then he let go and crossed the room.

The volume knob on the machine balked as he turned it on. He snapped the cassette magazine closed and punched the play button. The tape hissed awhile like a worn old record. Then it clicked and huffed as his father fiddled with the microphone—tapping on it to make sure it was alive. Nolan could hear his father shuffling papers so furiously it sounded like fire. He could imagine him sitting there at the table heaped with books and gizmos, arranging his script and straightening his tie, coughing to clear his ravaged chest; for him, a thing was simply not worth doing unless it was worth overdoing.

"In case you were wondering," the small, pinched voice finally said, "this crap's my last tape."

His father paused for a laugh and got it. The joke was close to the wound, where he always played it.

When the voice came back, Nolan was aware of its odd cadence. It reminded him of the recording he had listened to at police headquarters. Something about the silences, the way they were paced.

"Somebody once said that there was no greater sorrow than in a moment of unhappiness to remember joy," said the voice. "Now I hope that isn't the effect of this little *memento mori*. All I can say is that by the time you hear this, things won't seem so great where I am either, so there's nothing to be sorrowful about."

Nolan shifted in his chair and balanced the wineglass on the arm. The machine ticked a couple of times as his father got off the line, then back on it again.

"Just catching my wind," said the voice. "Now, the point here is to have a serious talk this one last time. You two boys would never sit still for it before. Jake, you always had somewhere to go quick as the devil, and you didn't like it once you got there. Frank, lately I've had the feeling that whenever I talked about anything important you thought I was making what you lawyers call a gift in contemplation of death.

"Well, I suppose you were right, in a way. But just because a man removes his hat at the side of a grave, that doesn't necessarily mean he's being morbid."

The tape sizzled softly for a moment, and Nolan leaned forward to try to hear what his father was doing.

"Trying to find the right page in this book," said the voice. "Here. Here it is.

"Now, when I was a young man—a very young man, before any of you were born—I picked up this volume in a secondhand store. My blood was running then, you know, and the urgency of every damned thing just took my breath away. I guess I was still pretty much a romantic, and I wanted something that would give a shape to these formless yearnings. So I tried out Epicurus. Know of him? Whence the word 'epicurean.' Eat, drink, and be merry, or at least that's what I had been led to believe. Well, I read what I could of his work and found it haunting. It was not at all what I had expected, but it stayed with me. And lately I've gone back to it. You can find the book, by the way, on the desk in my study next to the stack of *National Geographic*s and the *Britannica* volume from EXTRACTI to GAMB.

"Here's the passage I was looking for: 'It is not the stomach that is insatiable,' Epicurus wrote, 'but the false opinion that the stomach needs an unlimited amount to fill it.' You can see what I mean. That's hardly sybaritic, is it? Wait, here's another one. You'll like this, Jake. 'Sexual intercourse has never done a man good, and he is lucky if it has not harmed him.'

"As you can imagine, when I was a youth I was not exactly ready for that kind of advice. I put the book neatly away on the shelf.

"By the time my mood and condition had prepared me for it again, I had learned the truth about Epicurus. Turns out he had a sour stomach—it finally killed him—and he couldn't eat anything richer than oatmeal or drink anything stronger than a sip or two of herb tea. As for merriment, you don't find a whole hell of a lot of evidence for that in his writing, either. His reputation stems from one maxim: that good things are those that feel good and bad those that hurt. He apparently followed his own advice about sex, and so he didn't leave behind a human line—just a few letters, some fragmented, aphoristic pieces, and a good number of disciples, sons by the accident of choice. And what he offered to others of dyspeptic gut and pounding head was nothing less than the consolation of philosophy.

"Here's a passage of advice he wrote to a friend: 'Become accustomed to the belief that death is nothing to us. For all good and evil consists in sensation, but death is deprivation of sensation. And therefore a right understanding that death is nothing makes the mortality of life enjoyable, not because it adds to it an infinite span of time, but because it takes away the craving for immortality.'

"I guess we've all learned from the French savants to dread something that isn't even there. But Epicurus saw it differently, and I've taken quite a fancy to his view. . . ."

The voice had faded to a whisper. Then it stopped. Nolan heard the tight, sibilant breaths. He could almost see his father taking them, jaw slung down, eyes all but closed, the whole frail body gulping, drowning. Frank did not know what else "insatiable" could possibly mean.

And yet all that was left now of that craving was a fragile trace upon the tape and an increased capacitance in the fibers of a son's brain. Nolan closed his eyes and pushed on them with his thumb and forefinger. Little hallucinatory lights burst and radiated like a kaleidoscope, then swirled toward the center, growing brighter. In the middle of the firmament, he saw his father's face inside the grave. His beard had grown in horrible, gray filaments. Something pale inched across his sunken cheek. And Frank suddenly understood what the poet had meant about the death of fathers: for the first time in his life, he felt nothing.

"By now, I suppose you are wondering what I think I'm doing. Good question. Very good. Well, a man's got to leave something behind. As I got to thinking about that I realized that you three are it. A damned good thing to be remembered by, too. But there are certain points that need to be made. I hereby leave them to you, jointly and severally, *per stirpes, res ipsa loquitur, ad hoc,* and *dominus vobiscum.* . . ."

"Amen," said Nolan in the pause his father left for it.

"You see, I worry about you fellas. Sometimes I think I paid too little attention to the important matters. The damnable thing about the spirit is that you think you might be able to do something about it. The body, well, it's just there: lumpish, unruly. It goes its own way. Whatever I've passed on to you in that regard, I can't do much to change. But the other part, maybe I haven't done enough.

"I get the feeling sometimes that maybe you expect too much and too little. Here, let me explain. Have you ever noticed, say when you are playing piano or trying to draw, that the harder you work at it, the worse you do? I mean, if the thing you're trying to accomplish is difficult, the natural inclination is to bust a gut getting as close to perfection as possible. No wrong notes in this nocturne, goddamn it! It's the quickest way to tie your fingers into a granny knot. On the other hand, if you go at a piece with fewer demands, well, then you just might make that old instrument sing. In other words, you have to get inside the music to appreciate it. You have to surrender, take the risk, accept.

"Acceptance. That could be the theme of this Chautauqua. Acceptance of the inevitable. A man in my spot, you might say, is naturally going to have that point of view. But, listen, a sense of limits might just be the source of all wisdom. You cannot know what you are unless you appreciate your end."

Nolan sprang out of his chair and hit the stop button. If he ever went insane and began to hear voices, this would be their sound: a wheezing little reed, vibrating up his spine.

He pushed another button and the cassette clicked up off the spindles. He pulled it from the magazine and turned it over and over in his palm. Then he slipped the tape back into the machine and started it up again.

It thumped, and all that came was a thin hiss like a slow leak or a snake. Then the sound deepened, went three-dimensional. His father coughed, tapped the mike, and said:

"It's morning again. Last night I was getting a little tired and probably was making no sense at all. Let's try something new."

Nolan loosened his death grip on the arms of the chair.

"I remember one time when you were in your teens, Jake. Your mother was very nervous because you were spending a lot of time in the bathroom. Far more than Frank had. She wanted me to talk to you about it. She had that look on her face, so sweet and tough. It was like a wall between us until I finally did what she wanted.

"You see, she thought that maybe you were confused about your urges. I have to laugh, thinking back on it. I mean, it wasn't too much later, if I'm not mistaken, that you had your initiation. Don't ask how I know. It's just something a father can tell.

"Now there are a lot of folks who think that when you left home, you were just tagging along after your nether proboscis. But I think something else led you away. By the time you went, you had enough experience to know, I suppose, that when it comes to the old tickle and rub there's not a whole lot of difference in the physical variables from place to place. Now that you've spent time in Asia, I imagine you've discovered that the old crack about the cant of Oriental women is wrong, too. In other words, you had the whole world of sexual possibility at hand right here.

"No, you were driven by something else. You were looking for a meaning that you had not been able to find. Hadn't because I hadn't let you. And now I want to try to set things straight."

His voice trailed off at the end. Even in death it was Jake his father worried about. Good old Frank was steady, even a bit of a grind. You could count on him to handle himself. Frank forgave his father's favor, as he had a thousand times before. The old man's feeling for Jake was a love like any other, inflamed by rejection. And Nolan felt a measure of the same thing, too, a surging need for his own impossible offspring, never so great as it was now, knowing that they would have reason to blame him for giving them life.

The voice started up again. "When you were a little boy, Jake, you were capable of holding a conversation with anyone. You asked such intelligent questions. You could quiz the doctor on how his equipment worked or what they did to make the drugs. Dr. Owen used to say that if he didn't know your folks, he'd have sworn you were a sheeny. You questioned the policemen about the law, the plumbers about joining copper with lead. Do you remember Mr. Mishkin, the butcher? He was the most ornery old fart I've ever known. But not to you. You treated him as if he were a surgeon. I remember one day I dropped you off at his shop while I went next door to the bakery for some bread. By the time I got back you were deep in study. He was, as I recall, demonstrating the proper way to sever a joint.

"Trouble was, you never got satisfactory answers to your questions, did you? Least of all from me. There was no alchemy in the plumber's soul. The cop's law extended no farther than the arc of his baton. The hog's joint was a mystery shattered but never exposed. And Dr. Owen's stethoscope took only the most insignificant soundings of your heart.

"It would have taken a genius to answer your questions properly, Jake.

They went that deep. We were not prepared for you. . . ."

The tape ran on in deep and regretful silence. Then his father blew his nose, coughed a few times, and returned.

"I remember Sunday mornings best. Every other kid in the neighborhood was off to church. So was your mother. After the cartoon shows, I had you captive, and I used to drill you on this and that. Science mostly. Excuse me just a minute. . . ."

Nolan heard the sound of his father's troubled breaths and recalled the sweetness of those Sundays. His father had told them about infinities and how to compare them. He had described the way men measured the speed of light. He had talked about the calculus and had them learn some simple problems. Sometimes they did experiments. Nolan remembered how they made hydrogen in bottles and filled balloons to send off carrying self-addressed postcards. They had grand plans to chart the winds by the postmarks on the cards as they returned. But not a single one ever came back. They did the experiment over and over again, and the children learned the importance of sending messages even when you knew they might never be read.

"I gave you curiosities enough, I suppose," said the voice. "And they certainly kept your mind off church. But when I taught you those things, I never showed you how to savor them. They were only things to play with, toys on Christmas morning, never the deeper mysteries a child wants to share.

"I never let you in on Heisenberg and Gödel. That way lay the altar, it seemed to me. So instead, I taught you that doubt was a method, an instrument to reach the heart of things. I led you to respect only what you could know for sure.

"But goddamn it, just because you don't believe in saints and bleeding hearts doesn't mean you don't believe in anything. There is a risk in believing. But there's risk in anything that's worth a damn. If the prehistoric fishes had considered the odds, they would never have pulled themselves up out of the ooze to test themselves against the air. And think of the utter daring of the first beast that ever had the nerve to haul itself upright and gaze into the sky. You've got to believe at least in the surface of things, their possibility. Pick up a nautilus shell someday. Look at the graceful logarithmic spiral shaped by the perfect instinct of a beast without a spine. Sure, it's as empty as a sanctuary, but why dwell on what is missing? Instead of reasoning about it, just feel the beauty of the thing. And if there is still room for doubt, then take it as a form of grace, opening out into wonder.

"Shit! I think I'm running out of tape here. If you want me to go on, you'll have to turn me over. It's a hell of a thing to be stuck on your back like a beetle. . . ."

Nolan let the machine run through the end of the leader in flat, empty silence. One finger tapped a senseless rhythm on the desk, not so much to cut the stillness as to give it a hard edge. He picked up the telephone receiver to call after Laura. Then he put it down again.

It wasn't doubt that troubled him now. It was the dumb half-certainty of the odds. The only spiral that mattered was doubled around him, binding him like a winding sheet. The tape clicked to a stop. He stayed at his desk, paging through papers, copies of indictments, police reports, statements of witnesses, motions, briefs. He turned page after page, reading a sentence, a phrase. Finally he went to the machine and turned over the cassette. He needed the voice on the reel, the mad whisper, the whirl.

It said: "I knew I could depend on you to rescue me."

Then: "I guess I got a little heavy last night, but I hope it made some sense. I'm no philosopher. Never wanted to be. They always seem to make God into an untranslatable German idiom. My point was supposed to be poetry. I should have made it to you long ago. . . .

"When I was talking about Epicurus a while back, I forgot to read you one special quotation. It bobbed up out of the pile on my desk this morning, so I thought I might as well stick it in here. 'Infinite time,' wrote the dyspeptic Greek, 'contains no greater pleasure than limited time, if you measure by reason the limits of pleasure.' Think of music for a moment. A performance is not judged on how long it is. It is a matter of quality, something outside of time. You see . . ."

The voice hesitated, tried again. Something hauled it up short. Then it broke into a harsh, wracking cough. Nolan had heard it often before, listened to it through the thin bedroom walls in the middle of the night. He had seen it often enough, too, the spasms gripping his father. A terrible, scared look would come over the man's face. His jaw would drop and his neck stiffen as he tried to resist the reflex. Then the painful hacking would come. And when it was over, his father would dab his mouth with a handkerchief, gasp, and try to pick up where he had left off.

"Let's forget about Epicurus," his father said. "Pretend it's Sunday morning again. I'll try to do it right this time. You may think you are too old for this sort of thing, but humor your old man once. I'm going to tell you about the stars.

"The first thing is finding the right attitude. A man has to pass through many stages before he can approach the night sky properly. A child will gaze up with instinctive curiosity. The sky is a land of infinite possibility, a reflection of all the other magic he is discovering for the first time. This is a healthy view, but transitional. He soon wishes to be done with discovery and to get on with life. His attitude toward the firmament is impatience.

"Later a young man stares upward and does not even see the bright points of light, only the darkness in between. The shadows frighten and lure him. They conceal and embody the new desires that stir his shame and pleasure. His attitude toward the heavens is carnal.

"Next the young man meets the sky as a problem. He wants to learn its workings, the mainspring that moves it. The constellations are points on a great coordinate system forming an equation he wants to solve. Though he may be concerned about his ability to do it himself, he does not question that the formula can be unriddled. His attitude toward the vast beyond is instrumental.

"But something always comes along to destroy this, a rude little voice saying, 'Psst, bub, you gonna die.' The sky retreats to infinity. Its solutions become paradoxical. The stars suggest no answers at all, only conundrums that isolate him, make him small. The universe is indifferent. The man gazing upward does so in an attitude of unholy terror.

"But you have to get past this stage. And when you do, the sky ceases to be the source of dim light upon a man and becomes a screen to be lighted up by the risky, uncertain projections of man himself. And it is the grandest goddam slate a fellow ever had to write on. The last and proper attitude toward it is pure and unequaled love.

"Despite all the astronomers' estimates of mass and distance, color and intensity, red shifts and the rest, the universe is still so immense and the human mind so narrow that the sense of inadequacy a man feels when he contemplates it has got to be the humility and love of God.

"But if I know you, Jake, you are probably drawn to the black holes. Here's a suggestion. Let your imagination soar. Black holes may open into whole other universes. I prefer to think so right now, thank you very much. And those universes may be joined together one with another in vast and infinitely complex matrices to form the atoms and molecules that make up the genes and chromosomes that transmit the information that electrifies the imagination of a man of whom this universe in which we and the black hole exist is a part so infinitesimal that his senses, magnified by the most powerful machine, would never detect it except through the sixth and most acute sense: his astonishment.

"Now," he whispered at the very end of his breath, "can you see what I mean? . . .

"But there is more. There are quasars and brilliant supernovas. There are gaseous clouds and firmaments—new galaxies waiting to converge. There are immense distances where time does not govern and space curves back on itself like a Möbius strip. Most important, there is an end and a beginning, and they are the same. You can hear all creation whistling like wind from beyond time. The sound was discovered not so very long ago, and the news went forth under the title 'A Measurement of Excess Antennae Temperature at 4080 MHz.' It is the finest scripture ever written."

He was becoming more animated now, working beyond his disease as if nothing could hold him back. Nolan leaned forward in his chair.

"You see," said his father, "the universe began with an enormous explosion, a conflagration in the heart of a nothingness so profound that it is still beyond our minds to conceive of it even in death. The inertia from that first fire still sends galaxies careening apart. But the outward expansion is slowing down. Eventually it will come to a stop and reverse itself in a cycle of birth and death and resurrection. It is the pattern of generations, the pattern of the universe.

"The instant the universe exploded and sent out the gases that later cooled to become the planets and stars and lives of men like you and me, the radiation was extraordinarily powerful. It was random, diffuse, the souls of children not yet born. And now, from so very far away in time that what we hear is the very beginning of time itself, the radiation sings to us of creation.

"A man can listen to it and hear Genesis and the apocalyptic promise of Revelation in one terrible, lovely moment and discover the voice, not of God in the shape of a man, but rather of the very essence of the marvelous that cannot be destroyed by science or tested by doubt but only acquiesced in like man's hope and most abiding fear.

"Three times in my life I have thought I heard that sound, the nights each one of you was conceived. Maybe it was the restless sound of your spirits surging from me, but Lord, it was a sweet sibilance. And a fine, fine farewell."

The recording flattened out. The voice was gone forever. Nolan sat with the tape's dead hum and hiss. He did not move until the telephone cut into the silence like a human cry.

22

Jake dashed to beat the yellow light as a taxi snuck into the crosswalk against the red. He slapped the hood and shouted as he stepped in front of it. The driver hit the brakes and cursed behind the windshield. Jake could read the words on his lips, so he stopped between the taxi's headlights and just stood there. The driver gunned his engine. Jake did not move. The light had changed and the traffic behind began to go for the horns. Finally the cab driver took his hands off the wheel and gave a resigned little shrug. Then Jake moved out of the way and smiled. The cab laid a patch of rubber as it pulled away.

The wind had finally eased up and the sky glowed with what his father at the telescope used to call Chicago borealis. The sidewalks were deserted, and Jake walked aimlessly, alone. He had been wrong to take it out on Laura. She hadn't been the one who had deceived him. She was in the dark, too. If only he'd paid attention to what she was saying . . . but he hadn't been listening, hadn't been thinking. He had been looking for a fight, and it didn't matter who or why. He had done it just because it was in him, burning.

He stopped in front of a cheap gallery with the inevitable Picasso bullfights and narcotic abstracts in the window. But what caught his eye was something from the bad place, a temple rubbing. Two graceful dancers stood poised in a delicate symmetry, their strange, beautiful eyes averted, their bodies round and inviting, like Luong's.

What was he going to do about her? He did not want to cause her pain. And the only way for a man like him to avoid that was to let her go. She said she wanted it that way, wanted it for fear of hurting him. He needed to go back to her, but only to make her understand that the shame was his alone, that she had done nothing wrong.

She would listen, of course. His voice would rise with her silence. She would turn away from him and say that it was all right, that she deserved no better. And he would insist that no one deserved to suffer him. The bad seed, he would say, is mine.

A bar up ahead was called Superheroes. He needed more whiskey to take away the chill, or to feed it, either one.

"What the fuck, buddy!" said a lummox, bumping into him in the doorway.

"Watch your step," said Jake.

The lummox just looked and stepped past.

"Come on, bitch," he said to his lady. "We got business." Then he lurched onto the sidewalk with a snow bunny who caught Jake's eye as she passed.

The decor inside the bar was straight out of Action Comics. The walls were covered with huge enlargements of Spiderman and Wonder Woman doing battle with all manner of Titans. Spotlights revealed something Jake did not remember from the originals. Spiderman's crotch showed the outlines of a big, semierect member beneath the tights, and Wonder Woman's nipples threatened to puncture the front of her tank suit. Jake made his way to the bar and ordered a shot and a beer.

The bartender returned with the drink and a telephone, which he plugged into a jack at the back edge of the bar.

"It's for you," he said.

"You're shitting me," said Jake.

"No way," said the bartender. "Young stud like you walks in, the lines always start humming."

"I don't know what you're talking about."

"You been here before?"

"Never."

"Every dive's gotta have a gimmick. Between you and me, this one's a pain in the ass, no matter how many people it gets laid. And when some broad gets a bad piece of ass or a guy walks out and finds himself with a cockteaser, they come back and act as if I sold them rotten meat."

"I still don't get it."

"Pick up the phone," said the bartender. "I call it Dial-a-Dick. She's calling from across the room. Some Enchanted Evening."

Jake picked up the receiver and put it to his ear, saying nothing.

"You sure took your time," said a small voice. "Sometimes that's good. You're not in any hurry."

"Who are you?"

"I'm not into names," the voice said.

"Where are you then?"

"You can't see me from where you're sitting. I watched you when you came in. If you want, I'll join you. After that, we'll just see what happens."

"Sure," said Jake. "Why not."

The line went dead, and Jake handed the phone back to the bartender.

"She's a hot one," the bartender said. "Doesn't come in here every night, but she never leaves alone. Cheeky broad, you ask me. But I wouldn't throw her out of the sack."

By the time the bartender had poured Jake another shot, the woman had taken a seat beside him. She was small, with angular features, athletic and trim. She wore a bulky sweater, jeans, and jogging shoes, and they did not quite hide the fact that she took care of herself very well. Around her neck hung a chain of tiny links that looked like real gold.

"The way we start is for you to buy me a drink," she said.

"Whatever you want," said Jake.

"A prince," she said, and Jake nodded to the bartender, who brought her a scotch and soda without being told.

Jake sipped his beer and then called for another shot. The whiskey was just beginning to take effect. It clarified the woman's features in the mirror behind the bar. Not half bad. He thought of Luong for an instant, of what he needed to prove. Then he threw the shot back into his throat like a rerun cowboy and looked at the reflection of her hard, steady eyes.

"So what was it you had in mind?" she said.

"Can't tell yet," said Jake.

"Ah, the sullen type."

"Look, I'll be back in a minute," Jake said and got off his stool.

"You could just tell me to get lost," she said.

"If I wanted to. I have to heed the call of nature. I'll be back."

The john was a decrepit affair off the alley. It smelled of mildew and air freshener. The window did not close all the way, and it let in a cold draft. He pissed into the cigarette butts in the urinal with almost no pain at all and was surprised at how quickly the gentle itch of desire came back to him afterward. He wasn't cured, but he was capable. And what the hell, he didn't even know her name.

When he returned to the bar, he found her going at her drink.

"Do you want to stick around or go somewhere?" he asked.

"Did you wash your hands?"

"You're kidding."

"It's important. Did you wash your hands?"

"Come on."

"Tell me or it's bye-bye."

"Sure," he said. "I washed them."

"You meet a lot of creeps," she said.

"Now do you want to go?"

"I think I need a little more of this," she said, tipping her glass and rattling the cubes to get the bartender's attention. "Buy me another. Talk to me. Tell me about your wife and kids and how you aren't appreciated."

"I'm a soldier," said Jake.

"Well, well. That's a new one."

"Home on leave."

"Going to Vietnam?"

"Been there," he said. "Going back."

For just an instant he saw something warm come into her eyes, like sympathy, then it was gone."

"Did you have to kill anyone?"

"That's how the game is played."

"But did you enjoy it?"

"Not as much as I should have."

"You're putting me on, aren't you?"

"A little," said Jake. "Now how about you."

"I'm a student," she said.

"Studying what?"

"Human nature, I guess. This is field work."

Jake found himself warming to her for some reason, and it began to tug him away.

"You here every night?"

"Nights are for Momma's pleasure," she said.

"Come what may."

"You're pretty sure of yourself," she said. "I like that."

"You take what you can get, I guess."

"Momma can get whatever she wants," she said, stiffening. And he felt it again, the sadness. "That's got to be straight up front. You either understand that or Momma moves on."

"Momma can do whatever she pleases," said Jake.

"Yes she can. And she definitely pleases."

"I bet she does."

Jake ordered another round to buy some time. He watched her breast where it nudged his upper arm. He was not sure of himself now, not sure at all. Then an older man sidled up to her and leaned his elbow on the bar.

"Well, hello, sweet thing," he said. "Remember me?"

He wore bell-bottom pants and a tailored shirt that was open to the sternum to show off his medallion and the gray, curling hair on his chest.

"I don't remember faces," she said.

"I've got something better than my face."

"Sorry," she said. "I don't remember that, either. Can't you see? I have other plans."

"Your loss, baby," said the man.

When he was gone, she turned back to Jake. He expected some embarrassment, some sweetness, some distinction to be made between that man and him.

"You did say that you were going back to the war, didn't you?" she asked. "You aren't going to hang around."

"I think maybe I'd better take a walk," he said.

And it wasn't because he didn't want her. He could feel the need creeping up inside him again. But something else pulled at him, too. He stood up and put a few bills on the bar to cover the tab and tip.

"You don't like me, soldier boy?" she said.

"I like you fine," he said.

"Then let's leave together."

"It wouldn't be right," he said.

Once out the door, he drew a cavernous breath. The music was at his back and he was light-headed. The itch was still in his groin, that nettlesome urge that drove him to all his folly. The old tickle and sneeze. But when you stifled it, you just felt another one coming on.

He walked toward State Street, where the bars were still open and the touts were out in the cold, bragging of the torrid climes inside.

"I got live ones here," one whispered to him. "Topless, bottomless, everything you want."

Jake walked on under the flashing signs, past big pictures of girls with silver stars on their nipples and mounds. He looked away.

But it did no good. It wasn't a feeling he could deny and be done with. The only way with a nettle was to grasp it, grasp it hard.

He stopped at a lavender door and went inside. The air was dark and yeasty. On the tiny stage a naked woman danced lazily. A record player scratched away at some drag-ass blues. Jake took a place at the bar.

"Show's nearly over," said the bartender. "I'll give you a pass on the cover until the next live act. Before that there's a film. Continuous performance. What'll you have?"

Jake ordered a bourbon and watched the woman swaying back and forth under the unforgiving spotlights. Two men down the bar were talking about their wives. Another studied the surface tension of his whiskey, only occasionally looking up at the idle, diddly-diddle syncopation of the dancer's breasts.

"The movies are better than this," said the bartender. "She's new. No talent. Hell, waiting for Mass to start on Sunday morning is better than this. Hey, bitch! Get your clothes on. You're fired."

The woman just kept dancing. The bartender blew his nose on a rag he pulled from behind the counter.

"I guess she's in love with her work," he said.

Jake asked for a refill and rubbed his forehead where the ache had concentrated. But the itch, unlike the ache, wasn't localized. It moved, grew, subsided, eluded you whenever you tried to find and appease it.

The music stopped. The woman stepped off the stage and bent over to pick up a terry-cloth robe that lay on the floor. The stage lights dropped, leaving only the dim glow behind the bar.

Then the bartender flicked on a projector, and a cone of light slashed through the smoky air. The image on the screen was blurred. Jake turned and took a sip of his drink. In the mirror he watched the shape congeal. It was a living room. A woman in a modest dress was vacuuming the rug. On the scratchy sound track, he heard her humming when she turned off the machine. He turned back to the screen as the camera zoomed in on her hand, which gently stroked the nozzle. The doorbell rang.

When she opened it, naturally enough there was a man. He was thin and dark, dressed in biker's leathers. He said something about being lost in the neighborhood, and she let him in. She was obviously flustered and nervous. Her fingers rubbed at her thighs, lifting the hem of her skirt. The man did not fail to notice. The words he spoke did not matter; they never did. Within moments she was leading him to another room, where he stripped her naked and strapped her to the bed.

"For Chrissake," said Jake.

"Something, isn't it?" said the bartender.

The film was no worse than the one-reelers they sometimes showed at LZ Condor, the projector splashing the pictures against the scarred old stucco. Sometimes at the LZ there would be a lizard on the warm, hard wall, and the men would cheer it on as it closed in on the woman's breasts or mound. But there was never any violence in those films. The fantasy there was peace.

Jake shifted on the stool as the man began to rough the woman up. He did not know where the anger came from, but as the woman grew excited at the abuse, the man grew bolder. He finally struck her open-handed across the cheek. Jake looked away and heard again the ambiguous smack of flesh against flesh.

"Kinda brings it all down to basics, don't it?" said the bartender.

But Jake could not bear to watch. His anger had sunk into a dull, painful clot in his chest. The heavy smell of the bar closed in on him, the darkness and the muffled laughter of the other men.

He could live with the emptiness of the tickle and sneeze, but this was something else. This brought home the hurt you could cause, the pain at the heart of it. And you could not just pick up and walk away and say that this was the remedy, because leaving simply made the wound go deeper. You had to go back and try to get right with what you had done. There was no other way.

Jake pulled on his coat and threw a few bills on the shiny surface of the bar.

"Next one's a little better," said the bartender.

But Jake was not listening. He was already at the door, and the sounds of the woman's moans and the man's brute grunts filled his ears, as harsh as conscience.

23

*L*aura was ready to give up trying to raise someone inside when the janitor opened the steel stage door a wary crack.

"Mrs. Nolan," he said, letting her inside. "Did you forget something?"

"I'm sorry to disturb you."

"Lucky I heard you knocking. Here. Come in and have some coffee. You must be cold, waiting out there in the wind."

"That's very kind," she said.

He led her to a tiny room where a glass pot was heating on a coil. She watched as he spooned the brown crystals into a paper cup and poured the water, which foamed up brown and steamy.

"Cream or sugar?"

"Black is fine," she said. "Thank you."

"I'll go open the dressing room for you. What was it you left behind?"

"Nothing," she said. "I just wanted to come back."

"You played real fine tonight, Mrs. Nolan."

"Thank you."

"You should be careful, out alone. Can I call you a taxi?"

"I was hoping you would let me use the piano," she said, sipping the coffee and letting the cup warm her hands.

"It's still on the stage," he said.

"I feel rather foolish."

"It's no bother to me," he said. "Are you all right?"

"A crazy whim," she said. "Forgive me."

She simply did not want to go home and see Frank just now. She was not ready. She had to work things out first. Whether this was the end or the beginning. How to tell him the way she felt. What she wanted now, knowing the truth.

193

The janitor led her to the stage, which was dark except for a few service lights. He rigged up a lamp from a music stand so it shone upon the keys.

"I'll be back here if you need me," he said.

"It won't be much of a concert."

"Hell, Mrs. Nolan," he said, "I usually just have this old radio to keep me company."

He moved into the shadows, and she began to work on the scales, tiresome repetitions, up and down. She took the notes through the changes, pity to anger, anger to sadness, loud and soft, opposing. It was not music. It was a mantra. She repeated it again and again. She had lost something, and she felt its absence like a physical void inside her, stillborn. The notes echoed and then were gone.

"Every man has a hidden vice," Frank's father had told her once. "I don't know Frank's, but I'll tell you this: nothing tells you more about a man than the weakness he chooses to hide."

And now she knew. He had hidden from her the reason for his reluctance to have children. And it seemed to her as grave an infidelity as if he had been having a secret affair. An affair with the most horrible bitch of them all. Stealing away the very center of Laura's life. Her husband's vice was his crushing refusal to trust. Laura's hands struck a tonic chord. The loudness of it startled her. She began again the circle of the scales, as softly now as a sunset raga.

When Laura lifted her fingers from the keys, she listened to the slow whisper of the steam from radiators. The janitor moved back onto the stage. He puttered around at the rear of it, then moved up to the piano.

"Something the matter, Mrs. Nolan?"

"It is odd to play to the darkness," she said. "It swallows up the notes."

"Sounded fine to me."

"Shall I play something else?" she said. "The scales must seem very dull."

"It's your concert," he said.

"What would you like to hear?"

"I'm kind of partial to Beethoven. But maybe that's a little tame for you."

"Tame," she said, laughing a little. "I had never really thought of Beethoven as tame."

It took her a moment to fix the sonata in her mind. And when she began, she threw herself into it. All the restraint and understatement fell away. She missed notes and did not care.

Yes, of course there was danger. There was always danger. The only thing that had changed was that now they could state the probabilities and give the peril's name. That was the difference between a dumb animal and a man. A sad, wonderful man who went to his death in love and longing.

Frank had known and she had not. That made everything else that had been going on between them suddenly clear. He had been bitter and withdrawn. But he hadn't left it at that. He had gone after all her tender spots, complaining that she did not have dinner waiting for him or that they had run out of scotch. He wondered out loud why it took so long to get his shirts from the cleaners. These were things she insisted on caring for herself. She wanted to feed and clothe him, as a proper wife, but sometimes when she was deep into a composition or rehearsing for a concert, her attention slipped. He had always been good about it before, but this time he overlooked nothing. The checkbook hasn't been balanced yet? You had to pay a finance charge just because you forgot to mail the payment? He was too clever to dwell on any single thing, but the incidents mounted up, and she began to ask herself whether she could really be a decent mother after all. And only now did she understand how deviously he had led her to that doubt.

The final chord came crashing down, notes out of whack, too loud, too quick. She dropped her head. The janitor clapped his hands and said, "Brava." When she looked up, she was weeping.

"I'd better go," she said.

"That was wonderful," he said. "From the heart. Please don't cry."

"All wrought up. So foolish," she said. "I'm sorry."

She found her coat and put it on.

"Maybe you'd better wait awhile," he said.

"I'll be fine."

He showed her to the front door. Snow had begun to dust the sidewalks. The wet street reflected the lights. The janitor stepped outside with her and flagged down a taxi. She thanked him and gave the driver her address. It was strange hearing herself saying the number so distinctly, as if she had never said it before.

"No hurry," she said to the driver as he sped through a yellow light.

FOUR
JUDGMENT

24

J ake passed the lobby door and went into the alley at the back. The wind whipped along the sheer stone face of the building, which rose straight up into the darkness like a monument. He counted up seven rows of windows and saw that the lights in Frank's apartment were on.

When he reached the street again he turned left toward the commercial strip where he thought he might find a pay phone to call ahead. Then he stopped and turned back. He had walked for nearly an hour, the alcohol evaporating like anger in the punishing wind, and he still did not know what to say.

The man inside the revolving doors was an off-duty cop. He stood at the desk and straightened the service revolver at his hip as Jake approached.

"I'm here to see Frank Nolan. I'm his brother."

The cop looked him over and seemed satisfied by the military haircut.

"You can buzz him over there on the right," he said.

Jake found the name and pushed the button. He glanced back. The cop was seated again, feet propped up on an open drawer of the desk. Jake pushed the button a second time. There was no sound but the rustle of the heater blowing from a vent. Jake flexed his hands back to life and rubbed at his raw, chapped lips.

The trouble was, he could not get a fix on the things the doctor had told him. And it confused him that Frank had kept everything secret. It wasn't as if this protected anybody. They either had the disease or they didn't have it. And if they did, they would find out soon enough. What was Frank thinking about, keeping them all in the dark?

Well, it wouldn't do any good to demand an answer to that right now. The only way was for Jake to take responsibility for the hurt he had caused and hope that together they could make peace with the living and the dead. But it was hard, very hard, reconciling yourself to what you'd been given as well as what you had done. The voice of conscience that had been so clear to him an hour ago had become confounded with others now, and he did not know which was worse, the guilt or the innocence.

The little speaker next to the rows of buttons ticked twice and then gave way to static.

"Who is it?" The voice was distorted.

Jake took a step back.

"Hello?" said the voice. "Who's there?"

It was no use trying to walk away. This was something you carried with you, deep in your flesh.

"It's me, Frank," he said.

"Talley?"

"No. It's Jake."

There was no answer at first. The speaker clicked off and then on again, and the static made it seem as though they were communicating from opposite sides of the universe.

"Frank?"

"Wait right there," said his brother. "I'll be down."

So Frank did not want him to see Laura. She must have been crushed by what he had told her. Oh, yes, Jake thought, I've really done it this time.

A few minutes later, the elevator door opened. Jake stood his ground as Frank emerged. He was wearing his trenchcoat.

"You might as well come along," he said as he pushed open the door.

"I need to talk to you," said Jake.

"In the car," said Frank.

"Laura, too."

"That'll have to wait," said Frank, brushing past Jake and into the main lobby. "I'm parked on the street."

Jake caught up with him on the sidewalk, and when they reached the car, he touched Frank's shoulder.

"Look," Jake said. "I'm sorry."

Frank bent over and unlocked the passenger door.

"Get in, Jake," he said. "We don't want to keep everyone waiting."

"Where are we going?"

Frank didn't answer. He went around to the other side and slid behind the wheel. The engine turned over sluggishly, but finally it caught. Frank let it idle a minute at the curb, playing the gas and fooling with the levers of the heater.

"I'd really like to talk to Laura," said Jake.

"She isn't home yet. She must have stopped somewhere. I thought she might be with you."

"You haven't seen her?"

"It's OK," said Frank. "She probably ran into somebody. They sometimes go on pretty late."

"Then you haven't talked to her," said Jake.

"She doesn't need to ask my permission, Jake. We don't have a curfew."

Frank pulled out of the parking spot and sped through a yellow light toward the Drive.

"I don't understand what this is all about," said Jake. His resolve was slipping away from him. If Frank hadn't even heard what had happened, Jake didn't know where to begin.

"There's been a break in the Tatum murder," Frank said. "Talley called just before you showed up. He was out on a raid of a smut arcade, one of those dives where you can see a movie or buy a companion by the quarter hour. They rolled it up and arrested the night manager and were doing an inventory on the take when Talley found a cache of really foul films, S and M, child porn, the works. They had to look at the junk just in case there was some question about the seizure later on. And one of them turned out to be a film of the Tatum girl."

Frank gunned the engine and roared past the traffic. Ahead of them the skyline poked up into the low cover of clouds.

"The guy kidnapped her to make a movie?" said Jake.

"I don't think so. It doesn't make sense. The kind of guy Williams was."

"I'm not following you."

Frank slowed down a little and turned to him.

"I just have a feeling," he said. "I wish I could tell you that I have a whole list of reasons, but I don't. What I do have just won't fit together right. First there's the physical evidence at the scene. They found the girl's body under a newspaper. A lady in the neighborhood had thrown it in there the night before. She was a drunk. The body was wrapped up in a blanket. The woman probably didn't even see it when she pitched her trash."

"What does that prove?"

"Stay with me now," said Frank. "The coroner said the girl had been dead for at least twelve hours before she was discovered. If she was in the can the night before she was found, then what was Williams doing there the next day? Forget what you've heard, Jake. Nobody ever returns to the scene of the crime.''

Off to the left, the lake was dark and empty. No moon or stars. Jake gazed past his brother into the night.

"But I couldn't find another explanation," Frank went on. "That was my problem. I didn't have a good suspect."

They slowed down some more to negotiate the S-curve bridge. Up ahead, the lights downtown still burned bright. Their reflection sparkled on the black, choppy water of the river.

"And now you do," said Jake.

"I'm pretty sure."

25

‘ ‘W hat would I want a lawyer for?”
"You have a right to have one, Mrs. Tatum. That's
all," said Frank.

"I heard you the first time."

She sat opposite him across the old Formica-topped table, alone on that side of the dingy interrogation room. Arrayed against her were a homicide dick, a court reporter, two uniforms, and a police matron, along with Frank and Jake.

"This is not exactly like the other time we talked, Mrs. Tatum," said Frank.

"I know," she said.

"Then you freely agree to answer our questions without exercising your right to an attorney?"

"I can handle myself all right."

"Just yes or no, Mrs. Tatum. For the record."

"Yes," she said. "Of course."

Frank glanced over at the court reporter, who struck a decisive chord on her machine.

"Where is your husband now, Mrs. Tatum?"

"Business," she said. "He left yesterday."

Linda Tatum was dressed like a woman whose husband's business is good. Her fur coat hung from the back of the chair. The matron said she had taken an hour getting ready when they picked her up after midnight. This one could be trouble, Frank, the matron had warned him. This one's got something behind her.

Well, she certainly looked as though she could have had heavy talent on her side if she wanted it. But she had not even called her father when they had given her the chance. For whatever reason, the woman wanted to go it alone.

"We're going to have to ask your husband some questions, too," said Frank.

"I'll tell you everything you need to know," she said, pulling the fur up around her shoulders.

"Would you like me to close that window?" said Frank.

"Can we just get on with it?"

The homicide dick who had driven her downtown had said he couldn't shut her up. Would she confess? Hell, it was like the day before communion, he said.

The sun was coming up now, gray against the window. Frank squeaked his chair across the asphalt tile and turned away from the glare.

"Do you want to tell us where the movie came from?" he said.

"I just knew it would get us in trouble," she said. "I told Nicky to throw it out, but he wanted to have it developed. Somebody must have made a copy."

"Can't trust anybody anymore," said Jake. Frank shot him a silencing look. This was no time to be sarcastic. You wanted to make yourself the suspect's last friend in the world.

"Please pardon my brother, Mrs. Tatum," he said. "He's not familiar with this kind of thing."

"You know," she said to Jake, "I didn't think you were a cop. Just didn't seem to be the type."

"Can we go back to the beginning?" Frank said.

"You mean my father," she said. "What he was like."

The homicide dick coughed to cover his laugh.

"What'd I tell you, Frank?" he said. "Hail Mary, full of grace."

"What's his problem?" said Linda Tatum.

"Envy," said Frank. "When he asked his mother who his father was, she could only give him three to five in a field of seven."

"Your ass," said the homicide dick.

"Maybe we can start with the film, Mrs. Tatum," said Frank. "How it came to be made."

"It was quite a while ago," she said. "Last spring, I guess."

"Were you present?"

This was the first trap. He did not camouflage it. He wanted to see whether she was one of them who was out there trying to be caught.

"I was in the room," she said.

"But it wasn't your idea," said Frank.

"It just sort of happened," she said. "I don't know."

Her voice flattened out the way it does when a person is telling you something she has prepared herself to say. Her hands braided and unbraided three strands of brightly colored cord she had brought with her in her purse.

"But it wasn't a one-time thing," said Frank. "Your husband had abused her before."

"It wasn't abuse," she said. "He would never think of hurting her."

"But you went along with it?"

"Look," she said, "you don't have to pretend to be so cool. I don't expect you to understand."

Frank leaned forward across the table and took her hand.

"I want to, Mrs. Tatum," he said. "I really do."

She withdrew from him, but he was not afraid of losing her yet. He could tell that she wanted to tell him the story first, start to finish.

"It was all very innocent," she said. "We wanted her to be free. She loved to show off. She wasn't ashamed. Sure, I had my own hangups. But I was trying to get over them. I really was."

"You didn't see anything wrong with it then," said Frank.

"Not the way you think," she said. "I had feelings. Sure. But not that kind. Sometimes I was jealous of her. I was trying to get over it. Look, we weren't a bunch of freaks."

The stenographer struck the dissonance silently on her machine. The uniforms were getting restless. Their watch was almost over, and it was becoming clear that this could take a while. The homicide dick shifted his feet and lighted a cigarette. Frank took a sip of coffee. It was lukewarm.

"What exactly happened the night you made the film?" he asked.

"Nicky had just come back from a trip. We did a little grass. A little coke. We got high, but nothing we couldn't handle."

"You used cocaine regularly?" said Frank.

"Don't be shocked," she said.

"It isn't that uncommon anymore," he said, bringing her along.

"Even in the best of families," she said, looking at Jake.

"How often did you use it?" said Frank.

"Once a week maybe. Twice at the most. When we had the money for it."

"And did it often involve Susan?"

"Not at all," she said.

"But that night it did."

"She was playing at a friend's place down the street. When I brought her back, she went in and took a bath. She came into the living room wearing a towel. Nicky thought she was so cute, he had me go get the camera while he set up the lights. Susan showed off for him and he filmed it, that's all. She had fun.''

"He didn't have to beat her then," said Frank. He put it as routinely as he could, just to see her reaction.

"He never touched her," she said.

"Then who did?"

Linda Tatum looked up from where her hands were tying and untying the cords. There were tears now, and they seemed to come from a place that had somehow remained uncorrupted.

"She was beautiful," she said.

Frank handed her some tissues, and she used them. When she was ready, he started in again.

"You said that when it was over you wanted the film destroyed," said Frank.

"The next day," she said. "I was worried that someone might look at it when they were developing it. I was afraid they would misunderstand."

"Maybe you had second thoughts yourself," said Frank.

"You want me to feel guilty about the way we were together, but I'm not," she said. "I was just afraid that somebody would get the wrong idea."

"It didn't bother you at all, what you had done?"

"There were certain things, yes," she said. "Do I have to say what?"

"I'd appreciate it, Mrs. Tatum."

"I mean," she said, "he never made a film of me that way, did he?"

"Why don't you tell me."

"No, he didn't."

"And you wanted him to?"

"I would have tried to perform," she said, "if he had ever asked."

"What are you doing, Mrs. Tatum? I mean with your hands."

She held up the three cords, which she had unknotted and was knotting again.

"My mother taught me to braid," she said. "She told me it helped a person to think."

"She died when you were very young, I understand."

"It wasn't her fault that I have problems," she said. "It was my father."

"Problems?" said Frank. It was such a modest word.

"I wasn't able to get off anymore," she said. "After I had Susan it was like I'd gone numb. Daddy's revenge. It isn't easy to talk about this. Do you really need me to say?''

"It would help us understand," said Frank.

She went back to the cords and worked at them, keeping her eyes on them, not looking up once.

"I remember the way he talked to me as a child," she said. " 'Don't touch yourself there. It'll make you crazy. It'll make you a slut.' He just couldn't stand the idea that I might be getting any pleasure. And when I had the baby, he started treating me like some simple mother.''

The word coagulated on her lips.

"Nicky didn't want me to, but I saw a shrink about it," she went on. "I mean, I wasn't very good for Nicky either. I tried to pretend, but it probably wasn't too convincing. If you want to know why he didn't put me on film, that's the reason.''

"A real eye for talent," said Jake. This time Frank did not even make a move to stop him.

"Father dear was the one who recommended the analyst," she said. "He blamed Nicky for messing me up. He was always looking for a way to pull us apart.''

"I'd like to advise you again," said Frank, "that you have a right to an attorney.''

"Let me tell you about lawyers," she said. "Daddy made me see his attorneys before I got married. I had to get Nicky to sign a contract. Daddy was afraid he would take us for all we were worth.''

One of the uniforms lighted up a cigarette, and the sulfur match put a bite in the air.

"Was he afraid for Susan, too?" Frank asked. "Is that why he wanted you to get psychological help?''

"He didn't know that I hit her," said Mrs. Tatum, and she wrapped the fur tightly around her shoulders. Frank felt the chill, too, a fever spiking, the body struggling to rid itself of something it did not recognize. "Nobody knew except for Nicky.''

"He saw you beating her?''

"He made me tell him," she said. "He saw marks on Susan and forced it out of me.''

Frank was beginning now to see something taking form in what she said, something he did not trust.

"Why didn't he stop you?" he asked. "Why didn't he take Susan away?''

"He loved her," she said. "You have to understand that. He loved us both. At first I guess he thought I was just spanking her, like anyone might. But then one time he found a bad bruise and got upset. He yelled at me, told me never to do it again. But I was . . . I blamed her for what she could do and I couldn't anymore. I was numb, and she made me that way, being born. Do you understand what I'm saying?"

"I'm not a shrink, Mrs. Tatum," Frank said. "But I've read the books."

"Then this must be where you ask whether I was beaten as a child myself."

"If you want."

"The books are wrong about that," she said. "There are other ways."

Her look was so hard now that Frank thought it had either to be genuine or a growth of callus to protect what was.

"My father wanted me to be special, and I wasn't," she said. "He smothered me with expectations. He hit me with them every day, and I still have all the marks. Do you know what it is never once to live up to what your father wants?"

"We all have fathers, Mrs. Tatum," Frank said. Jake was as inert as a stone.

"He wouldn't let me go my own way," she said. "He forced me to try to be what he wanted. But I didn't have it in me."

"Maybe he should have hit you," said Jake. "Maybe that would have helped."

"Yes," she said. "He should have hit me. It would have taught me to hate him sooner."

"And that was why you killed your daughter?" said Frank, leading her now to where he could see she begged to be taken. "You killed her because you saw yourself in her?"

"She was better than me. She made everybody happy."

"Your father."

"And Nicky, too."

"I saw the film," said Jake. "Your husband was making that little girl into a whore."

She flinched and then caught herself.

"He would never have hurt her," she said.

"She was a child," said Jake, leaning across the table. "Didn't you ever think of the harm you could be doing?"

"I'm not sure you should be asking questions, Jake," said Frank. "There may be problems later."

"What difference does it make who asks the questions?"

"There are certain procedures."

"I want the truth," said Jake.

"It's a matter of the means. I may have to ask you to leave."

"Hey look," said the woman. "I'll tell you if I want him to get out."

"My brother and I have some differences of opinion," said Frank.

"You're all the same to me," she said.

Frank got up and went to the window. He pulled down the blind against the sunlight.

"Do you want a cigarette, Mrs. Tatum?"

"Sure. Yes. That would be good right now."

"Give her one, will you, Joe?" he said to the homicide dick.

"Camel too strong for you?" said the dick.

"I can take it," she said, accepting the pack and shaking one out. Frank lighted it for her, and she reached out to steady his hand.

"I want you to tell us how often you beat her," he said.

"It started after we made the film," she said, and each word was a puff of smoke. "I don't know what came over me. At first it was just a little spanking, nothing more than that. But then it got worse. Nicky tried to stop me. He even threatened to tell my father. I didn't take that seriously. Daddy wouldn't have believed anything he said against me. But it made me angry anyway, Nicky taking Daddy's side. More and more I took it out on Susan. Finally one day Nicky walked out on me. I went crazy. I had a few drinks, quite a few. Then Susan started to cry. I told her to stop. She didn't and I hit her. Hit her until she was so scared that she stopped. I don't really remember very much. All I know is that she stopped and I put her in her bed."

"My God," said Jake, staring at her. But Frank looked elsewhere, at the restless matron and the uniforms, at the court reporter's fingers on the keys. He pulled out a notepad and wrote down a few words. Then he put it back in his pocket. He was suddenly very weary, the night without sleep, the relief of finally knowing what had happened and the sorrow at what he had to do.

"How long did it take you to kill her?" he asked.

"I don't know," she said. She was braiding the cords furiously now. "I put her in her room. Then I got even more spaced out. Pills, liquor, anything I had. She was alive when I left her. But when I looked in on her later, she was cold."

Frank thought she might weep, but she did not.

"What day was that?" he asked.

She caught her breath and looked up at him.

"The eighteenth. The nineteenth. It's all a fog."

"And who did you tell?"

"Nobody."

"How did you dispose of the body?"

"I carried her out the back way in blankets," she said. "Then I drove to that alley and put her in the garbage can."

"How many blankets did you have on her?"

"Two or three," she said, "but I brought most of them home and washed them at the laundromat. I only left one on her, an old beaten-up thing I found in the linen closet when we moved in."

Frank tapped a pencil on the table.

"How did you set up Monroe Williams?" he asked. She did not answer. "Somebody got Williams and the police to the body at the same time. It's got to fit together, Mrs. Tatum."

"What makes you think I had anything to do with him?" she said.

"He had been around your apartment asking after you. The doorman had seen him there. Then he shows up in an alley with your dead child."

"I told you what you wanted," she said.

"He dealt dope," Frank said. "He was easy to set up."

She looked around the room, trying out every face. Frank thought he already knew the answer, but he wanted to get it from her.

"It's a loose end," he said, softly. "It makes you wonder."

"All right," she said. "Sure, I'll tell you. It was simple to do. He sold me dope. That's how I got to know him. As soon as I got rid of the body I called him up. I told him the apartment was hot, but I needed some coke. I told him to meet me in that alley. When the time came, I called the cops."

"Where did you call Williams, Mrs. Tatum? What number?"

"How should I know? I had it written down. I threw the paper away so you wouldn't find it."

"Did he answer the phone himself, or was it somebody else?"

Her hands fumbled with the cords. She closed her eyes. When she opened them again, he could finally see the fear.

"He always answered," she said. "I think it was at his flat." She spaced her words carefully. "I never actually went there. He came to me."

"Where did you call the police from?"

"I left the apartment and used a telephone on the street."

"A busy street?"

"Sure. No. I don't remember."

"Did you disguise your voice, Mrs. Tatum?"

"I don't know."

"The tape you made to play over the phone, did your husband destroy it?"

"I don't know what you're talking about."

"Those electronic devices confuse you, don't they, Mrs. Tatum? You let your husband handle the machines."

"What's that supposed to mean?"

"We're going to take you upstairs and book you now," said Frank. But the relief had barely spread beyond her eyes before he went on. "You'll be charged with a number of things: criminal neglect, aiding and abetting murder. But you didn't kill her."

He stood up and turned his back to her. He did not need anything more from her now.

"You're wrong," she said. "It was an accident. It was me."

"Your father won't be able to save you this time, either of you," he said. "I hope you understand that."

"I don't know what to think anymore," she said, and she was weeping.

Frank faced her again and met her pleading eyes. His voice was soft and sad.

"You didn't want to lose Nicky, did you?" he said.

"I wanted another child," she said. "I wanted to try again."

"Even though he killed Susan," said Frank.

She sat back in her chair. Her coat fell open. Her hands hung at her sides, the brightly colored strands of cord dragging on the hacked-up tile.

"I think I'd better have a lawyer now," she said.

26

uth was just becoming accustomed to the itchy tweed of the young man's shoulder when the telephone interrupted them.

"They never give a man peace," he said.

"Sit," Ruth said. "I'll get it. At this hour it's probably just a heavy breather."

He laughed as she went to the kitchen. When she lifted the receiver, she heard Laura's troubled voice.

"I'm sorry to call so late. I hope I didn't wake you."

"I'm the one who owes an apology," said Ruth. "I should have been at your concert."

"It doesn't matter."

"I met this guy," said Ruth. "He's here now. Remember what we used to call a heavy date? Mmmmm. If I can just keep myself from assaulting him, we'll be all right. Did you bring down the house?"

"I can call some other time," said Laura.

"What's wrong?"

"Nothing. I'll talk to you in the morning."

"Come on. Tell me. He's cozy. He can wait."

Laura hesitated, then told her what Jake had said.

"It wasn't right, was it?" she said. "Tell me he was only being cruel."

"I wanted to talk to you about it myself," said Ruth, "but I promised I wouldn't."

"Maybe Frank wasn't absolutely sure."

"For a while he wasn't," said Ruth. "But after Dad died and they did the autopsy, they knew."

She could hear Laura's breath, nothing more. They had only the thin telephone line between them, a fragile circuit, weakly charged.

"I'm scared, Ruth," said Laura. "I don't know what to think."

"Why don't you talk to Dr. Erdman? He's the expert."

"I don't know if I can wait until tomorrow," said Laura. "It's so confusing."

"I'll put him on," Ruth said. "Dr. Erdman is right here."

"Oh, Ruth," said Laura. "You don't have to . . ."

But Ruth was already putting down the phone.

He was in her father's study, fiddling with the telescope. She sneaked up on him, watching him turn the instrument's calibrated mount.

"You don't play the cello, too, do you?" she said.

It startled him.

"I was just admiring all his things," he said.

The doctor lifted his fingers from the stainless-steel dial and gears.

"I'm afraid we've had a crisis," she said.

"The hospital?"

"My sister-in-law. She just found out what made Dad sick. Frank never told her. She wanted to have children very badly. Can you talk to her?"

"Where's the phone?"

"I'm sorry for this," Ruth said.

"Don't be silly," he said.

"You wouldn't love me so much if I weren't," she said and saw him draw away shyly from the word. She did not regret saying it, though, and she could tell that he didn't regret it either.

He talked to Laura gently, explaining the odds, the causes. There wasn't much else he could do.

Ruth moved up close to him. She touched his lapel and straightened the caduceus pin with its two twisting snakes. Then she put her hand on his shoulder and caressed it lightly. He did not pull away.

"Yes," he said, "well, it is true that the only way to be sure of not passing the disease on is to refrain from having children. But I have to say that this is a very personal decision. It cannot be made solely on medical grounds. Did you want to speak to Ruth again?"

He handed her the phone.

"Thank you," said Laura. "I don't know why I think it helped to talk to him. But it did."

"I like him, too," said Ruth, for his benefit. She thought he might even have blushed a little. "Have you talked to Frank at all?"

"I don't know what to say to him."

"He hadn't stopped hoping," Ruth said. "That's why he didn't tell you."

"I want to believe that," said Laura.

"Don't worry."

"I'm glad the doctor is there for you."

"Don't you just covet him?" Ruth said, and she was pleased to hear Laura answer with the faintest little laugh. "I mean, isn't it tantalizing to wonder what he's doing in my parlor past midnight? God, it's such wonderful gossip I almost wish it were about somebody else so I could whisper it around and make it seem like a scandal."

He closed his eyes and shook his head tolerantly as Laura said goodbye.

But when Ruth hung up, the sadness came. She looked at him standing there and maybe for the first time felt the full sympathy for what Laura wanted, what she had lost. And also the fear. In the presence of this man who knew all about it, she felt flawed for him, incomplete.

"It's better if they don't have children, isn't it?" she said.

"Nobody can say that for someone else," he said.

"Aren't you worried that I have the gene, too?" she said.

"Is it a medical opinion you want?" he said.

"Not at all," she said.

He looked at his watch.

"It's gotten very late," he said. "I didn't realize. I suppose I ought to be going home."

"I could come with you," she said.

"Not just yet," he said. "Let's just see what happens tomorrow. I have rounds, but if you're free we could have dinner."

She nodded and then kissed him. She had kissed him before, and he was not pressing the point. But still it was nicer each time.

27

O'Neill took it all in stride when Frank laid it out for him: first the anomalies in the time sequence, then the things that began to click into place when Talley called him and told him about the film.

"The woman confessed, Terry," Frank said. "But she lied."

"You nailed her," said O'Neill. "What can I say?"

"I wasn't holding back on you. I was too close to it. Until the end, I couldn't see what I had."

But now he could. All the odd details that had been nagging at him suddenly made sense.

"What made you think it wasn't the woman?" asked O'Neill.

"Tatum said he had called home as soon as he checked into a hotel in St. Louis. And sure enough there was a charge for it on the bill. I must have looked at that piece of paper a dozen times, but I couldn't figure out what was bothering me about it. Then it finally dawned on me, the items that appeared after the long-distance charge—a dinner and a movie. The guy's wife tells him his daughter has been murdered and he sits down to a thirty-buck meal and a show."

"That was it?" said O'Neill.

"The woman's story didn't make sense. For one thing, she said she knew Williams personally, bought drugs from him. She said he delivered them to the apartment. But the doorman had only seen him once. And a buddy of Williams said he never dealt with clients face to face."

"Pretty thin, Frank."

"Maybe."

"I've got to give you credit."

"There was one more thing," said Frank. "Last night I stopped by the police communications room and listened to a recording of the call that tipped off the police.''

"You recognized her voice?''

"I didn't know what to make of it,'' said Frank. "But something seemed wrong. It sounded hollow, unnatural. The rhythm was out of whack.''

"It wasn't on the Top Forty chart, Frank.''

"I mean, the woman wasn't responding to the cop on the other end of the line. The funny thing is, later on last night I was listening to another tape at home and there were pauses on it where I was supposed to laugh. But I didn't figure it out until I had her in front of me.''

"Because it was a woman's voice,'' said O'Neill.

"And because I'd seen all the electronic gear in Tatum's apartment—stereo components, mikes, tape decks, everything you could imagine. See, he didn't trust her to improvise, so they taped her call in advance. They left gaps for the cop to respond, disguised her voice electronically, then called the emergency number and played it over the phone.''

"You think the tech jocks could reproduce it with gear from the apartment?''

"If we need it,'' said Frank.

"We got anything on Tatum?''

Frank sorted through the files on his lap and found the thin manila folder he was looking for. The tab had Tatum's name on it, date of birth, SSN, court number, and the notation that the file was sealed.

"Nothing since he was a kid,'' said Frank. "I ran a check on him earlier. But his name came up blank. Then this morning when I got done with the woman, I had them check the sealed juvenile court files and found this. He was bounced around quite a bit, and he had a few minor scrapes with the law. But nothing you could hang your hat on.''

He handed the papers over to O'Neill, who paged through them and then put the file on his desk. "Foster homes,'' he said. "The kid had it rough.''

"I'd bet money he was abused.''

"It doesn't show in the file,'' said O'Neill.

"It didn't as much in those days,'' said Frank.

"You think Pricer or his daughter knew where this guy came from?''

"A thing like this can lie dormant for years,'' said Frank. "On the surface a person is absolutely normal. Then all of a sudden it shows itself. You heard from Pricer yet?''

"Give him time.''

"Look at it this way: at least the cops are off our backs."

"Do I seem worried to you?"

"You worry about everything, Terry."

Frank took back the file and put it on the stack, then he stood up and went to the door.

"Don't think this is going to get you off the hookers," said O'Neill.

"I'll want to follow through," said Frank.

"You can handle the whores with one hand. Look, we'll talk about it tomorrow. Go home and get some sleep."

Frank was not ready for that yet. He made a quick stop at the men's room and then spun by Talley's office to thank him. But Talley was in court handling the regular docket, so Frank left him a note.

The fatigue finally hit him as he stood there writing it, and he had to force himself through the words of praise. His head was heavy on his neck. It was a struggle to focus his eyes. And the morning still hung in his nostrils, the sour smell of exhaled cigarettes and sweat. It carried him back to other dawns when he had awakened early and padded into his parents' bedroom, gazing at their faces and breathing in the smells of their sleep, his father's Turkish tobacco, the tarry liniment he used to relax his back, the odor of life and loss that came from every pore.

When Frank reached his cubicle, Jake was standing at the window staring out into the yard. A north wind was blowing the clouds away, and the day was bright and clear, full of the false promise of warmth.

"We've gotten a goodnight," said Frank. "The boss is satisfied. There's nothing more to do here."

Jake turned to him, a silhouette against the gray, filmy pane. "You look beat," he said.

"Why don't you sleep at our place, Jake? It won't take a minute to make up an extra bed."

"Maybe I'd better not," said Jake.

"Suit yourself. I'll run you over to the house then."

"I fucked up, Frank."

Jake stepped away from the window and came close enough to touch Frank. But he did not reach out. He just stood there in the stark, slanting light.

"Don't worry about it," said Frank. "I was just kidding when I said there was a problem about your asking questions. I was on a roll with her was all. I had a hunch and I wanted to play it out."

"I don't mean that," said Jake.

"Sit down a minute."

Frank pulled a chair up next to the desk for him. The room was so tiny that they ended up knee to knee.

"Dad left us a tape recording," said Frank. "I listened to it last night before you came by."

"What did he say?"

"A lot of things. You know how he was when he got started."

Jake abruptly pulled himself to his feet.

"I let you down, Frank," he said.

"Come on. None of that now."

"Last night I told Laura what killed Dad."

Frank did not even blink. It was as if he had expected something like this all along.

"I didn't even realize she didn't know," said Jake.

"Ruth told you?"

"Dr. Owen," said Jake. "I was angry at you for keeping it from me. I thought Laura was in on it, too."

"I was going to say something to you before you left," said Frank.

"It hurt her, Frank, to find out that way."

"I just had to get my head together first."

Jake went back to the window and squinted into the sun.

"You knew I'd tell her if you told me," said Jake.

"I guess I did."

"That's why you didn't say anything."

"Maybe I was hoping they'd find some other explanation."

"What are you going to do?"

Frank lifted his feet to the edge of the desk and tipped back in his chair until the swivel reached the sticking point. "Nothing we can do except go ahead and live," he said, and he was surprised at how easily it had come out, how banal it seemed aloud, how perfectly obvious and right.

"I mean about Laura," said Jake.

"I'll have to do what I can to explain."

"I put you in a spot."

"Maybe you did me a favor," said Frank. "I was having trouble finding the words."

"She was awfully upset. I wasn't exactly gentle."

"It was wrong to keep you in the dark."

"I'm sorry, Frank."

Jake stood over him now, and Frank lifted his feet from the desk, rubbing the lines it had cut into his ankles.

"Maybe we ought to go home so you can hear that tape," he said.

"I think you should be with Laura."

"Most of what he said was for you."

"I guess with me he had more to worry about."

Jake got up and put on his jacket.

"Where are you going?" asked Frank.

"I have a few things to do."

"Don't be in a hurry to go back," said Frank. "I want you to stay with us for a while. I want you to listen to what Dad had to say."

"Maybe I should straighten myself out on my own first. Maybe then it wouldn't be so hard to listen to him."

Frank came around the desk, and Jake embraced him.

"So long, brother," Jake said, and then he left.

When Frank was alone, he began arranging the items in the file. He was almost ready to face Laura now and talk about the past and the future, what they owed each other in the continuity of blood and time. But he needed to sort this other thing out first. He went through the documents, arranging them chronologically, putting paper clips on the pertinent pages. Then he came across the picture of the little girl laid out on the slab.

The odds against her had been terrible, and yet she might have defied them. The burden that she had innocently inherited might have become the occasion of her greatest triumph, like the force that drove the first creature to pull itself onto land or walk upright in the sun. If she had escaped, the chain of abuse might have ended with her in an act of perfect will and faith. He closed his eyes and saw himself bearing her gently to the tomb, and when he had put her down on the soft silk, her eyes opened to him. Finally he wept—for love and trust and loss. And too it was a kind of knowing. Her eyes looked up at him, asking what was right. And for the first time he thought he knew the answer, had learned it from her, because it was the damaged ones who always showed the way.

28

The house was empty when Jake unlocked the front door, which stuck until he leaned against it with all his weight. It had been balky for as long as Jake could remember. His father had pulled it down off its hinges a dozen times and gone at it to no avail with sandpaper and plane. When Jake got inside, he pushed his shoulder into the door until he heard the click of the latch.

Ruth had done nothing to reorganize the place. Books still lay open on every surface. The old sweat-stained fedora and wool jacket hung on the coatrack. Music was stacked up on the piano, and it spilled from the bench onto the floor, yellow Schirmer covers detached from the signatures by long and ardent use, some pages so tattered they looked as though they might soon turn to dust.

Jake went to the bedroom he and his brother had shared as boys. On Frank's side composite pictures of his college fraternity hung on the walls flanked by diplomas and certificates of his achievements. The bed was neat, a university blanket as a bedspread, official seal neatly centered, corners tucked, as if it had been Frank who had been drilled in the arts of war.

Jake went to his closet and took out his uniform. Ruth had pressed it and done his shirt. She had tried her best to get the medals and brass back on right, but she didn't know all the little rules. He put them in order, then slipped off his jeans and flannel shirt and went to the bathroom to shave.

In the mirror he saw a face that looked as though it had seen weeks of duty in the bush. His hair was getting long; he would have to stop off at the barber shop at the airport and get a trim. He scraped the shadowy new growth of sideburn back up in line with the upper whorl of his ear, then lathered up again to get all the last little pinfeathers. When he dried his face, he dumped the hand towel into a hamper along with the washcloth and the rest of the set he had used during his visit. Then he went back into the bedroom and put on the uniform, straightening the gig line: shirtfront, belt buckle, and fly.

On the wall on Jake's side of the room, his father had left up the big motorcycle poster and an old cheesecake calendar. Jake took them down, folded them, and put them in the bottom drawer of the dresser beneath a tangle of underwear and unrolled socks. He did not remove the snapshot of himself and Spurgeon Whitelaw joking outside their hootch; it stood on the dresser in a dimestore frame. When he was finished, he took the government-issue things he had come home with and stuffed them into his AWOL bag with his dop kit.

Then he retrieved the bag from the pharmacy and the note Dr. Erdman had written to the medics. The doctor had seen him right away when Jake went to his office on the way back to his father's house. He had listened when Jake told him about the woman, who she was. He had said the treatment was simple enough and had given him medicine for both of them in case it should be unavailable to her otherwise. Jake put the pill bottles into his AWOL bag, carefully cradling the medicine for him and Luong among his clothes. He took one last look around to make sure he had forgotten nothing, then he pulled his army-green trenchcoat from a hanger and went back to the living room.

He rooted around until he found a gnawed pencil stub. He used it to write a short message for Ruth and Frank. There was no reason for him to stay any longer, he wrote. It was time for him to get on with his life. And there were certain matters he had to take care of in the bad place. But he would be back. They could be sure of that now. Soon he would be coming home for good.

Before leaving he went to his father's room one last time. The big oxygen tanks and respiratory therapy device still stood next to the bed. A picture of the five of them hung over the nightstand where he had kept his radio and medications. Their mother looked so beautiful and happy.

"Don't think I'm running away again," Jake said to the strong, merciful presence he felt in the room. And that done, he left the house and walked to the motel parking lot where the airport limousine made a regular stop.

29

When Laura finally came home from her concert, she found the apartment empty. Frank was gone, and though she found his note saying there'd been a development in the case he was working on, she suspected that he was just looking for another excuse to avoid her. She waited up for a while and then called his office. There was no answer, so she went to bed. She did not sleep well.

In the morning he was still gone, and she decided that the only way to keep her sanity was to work. There were errands to run and then lessons to give at the conservatory downtown. The papers had reviews of her concert, but for once the praise and quibbles did not touch her. She felt as if she had given the performance years before.

After she finished teaching, she went out for coffee with one of her students who was going through a crisis about whether to continue entering competitions or to give up the dream. She listened to the young woman and encouraged her, but the deepest part of sympathy was simply not engaged. She knew how such a decision could paralyze you, but now it seemed trivial, unreal.

As she returned to the apartment in the late afternoon, she prepared herself to confront him with what she had learned from Jake. She expected Frank to be so desperately sorry that if she wasn't careful she would find herself feeling sorry for him. That was the way it usually worked. But this time she steeled herself so that she would not let him avoid the central question. They had to deal with it now, both of them. They had to resolve this thing once and for all.

But when she arrived home, she found him lying asleep in the bed. He looked so exhausted that she did not have the heart to wake him. She rearranged the covers where they had become twisted. He did not stir.

Back in the living room, she listened to part of an opera on the radio.

When it was over, she began to putter around the room. His birthday was only five days away now. He had already heard the song, but she still had to record it and wrap it up with ribbons and a card.

She retrieved the recorder from his study and found a cassette already in it. It was a cheap tape, not the kind she used. The label had some writing on it, his father's awkward scrawl. She plugged in the machine and turned over the cassette. She felt a little guilty as she pushed the play button, but she wanted to hear Frank's father's voice. She listened to the tape from beginning to end.

When it was over, she sat there in perfect silence. The message had been for Frank and Jake and Ruth, but it had spoken to Laura, too. He had touched something deep and sure in her, and in the stillness she found herself repeating the words he had found to thank his children for being born.

She finally rose and put a fresh tape into the machine. After plugging in the microphones and setting the controls to the proper levels for the room, she pushed the record button and moved quietly to the piano.

She played the song to Frank without caution. The rubato could have been a setting for his father's testament. It was a gift and a plea. The first time she had conceived the piece, it had come to her in a rush, the way they said it happened with jazz. This time it came spontaneously again. And in the end it fell away to a hushed, resonant ambiguity that suggested, all the way up the abstract harmonic chain, every chord and melody she had ever played.

When she was finished, she looked in on him again, and his eyes were open. She bent down to kiss him.

"You should sleep," she said.

And he said: "Sleep with me."

She looked at the clock, which made him laugh.

"It is very chilly tonight," she said to him as she took off her clothes. Then she moved to the dresser and opened a drawer.

"Don't," he said. "Come to bed that way."

Again she did as he asked. She wanted to feel her flesh against his, to be warmed by him. He rolled over to meet her as she slipped in naked among the icy bedclothes. He held her, and she put her head deep into the hollow between his neck and shoulder.

"You're shivering," he said,

"You know the way I am."

He reached over and stroked her side, high up near where she could feel the tender point of her breast stiffening. He kissed her.

"Tomorrow is Saturday," she said, pulling away a little. "Let's stay home."

He pulled her back to him and kissed her again. His breath was sour from sleep, but there was an urgency, a need. And she thought that maybe this would save them. Maybe they had to go to the unspoken center and meet there before they could hope to put the thing into words. Still it made her frightened. She was afraid they would come upon the place and find a void. But this was not what her body told her. Her body wanted his touch. And so she kissed his shoulder and said:

"I ought to get ready."

And he said:

"Don't do that tonight."

She wanted to say it was dangerous. She wanted to say that it was her fertile time. She wanted to scream out in joy and terror and say there had to be some resolution and don't do it without thinking and consider the risk. But she said nothing. She just let him enter her unprotected for the first time in their lives. She felt herself more open to him than she had ever been. And it was as if he were finally open to her as well. He moved slowly and deeply within her. It frightened and excited her. She clasped her hands behind his back to pull him deeper still.

And when it happened, she cried out.

He did not roll away from her after it was over. They lay joined together in silence, and she wanted to ask him about the feelings she had now. Was there a living thing already awakening inside her? Did it really happen so quickly? Could a woman tell? The questions made her laugh and tighten herself around him.

He turned his head toward her on the pillow and whispered:

"Sweet, sweet sibilance."

And she wondered if he had been awake all along, even before she began playing his song, if he had heard her running his father's tape. She wondered whether he realized that in her warm, expectant silence she knew exactly what he meant.